The Body in the Bog

ALSO BY KATHERINE HALL PAGE

The Body in the Basement
The Body in the Cast
The Body in the Vestibule
The Body in the Bouillon
The Body in the Kelp
The Body in the Belfry

The Body in the Bog

Katherine Hall Page

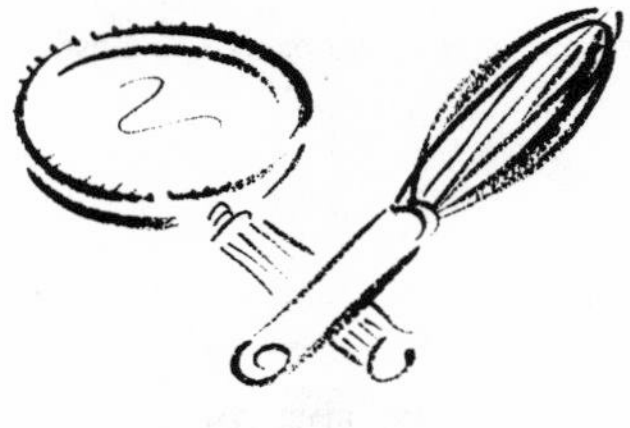

William Morrow and Company, Inc.   New York

It is the policy of William Morrow and Company, Inc., and its imprints and affiliates, recognizing the importance of preserving what has been written, to print the books we publish on acid-free paper, and we exert our best efforts to that end.

Printed in the United States of America

FIRST EDITION

1 2 3 4 5 6 7 8 9 10

ILLUSTRATION BY SALLY MARA STURMAN

BOOK DESIGN BY LAURA HAMMOND HOUGH

To my friend Mimi Garrett,

and in memory of her dear mother, Marion Mullison Ellis

Acknowledgments

I would like to acknowledge George Gabriel, "Captain John Parker," of the Lexington Company of Minute Men, and David Hackett Fischer, author of *Paul Revere's Ride,* for their help with the historical portions of the book. Thanks also to Robert Hilton for the title and sundry bog information. My special thanks to the best agent in the books, Faith Hamlin.

Accidents will occur in the best-regulated families.

—CHARLES DICKENS

Chapter 1

Seeing another woman in the Reverend Thomas Fairchild's arms was not a sight his wife, Faith, had expected. She'd flung open the door to her husband's study prepared to deliver an impassioned account of the infuriating selectmen's meeting she'd just attended this April evening. Instead, she stood frozen on the threshold, perversely embarrassed at having walked in on something. Then the anger so conveniently close to the surface veered toward another target and she made her presence known by slamming the door—hard.

As a matter of course, Tom had to comfort the afflicted in mind, particularly the bereaved, and Faith could only hope that the woman, whoever she was, had lost her entire family to the bubonic plague, or else there would be some serious explaining due.

While she was considering whether to grab said woman by the hair, wrenching her from the good reverend's grasp, Tom spoke.

"Faith, you're home!"

"Yes, dear," she replied, quelling the impulse to add, "obviously."

She'd no sooner spoken when the woman turned around and abruptly threw herself into Faith's arms. "I'm so glad you're here!" she cried. So was Faith.

It was Miss Lora, almost-five-year-old Benjamin Fairchild's beloved nursery school teacher and sometime weekend sitter for Ben and his younger sister, Amy. Miss Lora was crying. Miss Lora was upset. Faith patted Miss Lora's back, the fleeting earlier notion of clocking her one totally obscured. This was the woman who provided her son with quality care and—possibly more important—actually enabled the elder Fairchilds to get away for a few weekends alone together.

Faith looked at Tom over Miss Lora's heaving shoulders. It was a bit difficult to read his expression since, Janus-like, one side of his face was registering deep concern while the other displayed acute embarrassment. He repeated his earlier cogent remark. "Ah, honey, you're home," adding, "and early. Good, good, good."

Faith again opted for brevity. "Yes," she replied, trusting that after six years of marriage, Tom could read the volumes between the lines, volumes entitled, "What the Hell Is Going on Here?"

"Lora came to discuss a problem, and I've been trying to convince her that it really is a police matter."

Things were looking up. Faith loved nothing better than poking her nose into police matters. But Miss Lora? What on earth could be going on?

"Absolutely not! No police," Lora said, fishing around in her pocket for a tissue, with which she proceeded to blow her already-red nose noisily.

Faith regarded the teacher and thought, not for the first time, that Miss Lora needed to look to a fashion beacon other than Raggedy Ann. Lora wasn't wearing red-and-white-striped tights and a ruffled apron at the moment, but these were staples of her wardrobe, which also included a number of shapeless denim and corduroy jumpers, gingham blouses, and the like. She had an abundance of mousy brown hair, worn pulled back with a scrunch. Unlike the doll, however, she did not have even a hint of red on her lips or cheeks. What paint there was lay under her fingernails, the result of active participation with her young charges.

"Why don't we go into the kitchen and have something to eat while you tell me all about it?" Faith suggested. The makeover could wait. "I assume," she said to Tom, "that the children are asleep."

"Naturally," he replied, adopting an attitude of injured dignity as he led the way into the parsonage kitchen.

A parsonage was the last place Faith Sibley Fairchild had expected to be spending her adult years. It had been bad enough growing up in one. Tradition-bound, Faith's father, the Reverend Lawrence Sibley, donned the cloth, as had his grandfather and father before him. He also clung to Sibley family mores by naming his daughters Faith and Hope. Charity might have followed had not his wife, Jane Sibley, a real estate lawyer, put her well-shod little foot down. Enough was enough.

Faith had chafed at the fishbowl existence as a "preacher's kid"—the freely offered, "well-meant" remarks at the way the Sibleys raised their children, ate, drank, even slept, if it was too late. The fishbowl was, however, nicely located on Manhattan's Upper East Side, and that had helped.

Spurred by her younger sister's meteoric rise in the world of finance, Faith had finally found her own true calling—as a caterer—and Have Faith was born. After glowing reviews and by much deliciously satisfied word of mouth, she became the caterer of choice for the Big Apple's glitterati. Have Faith jams, jellies, chutneys, and sauces followed. Then, at a wedding reception, while checking to see whether a tray of the smoked trout wrapped in an herbed crêpe topped with a soupçon of caviar and crème fraîche was holding out,

Faith met Tom Fairchild. He'd changed collars, and it wasn't until they'd talked into the wee hours of the morning that the fact that she'd fallen head over heels in love with a minister hit her full force. It hit her again when she found herself in the small village of Aleford, Massachusetts, after their own wedding. She was acutely homesick—and bored.

She was determined not to sacrifice her standards, and kept her wardrobe and haircut up-to-date. At present, her thick blond hair was chin-length, parted on the side, enabling her to let the curtain fall strategically across her face. Trips home always included the three *B*'s—Barneys, Bergdorf, and Bloomingdale's—along with two others—Bendel, and Balducci's for food, if she had time.

Yet, the years in Aleford had proved more eventful than she could have predicted. The place was beginning to grow on her, like the ivy and old mosses attacking the brick parsonage walls. Not only had she produced two children and started Have Faith again, but she'd also demonstrated an uncanny knack for getting involved in crime. Getting involved after the fact, that is, having literally stumbled across several bodies and, as she liked to remind herself, in each case beaten the police to the denouement.

Police matter. The moment Tom referred to the boys in blue—although Chief Charley MacIsaac, thirty-four years in Aleford alone, could scarcely be referred to as a boy—Faith found herself drawn to Miss Lora as never before. Certainly it was interesting to hear that Ben was truly gifted when it came to block building, but nowhere near as riveting as the possibility that Miss Lora might need Faith's detective skills.

All in good time. Faith made fresh coffee, the drug of choice in places like Aleford, and cut some thick slices of the Scandinavian cardamom raisin bread (see recipe on page 271) she'd made the day before. Cardamom and coffee went well together and transformed the kitchen into an instant replica of the one in *I Remember Mama.* Faith had to watch that she didn't start to nod at Lora's every word and say, "Ja." It was an atmosphere calculated to encourage confidences.

Miss Lora was hungry and slathered her bread thickly with sweet butter. Twenty-two-year-olds didn't worry about cholesterol, Faith reflected from her vantage point ten—soon to be eleven—years ahead. In your early twenties, you didn't worry about much. Maybe boyfriend/girlfriend troubles, finding a job, small stuff, but nothing like clogged arteries. So what was Lora worried about? She was eating heartily, yet her face, kittenlike behind the huge horn-rimmed glasses she wore, was still troubled.

Tom, bless his heart, got right to the point.

"Lora has been receiving some threatening phone calls."

Faith turned to the young woman. "What do they say?"

Lora swallowed hard and took a gulp of coffee. "The third one came about dinnertime. They've all been the same. A man's voice tells me to get out of Aleford if I want to stay healthy. Tonight he said, 'Get out soon.' I was sitting in my apartment and I suddenly got so scared, I had to talk to someone, and Reverend Fairchild was the only person I could think of."

Faith wondered why Lora had not sought solace from her own spiritual leader, Father Reeves. At well over sixty, he was balding and paunchy, no match for Tom Fairchild's good looks, but a resource that should have occurred to Lora. Tom, the only one? Faith knew she hadn't spoken out loud, but Lora volunteered the answer as if the question had been asked.

"I couldn't go to Father Reeves, because—and I know this is an awful thing to say about a member of the clergy—I wasn't sure I could count on him not to tell my grandfather. I knew I could trust you not to repeat what I said to anyone."

Well, it made sense, and it also put the kibosh on any inclinations the Fairchilds might have to go to the police, or to Lora's grandfather, for her own good.

Lora Deane was from an old Aleford family. Not old in Millicent Revere McKinley's book—she traced her ancestors to the famous silversmith's door and beyond. According to Faith, Millicent's ancestors were the forward-thinking ones who had adopted Puritan garb and Congregationalism well before the Flood. Lora's family had come to this country from Germany in the mid-nineteenth century and had headed straight for Aleford, where they found employment as farm laborers and servants. Named Deane when the original name was misspelled by some official along the way, they weren't too sure where in Germany the family had originated. Nor did they much care. They were Americans and eager to make the most of their new country through hard work. They put their money into land and now owned a few good-sized chunks of Aleford, besides several businesses, mostly in the building trades. Lora's grandfather Cyrus Deane, called "Gus" for so much of his life that only his wife, Lillian, ever used Cyrus, ruled the current clan with an iron fist—never mind the velvet glove.

"If my grandfather found out, he'd go nuts and make me move in with them. He wants me to, anyway," Lora explained further.

Faith was firm. "But you have to take these phone calls seriously and find out who's behind them. If you tell the police, they can help you get the phone company to put a tracer on your line."

"I know that, but I can't believe anyone would really want to hurt me. Besides, I'm pretty sure I know who it is."

"Who?" Faith and Tom asked the question simultaneously.

"Well, actually two people."

Faith's image of the nursery school teacher was becoming seriously skewed. Two people who might be threatening her?

"One is my boyfriend, or I should say ex-boyfriend, Brad. Brad Hallowell. Do you know him?"

"I've met his parents at various functions. They moved to Aleford shortly after I did, almost six years ago. He was in college at the time. I think I know who he is, but I'm not sure."

"You're not missing much," Lora said bluntly. "He's good-looking. I think that's what attracted me, but all he can talk about are his computers or whatever cause he's latched onto at the moment—Save the Field Mice, whatever."

If Faith was surprised to discover the teacher more interested in the life of the flesh than the life of the mind, she did not show it. Only her husband might have caught the one eyebrow raised a millimeter.

"He was very upset when I told him I didn't want to see him anymore. If you can believe it, he backed his car right over the cold frames where I was starting the children's flower seeds. He isn't much for children. That was another problem—but he could have respected their work!"

Respect was a key concept in Miss Lora's room, appearing on banners, spelled out in dried legumes, and on the leather key ring Ben had made Tom for Christmas. Faith had received a slogan-free looped pot holder.

"But why would he want you out of Aleford? It sounds as if what he really wants is to get back together," Faith said.

"Oh, he knows I'd never go back with him, so now he goes out of his way to be nasty. You should see the looks he gives me. It sends chills down my spine. He'd just love to mess up my life and get me all upset."

It did sound plausible, and if it was Brad Hallowell, perhaps Tom could have a quiet word with him. Faith made a mental note to make some discreet inquiries about the young man.

"You said there were two," Tom prodded in a low, sincere voice. Lora looked at him adoringly. Faith was used to this.

"The other person is my brother-in-law, Joey. Joey Madsen."

Now this *was* a surprise. A scorned lover was one thing, but a member, albeit by marriage, of the Deane family!

"Why would you think it was Joey?" Tom asked. Faith was too surprised to talk. Joey Madsen was the prime cause of the fury she'd felt when she'd come home from the selectmen's meeting. If there was one person in town Faith herself was tempted to threaten, by phone, letter, or eye-to-eye, it was Joey Madsen.

Lora's father, Cyrus Deane, Jr., had been married twice. Over twenty years ago, as a relatively young widower with four children ages eight through twelve, he'd immediately remarried. Lora was born a year later, and the second Mrs. Deane decided she had more than enough children to raise. After Cyrus's untimely death two years ago, Carolyn Deane had moved to California to escape the cold of New England, much to the Deane family's bewilderment. They couldn't imagine living anywhere else. Carolyn had recently remarried.

Joey Madsen had married the oldest daughter from Cyrus's first family, Bonnie. He's joined one of the family businesses, Deane Properties, and had recently formed his own company, the Deane-Madsen Development Corporation. Tonight, his presentation of Deane-Madsen's latest project before the selectmen had been the reason for a packed room—and Faith's subsequent agitation.

Despite their climatic partisanship, New Englanders started looking for harbingers of spring in February. Faith's friend and next-door neighbor Pix Miller had called her excitedly one late-February morning to announce the sighting of her first robin—quivering on a telephone wire that was encased in solid ice from the latest storm. Spring meant the turning over of new soil, and the turnees fell into diametrically opposed camps. On one side were the passionate gardeners, armed with tools from Smith & Hawken, clutching the latest book by Roger Swain, the *Victory Garden* man. On the other were local developers who started digging foundations and framing as soon as nature permitted, anxious to get their houses up and sold before the killing frosts of autumn. One group hearkened to the *ping!* sound of a shovel hitting a rock in the unforgiving loam of the region; the other to the chorus of chain saws clearing the way for naturalistic foundation plantings. Good hedges, preferably fast-growing Canadian hemlocks, made good neighbors.

Joey Madsen had purchased a large tract that most of Aleford had mistakenly assumed was town conservation land. It included a bog, woodlands, and meadows. Joey planned to reduce them to one common denominator—enormous houses on postage stamp–sized lots. Five and six bedrooms, baths to match, exercise rooms—and gazebos. "California colonials," he called them, clustered in a planned community with shared pool, cabana, and tennis courts. In short, Alefordiana Estates.

And the new access road would pass between the parsonage and the church, an existing—though unused—right-of-way discovered by Joey. Like other developers, he viewed the town ordinance maps much the way Long John Silver did Captain Kidd's.

Faith fast-forwarded past her own irritations and leaned toward Miss Lora. "Yes," she asked the teacher, "why Joey?"

"Well, you know he's going to be building all these new houses out behind the church?"

"We have heard something about it," Faith said, muttering under her breath, "and if he does, it will be over my dead body."

"He needs a lot of money up front. You know, to pay for the land, put in the roads, and the houses themselves. Once he starts to sell them, he'll be okay. Anyway, he's been after me to put money into the Estates, but I don't want to, and he's hopping mad."

Faith's curiosity was beginning to resemble Alice's. And Lora's tale was making Faith feel as if she were growing and shrinking in turn. Where would Lora, a nursery school teacher—and Faith knew exactly how underpaid she was—possibly get the kind of money Joey would be interested in? This wasn't a question of piggy banks.

"You see," Lora continued obligingly, "Grandfather gave us all a lump sum of money when we turned twenty-one. We're supposed to use it to make more—that is, start a business, whatever. My dad used his to buy the dealership."

Deane Toyota was now in the hands of Cyrus junior's son Bobby, and it had always been a profitable venture. Faith was beginning to get some idea of the size of the nest egg. She'd found that New Englanders were remarkably reticent when it actually came to discussing dollars and cents in figures, as opposed to thinking about them, and she doubted Lora would tell them how pretty her penny was, but there were ways around this. Millicent probably knew.

"I have told Joey a million times that I need the money for tuition. I want to get my master's in early childhood education, but he thinks that's not what Grandfather had in mind when he started the whole thing."

"But that surely wouldn't cause him to threaten you."

"It also goes back to my mother. I get along fine with Bonnie. She was almost like a little mother to me when I was growing up, since she's so much older. But she never liked my mother." Lora put on a professional air. "For a child to lose her mother at that critical age—the onset of puberty—is particularly devastating, and especially since my mother was so young. I'm sure Bonnie resented her and saw her as trying to take her own mother's place." She went back to her conversational tone and reached for another piece of bread. "But what they're really angry about, all of them, is that Daddy left his money to Mom—except for what had to go back into the family pot."

"The family pot?" Faith was learning more about the Deanes than she had ever imagined possible, and it was fascinating.

"You have to give Grandfather back what he gave you, plus five percent of the profits you've made by the time you're forty."

"But what if you don't make a profit, or lose the money?" Tom asked.

Lora was aghast. "I have no idea. That's never happened."

Faith steered her back to Joey. "So your brother-in-law thought your father should have left some of his money to his family and not just to his widow?"

"Yes. Daddy left some money for me to finish college, and my mother has loaned me some more. Nobody liked that, either. But after all, she was married to him for all those years and raised them. I would have thought they'd be grateful to her."

Faith was beginning to think it was more than the climate that had attracted Carolyn Deane to California. Something about being on the opposite side of the country. With a chorus of disapproval, or worse, every time you bought a new pair of panty hose, it was no wonder Carolyn wanted to put as much distance as possible between herself and these serpent's teeth.

"You didn't want to move with your mother?" she asked.

"No. Aleford is my home, and I'd miss my family. I'm especially close to the twins."

Cyrus junior's youngest children by his first wife had been twin boys, Cyrus III and Eddie, now thirty years old. They were Deane Construction Company with their grandfather, having purchased partnerships with the eggs in their nests. This Cyrus was called "Terry"—short for *tertius*, meaning "third" in Latin—to avoid any possible confusion over two men with the same name in one family. He couldn't be called "Gus"; everyone knew there was really only one.

"Maybe I'm not getting this," Tom said, shaking his head. All these Deanes were beginning to addle him. "Why would Joey want you out of town if he wants you to give him money? Wouldn't he try being nice to you?"

"Oh, he did do that. Remember when he let the kids climb all over his excavator, his steam shovel, after we read *Mike Mulligan*? And he was always inviting me over to the house for dinner. But once he understood that there was no way he was getting my money, he stopped. Telling me to get out of town is the threat. He wants to scare me into giving in."

Faith thought back to some of the scenes she'd witnessed in the past. Joey Madsen was noted for his violent temper. At last year's Town Meeting, he'd started screaming at a fellow member over a line item in the budget and then later, outside, he'd engaged in a shoving match with the man. It would have gone further had Charley MacIsaac not promptly put a stop to it.

"I'm afraid Lora does have a reason to be afraid of Joey. You should have heard him tonight, Tom. This project means everything to him, and he already must have sunk a fortune into it."

Faith made a note to herself to find out how close Joey was to forty and how soon he'd have to be thinking about putting his percentage back into the pot. It could be he was in need of cash for more than Alefordiana.

"We can't talk you into going to the police, Lora, so we have to come up with something else. I'd like to think there won't be any more calls, but that's not how people like this operate. Whoever it is will keep on." Tom looked solemn. After a while, calls did not satisfy whatever aberration was motivating the caller, and the next step was something he didn't want to think about. He wished the young woman would be sensible.

"Okay. Since I'm not going to the police, what should I do?"

Faith answered. "I'll try to find out more about Brad. Maybe we can get an idea of how badly he really is taking the breakup."

"Badly. Believe me." Lora seemed more than a little pleased.

"And you should go to your grandfather and tell him you suspect Joey is harassing you. I know Gus, and he wouldn't be at all pleased at Joey's behavior—if it is Joey," Tom advised.

"Grandfather! No way! He'd go through the roof and be mad at *me* for causing problems. We're supposed to be the perfect all-American family with no disagreements. In fact, if he knew I was telling you about this, he'd be furious."

Faith had suspected as much. The Deanes were not known for airing their dirty, or even clean, linen in public.

"How about Bonnie?" she suggested. "You said that you'd been close growing up."

"That's possible," Lora said slowly, mulling it over. "Bonnie's the boss in their house, and if it is Joey, she'll put a stop to it right away."

"I think you ought to talk to her as soon as possible," Tom said. The seriousness of his tone seemed to impress the young woman.

"Tomorrow's Thursday and Joey will be off working somewhere. He still hasn't finished that house on Whipple Hill Road."

Faith knew the house. It was an eyesore wedged between two beautiful turn-of-the-century grandes dames, completely destroying one of Aleford's prettiest corners. Now instead of a long stretch of rolling lawn with huge ancient oaks and locusts, you saw a two-car garage almost as big as the house itself—a house boasting two decks *and* a gazebo.

"Bonnie is home with the baby for a few more weeks." Lora was thinking out loud. "And I can go over there after school. I haven't seen the baby in ages."

"Good." Tom sounded satisfied. He wasn't convinced Joey Madsen was making the calls, but this way, someone related to

Lora would know about them and perhaps be able to get her to take action. If by chance it was Joey, Bonnie would indeed put a stop to it immediately. Bonnie Madsen resembled her patriarchal grandfather. And there was no question who would assume his role in the future, despite the number of aunts, uncles, cousins all within shouting distance. Bonnie worked for Deane Properties, too, and her latest coup was a new mall development project in nearby Byford. She'd gone into labor an hour after the papers were signed. Gus was still telling the story proudly all over town.

"I'm sure she'll understand," Faith said. "Women have moved far beyond the stage where their financial decisions are dictated by men. If you don't think Alefordiana Estates is a good investment, then you shouldn't be pressured—even by someone in your own family."

"Oh, I think it's a good investment," Lora said. "Joey's going to make a ton of money. I have nothing against the idea personally. I just don't want to put my money there right now."

Faith looked at Tom dismally—a politically incorrect damsel in distress.

Lora left, thoughts apparently back to circle time and "If You're Happy and You Know It, Clap Your Hands." Faith and Tom were less sanguine.

"Were you being discreet or do you really not know much about Brad Hallowell?" Tom asked his wife.

"I really don't, but the more I think about this whole thing, the more likely it seems that the calls are from him."

"Hell has no fury—in this case—like a man scorned?"

"Exactly, and I'm worried about where that fury might lead next. Eventually, he's going to be driven to make good on his threat," she added.

"Lora was genuinely frightened when she arrived, quite hysterical."

"But you calmed her down," Faith commented somewhat archly.

Tom thought it was time to change the subject. He was getting a little tired of Miss Lora. He yawned and reached for Faith. "It's getting late. Sleepy?"

"Not all that much," she answered, fitting her head into the place just below his chin that seemed to have been designed for it.

Later, when she was drifting off to sleep, Faith realized she hadn't told Tom much about the selectmen's meeting. Now that Town Meeting had adjourned, Aleford, formerly glued to the local-access cable channel, had had nothing to watch on TV. *Seinfeld* was into reruns and all those stacks of must-read books next to the bed weren't as enticing as they had seemed during the cold of winter. It was the itchiness of spring.

Then, just when Aleford was ready to give up and pick up their tomes, Alefordiana Estates came along. As a saga, it was more riveting than *Melrose Place* and the *Nibelungen* rolled into one. It was enacted not just at selectmen's meetings but also at the planning board's. Then there were all the behind-the-scenes scenes at the Minuteman Café, Shop 'n Save, the library, Patriot Drug—wherever two or three Aleford residents happened to gather. Tonight's selectmen's meeting was the first of Joey Madsen's final presentations of his plans, his dreams. He'd already run the gauntlet of the planning board and various town commissions. Even he was not naïve enough to think they would be approved on the first go-round, and he was right.

Joey and his lawyer had dressed appropriately in dark suits. But the resemblance ended there. Joey was a large man with a thick mat of curly brown hair, beginning to show a dusting of gray. His round face was tanned and his skin was rough. He always seemed to need a shave, even tonight, when a fresh nick in his chin had indicated a recent encounter with a razor. But it was his hands that stood out—enormous hands, with fingers easily equaling two of Faith's. Strong, very strong hands. His lawyer had the look of an old Yankee family in need of fewer cousins marrying. Everything about him was bleached out, from his complexion to his thinning blond hair. He wore a signet ring. Joey's hands were conspicuously bare of even a wedding band.

Joey had done the talking, flinging over the large blueprints, citing drainage studies, setbacks—all according to code, and with minimal wildlife impact. At home, he'd said to his wife, Bonnie, "When the raccoons are in their garbage, they're on the phone to Charley MacIsaac right away. But put them in a godforsaken bog that nobody's thought about for years and suddenly it's like they're about to become extinct or something."

In front of the camera at the meeting, however, his tone had been measured and controlled. He spoke in glowing terms of the new families the Estates would bring to Aleford, contributing their talents to the community and enriching everyone's lives. At one point, he seemed to get a bit choked up as he spoke of "a new generation of children waiting to enjoy the riches of our historic community." Viewers at home were able to hear, although not see, a speaker who commented audibly that there weren't too many families with young children around who could afford $900,000 mansions. Of course, it was Millicent Revere McKinley's unmistakable voice, and people began to get excited. The show was about to begin. Joey had frowned but hadn't missed a beat as he segued into a paean to those older occupants who had worked hard all their lives just so they could spend their golden years in a place like Alefordiana. "And their gold," said the voice. The chairman called for order.

When Joey's presentation was over, it was time for questions from the board, but before any of them could open his or her mouth,

Millicent hopped up and cried, "Point of order!" in a manner worthy of her "The British are coming" ancestor, if indeed that was what he'd said. As with most things, there were several opinions on this in Aleford.

Penelope Bartlett, the current chairman of the board, looked a bit piqued. Millicent was a friend, but toying with the selectmen's agenda was pushing the boundaries of friendship.

"Yes, Miss McKinley?"

Citing precedent, a 1912 discussion of new shrubbery on the village green, Millicent demanded equal time.

"But equal time for what?" Penny asked. "It is the understanding of the board that only Mr. Madsen is submitting building plans tonight."

"Equal time to oppose his plans." Millicent had been Penny's campaign manager, and now she shook her head sorrowfully. Once they get in power . . .

"Madam Chairman," Morris Phyfe, one of the two liberals on the board, spoke up, "I believe Miss McKinley is within her rights." Historically, the board comprised two liberals, two moderates, and one conservative. This kept things nicely in balance, the town believed, and campaigns not in accord had little chance.

Millicent made a motion from the floor to vote on the issue. Penny was now seriously annoyed and forgot her *Robert's Rules*. "Millicent, you know you can't do that."

Morris came to the rescue and made the motion himself that the board vote on Miss McKinley's point. Faith noted that Morris was fulfilling his duty not only as protector of free speech but perhaps also as protector of his own property, which abutted the land in question. It could well be the Phyfes were not eager to have a multimillion-dollar complex-cum-pool and putting green in their own backyard.

To no one's surprise, Morris's motion passed. Sanborn Harrington, the conservative, voted against it. Penny abstained—and would hear about it, she knew. The rest voted to let Millicent offer a rebuttal before the board. Joey Madsen swept the room with a look that had it indeed been daggers would have resulted in wall-to-wall gore. He acidly asked again for questions from the board and Morris Phyfe spoke, after taking an unusually long amount of time looking for a single sheet of yellow lined paper upon which he had apparently written his query.

"Mr. Madsen, it is my understanding that a building of historic significance, known as the Turner farmhouse, is included in this parcel. Parts of the structure date back to the early eighteenth century and it is listed on the town's Historic Register. What are your plans for the dwelling?"

Joey smiled. Faith had wondered why he seemed so relieved. Perhaps it was not one of the questions he'd been dreading? She, for one, planned to look at his proposal with whatever the visual equivalent of a fine-tooth comb was to ferret these out.

"The whole premise behind our proposal is uniting the best of the past with the best of the present to create a perfect future." Was the man running for office or trying to build some houses?

"The Turner farm is what drew me to this treasured part of Aleford in the first place. The farmhouse will be lovingly restored as living history, not an inch of the original structure changed in any way. It will form the jewel in the crown of the community, its simple clapboard reminding us of those who toiled here before we did."

Morris interrupted Joey before he started reciting Longfellow. "So it is not true that you plan to appeal to the Historic Commission for a waiver to raze the house?"

Joey looked for a moment as if he might lose it. Millicent smiled a slow, little smile that did not show her teeth. "Absolutely not," he shouted, "And if that's what's being said in town, it's a damned lie."

Penny rapped her gavel. "I must remind the speaker to contain himself."

He did, quickly. "The plans for the preservation of the Turner farm are included in the packet the board has received. Over the years, certain necessary repairs haven't been made and I could not in good conscience put the house on the market without these, but I repeat, nothing of a historic nature will be altered. And you can stand and watch us if you want."

Joey was still fuming and barely in control. He bumped into the easel he'd been using and the fancy visuals the company had prepared slid to the floor. While he and his lawyer were on their hands and knees picking things up, Morris Phyfe spoke again.

"Madam Chairman, I'd like to review the material Mr. Madsen has prepared for the board and request that I be allotted additional time for questions at the next meeting."

"I'm sure we shall all benefit from reviewing these documents, and it is not my intent to limit questions to this evening." Penny sounded cross. Millicent had already stood up in readiness for her presentation—or assault. Joey sat down. Both the audience at home and those in attendance took a deep breath. Millicent had marched to the front and was staring directly into the camera.

"Madame Chairman, in view of the lateness of the hour, I suggest we adjourn the meeting until next week, placing Miss McKinley's item of business first on our agenda," Sanborn Harrington spoke sternly, in a voice that was oddly languid and nasal, the mark of his Boston Brahmin upbringing. He was determined to carry the day in this one regard, at least.

Bea Hoffman, the only other woman and a moderate, seconded the motion. She felt sorry for Sanborn, who was almost always all by himself when he voted, so whenever she found justification to join him, she did, thus unconsciously fulfilling her Aleford-appointed role. Occasionally, the system worked.

The ayes had it, and if Aleford was slightly disappointed, they were mollified by the prospect of another great show next week. It could have been sweeps time.

Faith was drifting off to sleep after running the scenes through her mind. Millicent had handed her a flyer as she'd left. Millicent had handed one to Joey, too, who'd torn it up into confetti, throwing it into the nearest wastebasket with what could only be described as a snarl.

The paper was still in Faith's coat pocket. Miss Lora and later dear Tom had driven thoughts of what Millicent and her supporters might be up to from Faith's immediate consciousness. She resolved to retrieve it immediately in the morning, or else she'd come across it in a few weeks, the way she did with shopping lists or coupons long expired, similarly shoved away. She also decided to take the kids on a nice long nature walk through the land surrounding the bog—while it was still there.

A spring walk. An April walk. Her mind would not shut down and she was wide awake. April. Chaucer may have thought it "perced the droghte of March" with its "shoures soote," but around Aleford, the month stood for something entirely different.

For those U.S. residents not fortunate enough to live in Massachusetts or Maine, the third Monday in April, Patriots' Day—if it means anything at all—is connected to the Boston Marathon. Since 1896, runners have gathered for the 26-mile 385-yard race from Hopkinton to Boston. Aleford residents, although taking note of the race, especially if someone from town was competing, focus instead on the past. While the runners load up on carbohydrates and listen intently to the weather reports, hoping to hit Heartbreak Hill under sunny but cool skies, Aleford goes to bed content in knowing there has never been a downpour on Patriots' Day and never will be so long as God's in his heaven. The only food crossing local minds is breakfast, specifically the pancake breakfasts run by various churches and civic groups after the reenactment.

The reenactment. That's the whole point of Patriots' Day, a day marked in some way each year, with only a few exceptions, since the whole thing kicked off in 1775, assuring Aleford a place in history, not merely as a footnote but worthy of entire books. The local Patriots' Day events meant many things to many people: a tribute to those fallen on the green that famous morning, a reminder of what they were fighting for, a celebration of continuity and survival, and, to people like Millicent, a great big thank-you for putting Aleford so deservedly on the map. Literally and figuratively, the town was swathed in bunting days before, flags lining Main Street, the green, and hanging from every patriot's window.

Faith had heard of the Boston Marathon before she moved to Aleford, but Patriots' Day itself had come as a surprise and was certainly not something she had associated with other major holidays, such as Thanksgiving. Tom had been quick to fill the gap. For weeks before Faith's first celebration, he primed her with detailed accounts of the battle, names of the participants—with which she was already familiar, since they tended to be on streets, schools, or town buildings, as well—and accounts of the parade in the afternoon. Faith shelved her skepticism and looked forward to waving the red-white-and-blue along with the rest of the town.

That is, until Tom told her she would have to get up at quarter to four in the morning.

"You can't be serious. No one gets up at four o'clock in the morning unless the house is on fire. Are you telling me all Aleford turns out at this hour to begin the revelry?"

"In a word, yes. We Minutemen have breakfast together over at the Catholic church's hall while we're getting ready. The British troops join us there; then we head over to the green around five. The bell in the old belfry starts to ring at five-thirty. We muster and everything gets under way at six."

Tom was a member of the Aleford Minutemen, playing the role of the Reverend Samuel Pennypacker for the reenactment. Faith had been relieved to discover he was not one of the ones killed, although for some time, Samuel had risked being blown sky-high during particularly inflammatory sermons, since a sizable cache of gunpowder was secreted below the pulpit—the same pulpit over which Tom now presided.

The reenactment had been the idea of several history buffs in town some twenty-five years ago, Millicent prominent among them. It had become such a popular event in the Boston area that Chief MacIsaac had to call in his auxiliary police to help with crowd control.

"If the whole thing doesn't start until six, why can't I come a little before then?"

Tom had been crushed. "I thought you'd join me. After the battle, our women and children rush onto the green to tend the wounded, weep, and wail. You have to be in place ahead of time. And you could also ring the bell."

Faith had already rung the historic bell, cast by Millicent's great-great-great-grandfather Ezekiel Revere, in real alarm. It had seemed the sensible thing to do upon finding a still-warm dead body in the old belfry, but many in the town did not agree. The last thing Faith wanted to do was ring the bell, even on the proper occasion. One not-so-sotto voce "Look who's at it again" might send her packing, and she was becoming, if not fond of, accustomed to Aleford.

She focused back on Tom. "All right, I'll be your camp follower."

Tom appeared slightly scandalized, "You'll be my wife, Patience Pennypacker." He leaned over to kiss her. "It's fun. You'll have a great time. Then later we march in the youth parade and the big afternoon parade."

March. Parades. "Period dress, right?"

"Of course. By the end of the day, you'll actually feel like Patience."

Faith knew what she was going to feel like, and it wasn't Patience.

Yet she had done it every year since, dragging out the multitude of petticoats, full-skirted dress, and scratchy linsey-woolsey cape. She'd better check to make sure the moths hadn't gotten to it.

Before she could say "Yankee Doodle," she was asleep and dreaming.

Chapter 2

It was after ten o'clock when Faith remembered to go into the coat closet to retrieve the piece of paper from her pocket that Millicent had thrust at her the night before. Mornings had a way of slipping out from under Faith, despite the fact that the Fairchilds, particularly the children, were all up and about at an ungodly hour. First, Amy would appear, her sleeper bulging with what Faith knew was a sodden night diaper. Tousled, smiling, cute as a button, their daughter at this moment held little charm for her parents and their first words of the day tended to be, "I did it yesterday; it's your turn." It had been Faith's turn this morning and returning to snatch a few more minutes in the cozy warmth of bed, she had not been surprised to find Ben with roughly forty of his stuffed animals occupying her space. Tom was sound asleep.

"Mommy!" he cried in delight. "Can we have waffles for breakfast?" Thoroughly awake now, "Mommy" managed a weak smile. Food. At least he had his priorities straight.

Breakfast over, Tom out the door to the church office, kids

dressed and deposited at school and play group—Faith reminded herself it was her turn Monday, another task that had been known to slip her mind—she stood still and savored the moment. The house was quiet. She could have a peaceful cup of coffee. She could read the newspaper. She could phone a friend. Instead, she went to the closet.

She'd worn her pale gray shearling—a Christmas gift from Tom. The night air had been cold and she was as tired as everyone else in Aleford of bulky down parkas. The House of Bauer and Bean tailoring left much to be desired on Faith's part. Its resulting fashion statement looked more like the House of Michelin. She'd tried to get through her first winter in something less warm and more chic, but she had given in around January, before doing permanent damage to her circulatory system.

The paper she retrieved was bright orange. Its message was spelled out in a variety of eye-catching fonts, complete with shadowing and clip art. What did people do before the advent of computers, Faith wondered, when mere words had to convey one's passion? She regarded Millicent's work. It had all the subtlety of a punch between the eyes.

POW!

PRESERVE OUR WETLANDS!

Aleford, arise! Over two hundred years ago, our ancestors risked their lives for independence. They were not afraid to stand up for what they knew to be right. Desperate times called for desperate measures.

Once again we face a crisis. **Aleford, are you ready!**

The area known as Beecher's Bog is under attack. Only **we** can save this historic habitat from destruction by greedy land gobblers. Only **we** can preserve what's left of Aleford's natural beauty for future generations before it's too late!

POW! will have its first meeting on Friday, April 5th at 7:00 P.M. in Asterbrook Hall. Call Independence 2-7840 for more information.

You couldn't help but admire the woman. As incendiary literature, the broadside was pithy. No names were named, yet Millicent's John Hancock was all over it—as was her phone number. She and several other diehards still used the exchange's full name rather than simply the letters *IN* or the numbers 46. Faith knew New Yorkers like this—stubbornly clinging to Algonquin and Murray Hill. Millicent also hadn't named Joey Madsen, but the "greedy land gobbler" appellation, identifiable to all, was bound to infuriate him. For vastly different reasons, each of them was the self-proclaimed guardian of Aleford: Aleford's quality of life. Whatever that meant. Faith noticed whenever people used the term, it tended to mean the quality of their own particular lives—backyards, streets, wallets—and not necessarily their neighbors', next-door or global.

Still, she'd see if Samantha Miller could baby-sit. Tom wouldn't want to miss the meeting, and Faith had already decided to become a charter member. Fonts or no fonts, POW! had a point. The bog *was* a wonderful place.

Plus, the access road would most assuredly wipe out the parsonage lilac hedge.

An hour later, Faith turned from her recipe notebooks. *Have Faith* was catering a large dinner party on the "real" Patriots' Day, Friday, April 19, and she had been instructed by the hostess to prepare traditional New England favorites. Favorites of whom? had been on the tip of Faith's tongue, but she bit it and was now searching through her files to find palatable fare. A region best known for baked beans, boiled dinners, and scrod was not exactly a culinary paradise on a par, say, with Provence, Tuscany, or New Orleans.

Baked beans—what could she do with them? (See recipe on page 269.) Sweeten them with the thick grade B maple syrup she preferred for its strong flavor? She'd give New England maple syrup. Also Maine lobster.

Or should she spice up the beans with a kind of mustardy barbecue-type sauce? The dinner was to be a buffet, and she'd already decided to serve her version of Yankee pot roast (see recipe on page 268) as the main course. Desserts. She sighed. They no doubt expected Indian pudding, a concoction that always tasted like porridge to Faith no matter how much vanilla ice cream she heaped on top. Besides, it should probably be called Native American pudding, and someone at the party was bound to object. Fortunately, Tom, partial to everything else springing from the rockbound soil of his birth, did not care for it. "Cornmeal does not leap to mind when dessert is mentioned," he'd observed. "Chocolate does." Faith had never heard of any New England chocolate desserts. It was time to get out her venerable 1915 Fannie Farmer, a volume she normally reserved for light reading in bed due to its wonderful photographic illustrations—a doily for every dish—and the recipes. She never tired of reading about things like Syracuse Five o'clock Tea (five o'clock tea sweetened with red or white rock candy—was Syracuse known for its sweet tooth?), Mock Sausages with Fried Apple Rings (the sausages were made of lima beans), and Lobster Boats (complete with instructions for sails made of rice paper). Then there were Little Brahmins—cooked rice flavored with catsup, shaped into the form of chickens, crumbed, and deep-fried. The photograph showed them nestled on a bed of parsley. One is facing in the opposite direction from the rest, the poultry equivalent of a black sheep, or an obscure reference to J. P. Marquand? Faith also ardently subscribed to Mrs. Farmer's introductory quotation: "We grow like what we eat; Bad food depresses, good food exalts us like an inspiration." Usage aside, Faith found comfort in the words and had suggested more than once to Pix, who did things like this, that an embroidered hanging for the Fairchild kitchen would not be ill received. Fannie would have something Faith could use for dessert.

She'd been completely concentrating on her work, or so she

thought, but she hadn't accomplished much and was feeling out of sorts. There really wasn't any reason why she should be. Her life was going well. Second children were supposed to be more easygoing than firsts, although Faith had greeted this remark with the same skepticism she'd rightly reserved for second deliveries being easier. But this maxim was proving true. Amy slept through the night—technically, it *was* morning when she got up and out—as opposed to Ben. He had nearly sent them round the bend with his nocturnal wanderings once he'd mastered the parent-defying art of climbing out of the crib.

Amy had also virtually toilet-trained herself, needing only the diaper at night, and was thereby saving them enough money in Huggies so that college tuition was once more a possibility. She had an interesting and sunny temperament, although, as Ben had been at the same age, she was a child of few words—approximately fifteen at the moment. Faith attributed this to her own parental failure to offer adequate stimulation. She could read to her children endlessly, but talking to someone who did not talk back or replied with one word, occasionally two, as in "Want Daddy," was not her idea of stimulating conversation. She firmly classified it with playing most games. Happily, Tom was good at that and could spend hours spinning spinners and moving brightly colored pieces about in circles with Ben. Watching them, Faith had had to concede that there are some things that passeth all understanding.

No, it was not her family. Like Amy, Ben was as easy as a child could be, which is to say he had the capacity to consume most of the oxygen in the room yet was willing to share when reminded. As for Tom, husbands are never easy, but she loved him very much and that went a long way, especially when the seat was left up in the middle of the night.

The scene with Miss Lora flashed in front of her. What would she do if Tom really did have an affair? Never mind the logistics.

He barely had time to brush his teeth, what with parish duties and family life. She'd warned him once when Amy's bout with colic coincided with Ben's discovery of how to release the car's emergency brake that if they ever divorced, he'd have to take the kids, any pets they might acquire, as well as the cottage in Maine. If she was getting out, she wanted *out.* He'd laughed, but not heartily. He knew she meant it.

But she had been jealous when she'd seen another woman in Tom's arms. And Lora Deane was not exactly a threat. When Faith had dropped Ben off this morning, the teacher had a voluminous smock over what appeared to be adult-sized Osh-Kosh overalls and an old turtleneck. No, Faith wasn't seriously worried about Tom and any possible dalliance along Sesame Street. She was, however, worried about Lora herself.

Stalked, being harmed, or even being murdered by an ex turned up in the news every day. She hoped that Lora really was going to speak to her half sister immediately. If Joey was eliminated, as Faith suspected he would be, then they could turn their attention to Brad Hallowell before it was too late. It might make sense to find out more about him now. Faith remembered she'd said as much to Lora last night.

Brad had been at the selectmen's meeting, standing in the back of the room. Faith had wondered what he was doing there. Joey's presentation had been the third and last item on the agenda. Brad had certainly not come to hear the Minuteman Café's request for permission to change the color of its awning from green to maroon when it ordered a new one. Nor would he have been interested in Norma Parkington's spirited reading of the most recent letter from Aleford's sister city in Iceland, Hafnarfjördur. So far, Hafnarfjördur officials had been to Aleford, but Town Meeting systematically voted down a request for funds for a similar junket by Aleford officials. Said officials did not seem to mind much, although, as Millicent tartly observed, if Aleford were twinned with Paris, France, they'd find the money. She was of the belief that an exchange meant an exchange and Aleford should return the call, albeit at said officials' personal expense.

Brad must have been at the meeting to hear Joey, but didn't the young man have better, more interesting things to do with his time? Faith certainly had had at his age, which, after all, wasn't that long ago. She closed her recipe books and decided to talk to Pix. Pix had grown up in Aleford and was seemingly born with all ten of her capable fingers in various town pies. Millicent might know who everybody in town was, and their mothers and fathers before them, but Pix knew what they were doing. Faith went to the phone.

"Faith! I'm so glad you called. I was about to call you. Can you come over for a quick cup of coffee? I know you have to pick up the kids soon."

"I'd love to—and I have something to ask you, too." Faith wanted to be sure she got equal time. Pix might be her dearest friend, but she could exhibit a single-minded sense of purpose that sometimes prevented getting a word in edgewise.

When Faith arrived at the Millers' doorstep, it appeared that today might be one of those days. Pix, normally unflappable, was in a quandary about not one but two of her children. The oldest, Mark, had been safely launched, a college sophomore majoring in political science, with his sights set on Washington. This did cause Pix an occasional twinge. "You don't think he wants to be president, do you?" she'd asked Faith once. "I would make such a dreadful campaigner. All those speeches and dinners. I don't know how Rose Kennedy ever did it." Pix had no doubt that if Mark did aspire to the Oval Office, it was his for the asking. No, today Pix was not worried about finding a pair of pumps that matched her purse in a wardrobe consisting mainly of clogs and denim wraparound skirts.

It was Samantha, a high school senior, and Danny, a seventh grader, who were on her mind today.

The Millers' kitchen had been remodeled when they moved into the Federal brick house many years ago. The spacious room was geared more to the family's various pursuits than to food preparation. Faith correctly assumed the stove, refrigerator, and so on were categorized more as "things that go in a kitchen" than "things we want to use." There was plenty of room to sit and chat—if you removed the hockey skates or quilt Pix was piecing. Pix now worked part-time for Faith, keeping the books and handling the ordering. She had agreed to this employment with the strict understanding that she would not be expected to do any food preparation whatsoever. "I could possibly peel carrots or potatoes," she'd said, "But then I might do them wrong." Pix's kitchen cabinets tended to be stocked with things that had the word *Helper* in the title. Yet the house always smelled of freshly baked bread—and, of course, coffee. The coffee, Faith could see. The bread smell mystified her. Pix offered her a steaming mug, pretty much a reflex action, cleared a pile of magazines she'd been meaning to read since last year, and the two of them sunk into the comfortable old sofa that overlooked the yard. One of the dogs immediately lumbered over to join them. Pix made more room.

Faith correctly guessed that any conversation about Samantha must involve college. She was right.

"Has Samantha heard from all her schools yet?" Faith had already been through the application process, during which Samantha had winnowed her choices from sixty down to fifteen at her father's insistence. "We could pay her freshman tuition with what it would cost in application fees if I let her apply everywhere she wants," he'd told the Fairchilds.

"That's the problem. She's heard from every place except Brown and Wellesley." Samantha was not only an extremely good student, but also something of a softball legend at Aleford High. Little kids asked her to sign autographs after games.

"And?"

"She's gotten into all of them." Pix sounded as if she'd just heard that one of the Miller family's golden retrievers had heartworm—and it didn't get much worse than that.

"But that's terrific! Congratulations!"

"Oh well, yes, but how is she going to make up her mind? Coaches are calling her. Her friends keep giving her advice. One day, she's definitely going to Stanford—which is too far away—the next it's Bowdoin, because of marine biology." Unlike her politically minded brother, Samantha's future constituency consisted of the inhabitants of tide pools.

"I thought she wanted to go to Brown, continue the family tradition." Pix had gone to Pembroke and her husband, Sam, to Brown. They'd also grown up together in Aleford. Thinking of this, Faith consoled her friend. "At least she's not involved with anybody, so she can make an independent choice. You and Sam are unique. Most people I know who went to the same schools as their high school honeys had broken up by the end of Orientation Week."

"Sam and I don't want to say too much, or too little. It would be nice if she went to Brown, but only if it's what *she* wants."

"Knowing Samantha, I don't think you have to worry about that. Now tell me quickly what's going on with Danny, because I want you to tell me everything you know about Brad Hallowell."

Pix was immediately diverted, as Faith hoped she might be.

"Brad Hallowell? Why do you want to know about him? What's going on, Faith?"

Pix looked her friend squarely in the eye. If Faith had ferreted out some new intrigue in Aleford, Pix didn't want to be left out. Faith had been far away when Pix had solved a murder up on Sanpere

Island, off the coast of Maine, last summer. She felt that she had proved herself. If only her family would take up less time and mental energy!

"I can't go into it yet. It was told to us in confidence. As soon as I can, I will."

"Hmmm, 'us,' you and Tom, I assume. A parishioner? Well, all right. I understand, but I'm afraid I can't help you too much. You really should be talking to Millicent."

"Millicent!"

"Yes, Brad Hallowell is POW!'s most loyal follower. You do know what POW! is, right?"

"Preserve Our Wetlands!—I got the leaflet last night as I was leaving the selectmen's meeting."

"I thought I saw the back of your head on TV. I wish I had been there in person, but Danny had so much homework, and if I don't sit with him, it doesn't get done. I just caught the tail end. Maybe next week."

Before Faith lost her advantage, she pressed Pix further. "But don't you know any more about Brad?"

"His parents seem nice. His mother is an Evergreen." Faith knew this meant a member of the Aleford Garden Club and did not refer to a possibly more exotic pedigree. "I do have the feeling that they regard Brad as someone from another planet. She's often said things like, 'I don't know where he came from.' Of course, many parents feel this way," Pix added.

"Then what do you think she means? Has he ever been in trouble—with the police, for instance?"

"Not to my knowledge, but they haven't lived here all that long, and he was in college until he moved home last year." Children were doing that with distressing frequency these days, Faith noted. Pix, on the other hand, would greet a returning nestling with a brass band. She still occasionally forgot and set a place for Mark at dinner.

"I think she's referring to his interest in computers," Pix commented. "He's always been some kind of whiz kid, and his company sends him all over the world as a consultant. She told us once that he's had an eight hundred number since he was nineteen and carries a beeper so if someone needs help with a program they can reach him day or night. He spends all his free time cruising the Internet. Samantha explained it to me."

Faith did know all about the Internet. Her sister had tried to convince her to hook up and get recipes that way. When Faith had discovered how much it would cost her to learn the secret of foolproof marshmallow rainbow Jell-O, that particular moment's offering, she politely declined. Although she'd heard a rumor that Julia might be posting her secrets.

So Brad was a hacker. He would certainly know about phones, but then whoever was threatening Lora only had to know how to dial.

"Besides computers, he's very, very ecologically minded. When Millicent found that out, she also probably figured he could do all their bulletins. You know Millicent."

Faith did.

Pix continued to talk. As Faith had expected, she had quite a bit of information. "He was seeing Lora Deane, but she broke it off. His mother was very upset. For one thing, it had been an interest in something that did not have a keyboard. But, even more, she was outraged that anyone would reject her perfect son. She had a few tight-lipped things to say about Lora."

"Did she indicate how Brad was taking it?"

"Very hard—and angry. 'I hate to see the boy like this,' she told us. He was taking long walks in Beecher's Bog; maybe that's what got him started with POW! And Maureen Farmer told me he put his fist through his bedroom wall, or at least made a hole in it."

"How on earth did she find that out?" Maureen lived on the opposite side of town.

"Same cleaners. They were there when it happened, and they arrived at Maureen's house pretty shaken."

This act, coupled with the destruction of the cold frames, indicated the kind of temper that could goad him into making the calls. Faith was beginning to form a picture of an adored child who was also used to praise and success in his adult life. A volatile nature. Someone who became passionately committed to various causes. She remembered Lora's remark about the field mice.

"He *is* good-looking. Samantha had quite a crush on him in the beginning of the year. He was helping out in the computer lab at school."

Faith didn't want to hear about Brad's good looks or good works. She decided she'd try to sit next to him at Friday's POW! meeting and gently plumb his depths. She'd mention Lora, as Ben's teacher, and watch his reaction. If all went according to plan, Brad Hallowell could be in Tom's study Saturday morning having the fear of God and Charley MacIsaac instilled, and then Lora's troubles would be over.

"Now what's going on with Danny?" Fair was fair.

As Faith crossed the Millers' yard back to the parsonage, she wondered if she might be able to get a moment alone with Miss Lora. She doubted it. Pickup time at the nursery school was chaotic at best. If Ben wasn't waving a dripping-wet finger painting, he'd have a fragile toothpick construction that would demand more care than a Fabergé egg. Lora would be in the thick of things as every mother sought a word. The two questions Faith wanted to ask—Have you received any more threatening calls? and Did your boyfriend ever hit you?—would not go unnoticed among "How was

Bryant at circle time?" and "Does Katie have her blankie?"

She was right. Miss Lora was surrounded by a swarm of children and mothers, yet she did manage to give Faith a knowing look and say, "I'm on my way to my sister's. You know, the one with the new baby." If the other mothers noticed that the last few words were enunciated rather precisely, as if they were the day's password to get past the guard, they did not let on. Faith nodded and replied in kind, "Let me know how the baby's doing. Tom and I are eager to hear."

Feeling vaguely like the spy about to go out into the cold, Faith scooped up Ben and today's project—a chalk drawing that had already left telling smudges all over his face, hands, and clothes and would soon, no doubt, on hers. They would just be on time to pick up Amy. Some of the mothers in the play group were more relaxed about hours than others. Today's was not one of them. Early in the fall, Ben had started calling her "The Grouchy Ladybug," after the character in the book, and Faith had given up correcting him. It had become shortened to Ladybug and she'd adopted it herself. "We'd better hurry, or the Ladybug will be annoyed," she told him.

Both Faith and Tom were in attendance at POW!'s first meeting on Friday night. In fact, much of Aleford was there. Asterbrook Hall was packed. People were standing at the rear and along the sides of the basement in the town hall.

"How many people do you think are here to save the bog and how many to see what's going on?" Faith asked Tom.

"About fifty-fifty. You have noticed that the Deanes are conspicuously absent."

"Well, of course, but someone will report back, I'm sure."

Tom nodded. "Look, Millicent is going up onstage."

The room quieted instantly. "Thank God she tends to use her

power for good," Faith whispered to her husband. He crossed his fingers in reply.

Millicent was wearing the red Pendleton suit she normally reserved for special occasions, so Faith knew how serious the moment was. The brass buttons had lost a bit of their luster and the seat had bagged out long ago, but as raiment went, it was perfect.

"You all know why we're here." Millicent didn't need a microphone. Her voice reverberated out the door and up onto Main Street.

"If we don't put a stop to these developers, Aleford might just as well be Boston. They'll be putting up high-rises on the green next!"

There were rumblings of agreement.

"Unfortunately, Town Meeting has never passed an ordinance limiting the size of a house in relation to the square footage of the land it sits on or the number of houses in a subdivision. We'd have had a possible out if they had. Mr. Madsen has to build quite a large number of these houses in order to turn a profit."

Faith couldn't help but remember that when this had come up the last time, Millicent had been on the side of individual freedom and opposed the restriction along with virtually everyone else. But then, who could predict the future?

"Madsen is entirely within his rights. His plans are up-to-code and there is no way to stop him on those grounds."

The audience looked glum.

"Nor do I think we can appeal to the man's better nature."

Nobody needed subtitles on this one. The implication was made clear by her scornful tone of voice. For one swift moment, Faith actually felt sorry for Joey. He wasn't even here to defend himself.

"Fortunately, I was able to devise a strategy that may circumvent all this. But it will take hard work on all our parts. Are you willing?"

She had them eating out of the palm of her hand and there were several yesses shouted out, a most unusual display of spontaneity for Aleford.

"First of all, we have to reconvene Town Meeting. The easiest way would be to get the board of selectmen to do it, but I don't think we can count on that."

Penny Bartlett was the only member of the board in the audience, and from the look on her face, she was clearly sorry she hadn't stayed home and deadheaded her African violets.

"Which means we have to collect signatures. Sheets and clipboards with instructions are on the table at the back of the room for you to take as you leave. I don't have to tell you speed is of the absolute essence here! The timing is particularly bad, since Patriots' Day is less than two weeks away. I don't want to point a finger . . ."

Clearly, however, she did, and there wasn't a person in the room who didn't believe that Joey Madsen was trying to slip his plan through at Aleford's busiest time of year, thinking everyone would be sufficiently occupied elsewhere to organize any opposition. It hadn't occurred to Faith, but if this was what he was doing, it was pretty smart. Only, he might not have sufficiently gauged the enemy, like the poor British retreating from Concord. Millicent could run any number of things at once.

"But what do you expect Town Meeting to do?" It was the Town Meeting moderator, Susan Waters, and certainly a reasonable query.

Millicent frowned. "I was about to get to that, Susan dear."

Susan sat down, somewhat paler than she'd been upon rising. Maybe it was the way Millicent had uttered the word *dear.*

"Going over town records in the library recently, I came across an account of the passage of two ordinances that will help us. One involves the Historic Commission. It can vote to delay, and I quote, 'the significant alteration in character,' unquote, of any property falling within the Historic District until Town Meeting is satisfied that said alterations will not, and I quote again, 'significantly impact the district.' Now"—she turned a beady eye on poor Susan, impaling her in her seat—"I know Beecher's Bog is not in the Historic District, but the proposed access road between First Parish and the parsonage is." This last word was uttered triumphantly. Faith found her spirits rising.

"Once we have the special session of Town Meeting, it can vote on this and the next ordinance I uncovered. We shouldn't have any trouble getting these introduced and voted upon." Millicent was herself a Town Meeting member, so no trouble at all. She paused for effect. The whole room waited breathlessly. "In 1842, our ancestors had the prescience to pass an article that gives Town Meeting the power to block any proposal it feels would be, and I quote, 'detrimental to the quality of life in Aleford.' "

There it was again, Faith thought, "quality of life." It was obviously an article—someone's whim, or worse—that had been forgotten as soon as it passed, only to surface some 150 years later to feed the flames of what was going to be one of the biggest battles Aleford had witnessed since the long-ago events on the green.

A man in a dark business suit got up and left. It was Joey Madsen's wan-faced lawyer. He was reaching in his pocket—for his cellular phone, no doubt. Joey and Millicent were cut from the same cloth: Forewarned is forearmed.

Faith was both relieved and distressed. The bog would probably get saved, but it was not going to be a pleasant spring in Aleford.

"Now, I'm going to introduce some of my fellow committee members, who will be circulating sign-up sheets. Please indicate when you are available to leaflet, collect signatures, and don't forget your phone numbers." Millicent had several people rise from the audience as she called their names.

"And Brad Hallowell, who has graciously donated his time and expertise with computers to print the campaign literature."

Brad stood up. Faith took a good hard look at him. She had not been able to sit next to him. He was in the middle of a row, surrounded, when the Fairchilds came in. She'd have to figure out another way to talk with him. Computer advice? As Pix had said, he was attractive and definitely crush material for teenage girls—and their older sisters, too. He had thick black hair, pulled to the nape of his neck in a small ponytail. His eyes were deep brown. He was tall and broad-shouldered and wore a flannel shirt over a T-shirt and jeans. He didn't look like a stalker or like someone who might physically abuse his girlfriend. But then, the whole point was that such people seldom did. It was the boy next door, or the husband lying beside one in bed—not a crazed lunatic. She suddenly felt cold and realized someone had opened a window.

"Can we go now?"

Tom was getting restless. She tried to remember if there was a Celtics game on tonight. She had trouble keeping the sports seasons straight. Everything seemed to continue year-round.

"Wait, I don't want to be the only ones leaving."

Millicent wasn't finished. "The last two POW! members I'd like you to meet are welcome for their dedication to the cause and also for their extensive knowledge of the area in question. Come on, Margaret and Nelson, stand up. Margaret and Nelson Batcheldor!" It crossed Faith's mind that Millicent could have made a career for herself as a game-show hostess.

Margaret and Nelson, a childless middle-aged couple, were members of First Parish. Nelson worked as a reference librarian in Byford, and, as an amateur woodworker, he occasionally took small carpentry jobs. He'd spent the previous fall putting in shelves and cabinets for the preschool. Miss Lora was pushing for a playhouse next. Margaret devoted herself to birding, as well as a number of community activities. But birding was her true avocation, and she often came to church with her binoculars slung around her neck the way other women wore pearls. The Batcheldors looked much alike, either because of many years spent together or due to the simple Prince Valiant hairstyle each sported. Faith had the uncomfortable feeling they probably cut each other's hair—same bowl.

"To close our meeting, we have a real treat. Nelson and Margaret are going to show slides of the bog that they've taken over the years. When you see these, you will know exactly what we're fighting for!"

The Batcheldors and their neighbor, Ted Scott, struggled to the front, carrying a screen and several carousels filled with slides that Margaret started loading into the projector. The lights went off and a slightly out-of-focus frog face appeared. Tom nudged Faith and they ducked out.

As they left, they could hear Nelson's voice droning on. Margaret provided a kind of counterpoint, breaking in with a somewhat-desperate cry, "Extinct is forever! These eastern spadefoot toads used to be as common as dirt. Now we're lucky to see one at all. Who will save them if we don't!"

Walking hand in hand down Main Street toward the parsonage, the Fairchilds had the carefree, slightly hilarious feeling escape engenders. "Race you," Tom challenged. Faith looked around. Aleford had taken its toll. If it had been Eighth Avenue, she wouldn't have cared. But they were alone, so she took off, and they collapsed, laughing, in a heap next to the flagpole on the Common.

When Faith had caught her breath, she asked, "What did you think of the meeting?"

"Millie was in fine form," Tom was one of the few people allowed to use the diminutive. "It was pretty much as I expected, except for those old bylaws. I'd be pretty worried if I was Joey."

"Yes, especially since he's already spent so much money on surveys, lawyers. He almost has to keep fighting to try to recoup his loss."

Tom agreed, "And the Deanes still haven't sold that big house on Whipple Hill Road. You know the one."

Faith did. It was around the corner, and she'd been watching it go up with the children. The construction company had been able to do a considerable amount of work during a freak February thaw, but the house was still nowhere near completion. It was a slightly scaled-down version of what Joey was going to put up in Alefordiana. The neighbors had been aghast at its size. "Something of a cross between Tara and the Flying Dutchman," one had complained to Faith as they stood gazing at it silhouetted against the horizon. It was the house Lora had mentioned, and Faith was pretty sure that every abutter had been at tonight's meeting. They hadn't been able to do anything about the Whipple Hill house, but blocking Alefordiana was a way to get back at Joey.

"Tom, this does have the potential for becoming extremely ugly, doesn't it?"

"I think it already is. Anything that polarizes the town like this is bad."

"I feel a sermon coming on," Faith remarked.

"Well then, I wish you'd write it." The Reverend Fairchild tended to get a little testy on Friday nights.

Faith stood up and straightened her skirt. In deference to the event, she'd changed. Tom looked at her approvingly. "My father said he'd never thought short skirts would come back in his lifetime, which just goes to show . . ."

"It just goes to show you need to have faith," she said, well aware of her atrocious pun, "and buy good clothes. If you wait long enough, everything comes back in style—even things that were awful the first time around, like go-go boots and fringed vests."

"How much did that tiny little skirt cost, anyway?" Tom asked, eying the black wool Donna Karan swath Faith had now adjusted to her satisfaction.

"None of your business. Besides, Amy will probably be able to use it. Now, shall we go home?"

"Given that the sole place open in Aleford at this hour is Patriot Drug, and that only for fifteen minutes more, I'd say yes."

Faith looped her arm through Tom's. "It may not be the Stork Club, but I think I can find a nice bottle of something Chez Nous. And if we're lucky, there won't be any floor show."

Saturday was always the most relaxed day of the week. No morning rush. True, Tom was usually putting the finishing touches on his sermon, but he tried hard to finish it early in the day.

It was cold but sunny. The only clouds in the bright blue sky were appropriately white and puffy. Faith decided she would take the kids for that walk through the bog. They weren't into mud season yet, so she didn't have to fear that someone's tiny foot might get trapped in the ooze. The only terror the bog might hold today was prickly brush. By the time they got back, Tom would be done and they could do something.

Easter had been early this year. Somehow, holidays were always early or late, never on time. Tom had been flat-out since Fat Tuesday, the season culminating in last weekend's Easter marathon. She knew he was pretty drained and having trouble with this week's sermon. As he put it, after the congregation has pushed the rafters almost through the roof with "Christ the Lord Is Ris'n Today," all else pales for the next few weeks.

Taking each child by the hand, she set off, Tom waving cheerfully from the window. Amy was wearing shiny yellow boots with duck-shaped toes; Ben's were green with frogs. Faith felt like a greeting card.

"Now, let's look for signs of spring," she told the children.

"Signs of spring, check," Ben said. He'd recently adopted this way of speaking from whom Faith knew not.

"Check," said Amy, bringing the current word count to sixteen. Faith felt they'd made a good start.

Despite the cold wind that swept across them at intervals, the sun shone steadily and they did find some bright green growing things under last year's dried grasses. Just before they were into the bog proper, Ben discovered a patch of snowdrops. "I want to pick them for you, Mom," he cried.

"Thank you, sweetie," his mother replied. Sons were so nice. "But we don't pick wildflowers. We leave them to grow where they belong, and also so other people can enjoy them."

Ben seemed satisfied, and they continued on in search of pussy willows. The approach to the bog passed through a densely wooded patch. Thick vines hung from the still-leafless deciduous trees. Small pines were struggling to compete. Amy pulled back, and Faith was surprised to see apprehension on her daughter's face.

"Noooo?" Amy asked hopefully.

Faith picked her up. "There's nothing to be afraid of. Mommy will hold you. There are so many trees, the sun has a hard time peeking through. It will be a cool place to be in the summer." If Joey's chain saws haven't leveled it, Faith thought dismally.

"I'm not scared of a bunch of trees," Ben boasted. "Amy is such a baby."

"She *is* a baby," Faith reminded him.

Ben gave her a patient look. "That's what I said."

Faith decided to let it go. She was starting to train early for adolescence. Choosing one's battlegrounds was an acquired skill.

" 'The woods are lovely, dark and deep,' " she quoted from Frost, even though there was no snow, nor did she have a horse. She did, however, have many promises to keep. Amy was getting heavy; Faith took a deep breath—or it may have been a sigh—and hitched her up higher.

"What's that noise?" Ben grabbed the corner of Faith's jacket.

"I don't hear anything." Her respiration hadn't been that loud. "Probably an animal—a squirrel, or maybe even a deer."

Then she heard it, too. Definitely some creature was rustling in the leaves—a good-sized creature.

"Don't move, children," she whispered. "Maybe we can see it."

Like startled deer themselves, the Fairchilds froze in position, and such was the family grouping that presented itself to the two human creatures who came crashing through the brush. Human creatures in quasi-military dress with black ski masks pulled over their faces. For an instant, the whole forest stood still; then Amy opened her mouth and wailed. Quickly, the couple removed their headgear.

It was the Batcheldors.

Hugging her daughter tightly and repeating that everything was all right, while Ben twisted her jacket so tightly it began to resemble a tourniquet, Faith said shakily, "Goodness, Margaret and Nelson. Out for a walk?"

What she wanted to ask was what on earth were they doing out here dressed like *Rambo* extras, but she opted for a return to normalcy as fast as possible for the sake of the kids.

"Oh, yes," Margaret replied cheerily in the birdlike tones she seemed to have copied from the confusing fall warblers. "Such a lovely day, and we were up with the sun." She waved her binoculars at Ben. "He's certainly old enough to start his life list. I was three when Mother started me on mine."

Faith knew from Pix that said list referred to birds spotted and not some monstrous "To Do" resolutions or other New England folkway. She also knew if Ben was going to start said list, it was going to have to be with another mother or be limited to birds that could be spotted after nine o'clock.

"Nippy today." Nelson smiled at the children and waved the woolen helmet, so recently the object of fear. It worked again. Amy started to wimper. Having removed their hats, the couple still looked bizarre—hair standing on end from the static electricity and deep red circles around the eyes and mouth where the elastic had been too tight. Faith could feel Amy's body get rigid in preparation for another ninety-decibel eruption.

Faith quickly took refuge in the mother's standby, "I think the children are getting tired. We've been out for quite a while." Before Ben, who had been blessed—or cursed—with total honesty, could point out, as he was wont to do, that they had just started, Faith said good-bye.

Margaret had found a nest and was focusing her binoculars. She chirped something unintelligible, presumably at the Fairchilds. Nelson waved good-bye with another of his smiles, which seemed destined to have the opposite effect on her children, and Faith turned the troops about-face. She hoped Ben's clear, high-pitched queries a few yards later did not float back to the two bird-watchers, "But we just came. Why are we going back? I'm not tired. Why did you say we were tired? Amy doesn't look tired. You're not tired, are you, Amy? Why did you say we'd been out here quite a while? It doesn't feel like quite a while to me."

Faith stopped and put Amy on her own two feet.

"Believe me, it has been quite a while and *I'm* tired."

"Then you should have—"

Faith gave her son a look he knew, and he fell to studying the ground, kicking at small hummocks, muttering, "I'm not the tired one."

Faith hoped Tom had finished his sermon.

He had, and they decided to go to the Audubon Society's Drumlin Farm in nearby Lincoln after Amy's nap. Ben brightened up at the prospect of pigs and Faith was able to settle him in his bed with a book after lunch. She went back downstairs and found Tom putting the food away.

"I still can't figure out what Margaret and Nelson were up to," she said. The encounter with the Batcheldors had been the prime topic of lunch conversation, introduced by Ben as soon as he saw his father emerge from the study. Faith had endeavored to downplay the whole event, while punctuating the salient details with various dramatic facial expressions whenever the kids became distracted by the tricolored fusili with Gorgonzola sauce she'd made, Ben's totally unaccountable favorite.

"Are you sure they were ski masks, not woolen hats pulled down low?" Tom asked.

"Of course I'm sure. I thought we had stumbled into the middle of some crazed neo-Nazi maneuvers. When they got close, I could see they weren't wearing fatigues, but they were all in green. Now knowing how nuts Margaret is, I wouldn't put it past her to dress up like a particular bird she was hoping to add to her list, the olive-colored, black-capped bog sucker or some such thing. But given the mood of the meeting last night, I don't think they were birding today."

"But what?" Tom looked extremely troubled. Nelson Batcheldor was a member of the Vestry.

"Maybe they're planning some way to blow up the bog if Joey goes ahead with his plans."

"How would that help them?"

"I don't know, Tom. This is all supposition, and as far as I could tell, the only thing resembling a weapon was Margaret's heavy set of binoculars. Unless Nelson's camera is one of those James Bond types."

"You were in the woods, so they were coming from the bog itself. Maybe they're stockpiling things. Oh, this is too crazy. We know they're a little eccentric." Tom looked at Faith and amended his words, "Well, very eccentric, and they probably dress like that for bird-watching all the time. We've just never seen them before. And it was cold early this morning. I would have worn a ski mask, too, if I'd been out."

"You don't have a mask like that. Only robbers do. In fact, I wonder where you'd even get one." Faith was getting sidetracked into a realm of speculation she'd explored before. You're about to engage in criminal activity. Where do you shop? Walk into housewares at Jordan Marsh and ask for a good, long, sharp kitchen knife? And these masks. *Soldier of Fortune* mail order? For those necessities not covered by the Victoria's Secret catalog? She was about to expound on all this when the phone rang.

Faith answered it, and whatever she had planned to say about the Batcheldors' proclivities went clear out of her mind.

It was Pix and she was definitely agitated.

"Faith, is Tom home? I've got to talk to you both right away! You know Sam's in California; otherwise I wouldn't bother you."

This didn't sound either college- or middle school–related.

"What is it? What's happened?" Faith asked anxiously.

"I've just gotten a poison-pen letter," Pix answered, and burst into tears.

Chapter 3

Pix Miller was not a woman who cried without provocation—funerals, illnesses, seeing *The Yearling* once again. As soon as Pix had arrived, Faith put her arm around her friend and led her to the couch with only a fleeting thought to the number of females who seemed to be drenching the parsonage with their tears lately.

"It's the shock, I suppose." Pix reached around in her pocket, produced a crumpled handkerchief, and dabbed her eyes. "I was opening the mail and there was this thin envelope, and at first I thought, Oh dear, Samantha's been rejected. Then I noticed there wasn't a return address, and I opened it and . . . well, here it is."

She handed the envelope, which she had clutched in her other hand, to Faith. Tom leaned over the back of the couch, reading over his wife's shoulder. It was a plain white business envelope addressed in ballpoint pen, block letters, to "Mrs. Samuel Miller," with the address.

Faith paused and put the envelope down. "It's hard to get prints from paper, but I think we should be careful anyway." She went into the kitchen and returned with a clean dust cloth, which she used to hold the paper by one corner as she eased it out of the envelope.

There was no doubt. It was venomous—a classic of its sort, the letters neatly cut from magazines and newspapers. Occasionally, the writer had been fortunate enough to find an entire word. A few of the pieces were colored type, producing a collage effect. But it was not a work of art.

> "CINDY" 'S NOT DEAD. SAM IS BETRAYING YOU. DON'T TRUST YOUR HUSBAND.
>
> A FRIEND

"I know one thing"—Pix had given her eyes one final swipe and was giving an award-winning performance of her old self—"whoever wrote this horrible letter is certainly *not* a friend. The idea!"

Faith was staring at the letter.

"It really is strangely worded—'A friend' . . . 'betraying.' As if the person has some sort of quirky Victorian manual on how to write nasty letters—or watches a lot of daytime TV. And of course you don't believe it," Faith quickly reassured Pix.

Sam Miller had, in fact, had one brief, disastrous affair during his particularly bumpy ride into middle age, but that had been several years ago. The young woman, Cindy, with whom Sam had chosen to dally had later ended up as a corpse in Aleford's own historic belfry, discovered, in fact, by Faith. The suggestion of current adultery was horrible by itself. Bringing up the murder was particularly loathsome.

"Not for a minute," Pix said staunchly. "Still, I wish he was home." Pix was incapable of lying. Coupled with her tendency to speak her mind, it often resulted in revealing self-confession. Faith did not have this problem.

Tom sat down on Pix's other side and took her hand. "There's no question that Sam is totally devoted—and faithful—to you. But letters like this are intended to plant seeds of doubt. It's only natural to want him right here. When will he be back?"

"Tomorrow night. But don't worry. Of course I want to look him straight in the eye, but even more, I just want him home. Who would do this to us?"

"That's what we should be talking about." Faith thought it was time to get down to business. If they began to dwell too much on Sam, Pix would get weepy again and water those malicious seeds Tom had mentioned. "Do you have any idea at all?"

Pix shook her head slowly. "I never thought I had any enemies. You know, Tom, when you preached that sermon, 'Who Is My Enemy?' I thought it was going to be about what we fight against in ourselves. Oh, I agreed with what you said, that we can become our enemy—the thief, the slanderer, now the poison-pen wielder—if we don't forgive him, yet I truly can't think of anyone who would want to harm me."

Faith had to agree. Pix was one of the best-liked people in Aleford and one of the few about whom Faith had never heard a negative word. It was astonishing. Still volunteering in all sorts of organizations her children had outgrown—Pix had only recently stepped down as head of the cookie drive for the Girl Scouts, even though Samantha's uniform probably wouldn't even fit over her head—Pix was the person Aleford called for help, ideas, and comfort. Which reminded Faith, who said, "I heard you were running St. Theresa's blood drive this year? Are you switching pews?"

"My friend Martha Stanley was doing it, but you know she's scheduled for a hip replacement and she couldn't—"

"Find anybody else." Faith finished it up for her and they laughed. It was a welcome diversion.

Tom moved them back on track. Although he'd been pleased that someone not only remembered the title of one of his sermons, but had listened. Still they were ranging a bit far afield. "The point is that although we'd be hard put to come up with anyone who had a grudge against you, or Sam, you *did* get the letter, and the first thing we have to do is tell Charley. Do you want to call him or would you like me to?"

The offending object was on the walnut coffee table in front of them, next to a clear glass vase of anemones just past their peak—elongated stems with petals splayed out in bright silk colors. A bowl of pears completed the still life. The letter looked as out of place as a porno magazine.

"You, please," Pix said promptly, eyeing the missive with extreme distaste. "I don't mind Charley knowing. I suppose it is a police matter, but I'd just as soon not talk about it."

Faith thought it impolitic to mention that the moment Charley was on the scene she'd have to do a lot of talking. "How about a cup of coffee or tea while Tom is calling. Or are you hungry? Did you have lunch?"

Pix, a tall woman with a healthy appetite looked surprised. Certainly she'd had lunch, as had the rest of Aleford—at noon when you were supposed to, but coffee sounded good. "I'd love a cup of coffee, if it's made."

Faith went out to start a fresh pot and put some molasses spice cookies on a plate while she was waiting for the water to get hot. Chief MacIsaac might come here rather than meet them down at the station. She added more cookies.

"Charley's on his way," Tom told her when she brought the tray into the living room.

Pix bit into a cookie, "Where are the kids?" she asked. She'd been so involved in her own problem that she'd forgotten about the younger Fairchilds, as much a part of the parsonage landscape as her children—and she counted the dogs—were of hers next door.

"Amy's still taking a good long nap in the afternoon and Ben's upstairs resting. He's been awfully quiet, which either means he's dropped off, too, or he's taking apart the VCR." At the moment with no audible sounds, Faith was letting well enough, or the opposite, alone.

The doorbell rang. Charley must have left as soon as he hung up the phone.

"So you've gotten one, too, Pix," he said as he walked toward the plate of cookies.

Faith was oddly relieved. Pix wasn't the only one. Find the common thread linking the recipients and they'd have their noxious correspondent.

"Who else?" she asked.

"Now, Faith, you know I can't tell you that," Charley said, looking around for a sturdy chair. Unfortunately, the parsonage ran to spindly Hitchcocks. He lowered himself into one of the wing chairs flanking the fireplace. He was a large man, brought up on the stick-to-your-ribs traditional fare of his native Nova Scotia. Food had been sticking to his ribs ever since, although he carried it well. As usual, he was in plain clothes, very plain clothes. His Harris tweed jacket was due for a good pressing and it was doubtful his shirt ever had.

"Let's see it," he said.

Tom motioned to the coffee table. "We didn't want to add our prints; that's why the cloth is there."

"Hard to get good ones from paper, but we'll try."

Faith shot a forgivably smug look at her husband.

Charley read the words slowly, looked at the envelope, and, using the cloth, put them in a plastic bag he'd pulled from his pocket.

"They were mailed from Boston—Post Office Square, to be precise—and at the same time—Thursday afternoon. The miracle is that they all arrived yesterday or today and didn't take several weeks as usual. Maybe we should be looking for a postal worker." Charley was not above a little government-employee chauvinism.

"Post Office Square is in the business district. Who do you know who works there, Pix?" Faith asked.

"Could also be that our writer has a sense of humor," Charley interjected, on a roll. "Post Office Square, poison-pen letters—get it?"

They did.

"Every lawyer, CPA—all those kinds of people—not working here in town works there, as far as I know. Including Sam." Pix was depressed.

Faith forgot that Sam's law offices were on Congress Street. Yet surely he'd have no reason to mail a letter like this to his wife. Plus, he'd been out of town. Somebody in his office? But was there anyone who was familiar enough with Aleford to send the others, hoping maybe to divert attention from the intended target, if indeed Pix, or Sam himself, was it? It seemed unlikely.

"Does anyone else from town work with Sam?" she asked Pix.

"Only Ellen Phyfe—you know, Morris's wife. She's been the office manager for years. They moved to Aleford because she'd heard such good things about it from Sam."

Faith's mind began to work furiously. Could Ellen have something against her boss? Faith had to know who else had received letters, and if Charley wasn't going to tell her, she'd have to find out some other way. It looked like Tom was going to be avoiding cow patties on his own this afternoon at Drumlin Farm. She planned to make some parish calls.

"If you got permission from the others to reveal their names, it might help to meet and establish some common ground," Tom sensibly pointed out to Charley.

"Exactly what I've been doing. Okay with you, Pix?" Faith had finally put a mug of coffee into his waiting hand. He took another cookie. "I plan to get all of you together . . . by yourselves—sorry, Faith—later this afternoon."

Faith didn't think he looked very sorry.

Pix's face assumed a determined look. She'd been running her hands through her short, thick brown hair and one piece in front stood straight up like a visor. "Of course you can include me. Anything that will help to figure this out."

Charley stayed a little longer, finished his coffee, and managed to tantalize Faith further with references to the other letters. It was Pix who broke things up.

"I have to pick Samantha up at softball practice and take Danny to that skateboard place in Cambridge for a birthday party. And," she added, "I don't want the kids to hear anything about this. It was bad enough the last time, the Cindy time."

"Bad enough" was putting it mildly, but Pix did not tend to histrionics. In any case, "bad enough" in Aleford was generally understood to suggest major tragedy.

She left and Charley followed. Faith and Tom sat facing each other on the couch. Amy was beginning to call from her crib and they could hear Ben go into his sister's room. It was extremely unlikely that he had thoughts of brotherly love in mind. His idea of play with Amy consisted of making her animals "fly."

"So," Tom said, poised for intervention.

"So," said his wife. "We've got to get this settled. I know Pix seemed calm when she left, but that's for Samantha and Danny's benefit. Thank goodness she's got them to worry about."

Tom had never been enamored of his wife's investigative involvements, but for once he thought she ought to see what she could discover. These were the Millers—parishioners and their dearest friends.

"The first thing we have to do is call Sam. See if he can come back earlier. Pix said he was staying at the Fairmont in San Francisco."

"Good idea. You do that while I get the kids ready for the farm." She looked at Tom's shoes. "You'd better put your wellies on, too."

Tom assumed a forlorn look, "And where are you going to be while I'm having all this fun?"

"At Millicent's, of course—at least to start."

Faith was surprised he'd had to ask.

Millicent Revere McKinley answered her door immediately, confirming that Millicent had been at her usual post, an armchair perfectly angled in the bay window so as to afford the occupant a view of Main Street and the green. Millicent's muslin curtains provided just enough cover so that passersby could not be absolutely certain they were being observed. Millicent spent whatever leisure time she had ensconced in the chair, knitting enough sweaters, socks, and mittens to keep not only her own Congregational Church bazaars supplied but one or two others, as well. And she never looked down.

Leading the way into the parlor, she did not ask Faith the nature of her call. All in good time.

"Lovely day, isn't it?" she asked, not pausing for an answer. "Let's hope this good weather keeps up through Patriots' Day, although, as you may know, we have never had to cancel due to an inclemency."

"Yes, it has been a lovely spring." Now that Faith was there, her clever opening gambits slipped completely from her mind, as usual, and she felt herself rapidly falling under Millicent's control. She pulled herself together and sat down opposite Millicent's chair, presuming the woman would want to get back to her work—a baby sweater with little teddy bears around the yoke—and her surveillance. She presumed wrong.

"Oh, don't let's sit there. Come here on the couch."

Recalling other visits when she literally had had to grab the arms to keep from sliding off the singularly slippery and uncomfortable horsehair, Faith defiantly chose a chair next to it. Visits to Millicent abounded in thin-ice metaphors.

"Never mind. The couch is not for everyone," Millicent assured her. Another test failed. "Would you like some tea?"

It was a welcome reprieve. After refusing all offers of help, Millicent left Faith alone to regroup. Getting information from Aleford's prime source was more difficult than gaining access to the Beatles' uncensored FBI dossiers.

Millicent's parlor was crammed with objects, some good, some mediocre, yet all treasured. A veritable phalanx of Hummels stood imprisoned in a china closet like so many Hansel and Gretels biding their time behind the mullioned glass before the witch would bake them. There were small tables, tilt-top tables, one large trestle table beneath another window, and chairs everywhere. Looking at the worn but good Oriental at her feet, Faith suspected the furniture served several purposes, not the least of which was to cover the threadbare patches of the Hamadan. A mourning picture on silk, two braided-hair mourning wreaths, and a reproduction of Paul Revere as a very old man gave a slightly lugubrious air to the room. There was a fireplace, and Faith was surprised to detect a small curl of smoke. A fire in April? Had Millicent taken leave of her senses? No true New Englander burned wood out of season, no matter what the temperature outside—or storm conditions. Curious, she stood up and went over to look at what was left of the blaze. Whatever it was, it hadn't been much. It had been a paper fire and all that remained was the charred corner of an envelope—a plain white legal-sized envelope.

So Millicent had gotten one, too.

Faith resumed her seat quickly, fully restored. She had planned to say something about POW!. She'd thought of saying that she needed a clipboard to collect signatures, or some other ploy. Since Millicent was not a member of First Parish, although she interfered enough in church business to be considered at least an "inquirer," Tom had pointed out on more than one occasion, the parish-call routine would not do. Now she did not need subterfuge and could come straight to the point.

She let Millicent put the tray down on a wobbly Shaker-type table and waited while the older woman fiddled with a piece of cardboard shimmed under one of the legs. Finally, all was in place and Millicent was "mother," pouring the strong tea she favored into delicate Limoges cups that she invariably mentioned were a throwback to the Reveres'—Rivoires'—French beginnings.

Teacup in hand, Faith declared, "You've had one of those nasty poison-pen letters."

Millicent cast an involuntary glance at the hearth and then back, her piercing gray eyes matched by the iron Mamie Eisenhower fringe above them. Never a hostage to fashion's whims, Millicent—and Mamie—had found a hairstyle and stuck with it.

"What makes you say that?"

Faith noticed it was not a denial.

"Because you've burned it in your fireplace, which was really not the best thing to do. We need all the evidence we can get to discover who's behind this."

Millicent gave Faith a world-weary smile—Oh, the impetuousness of youth. "I had a very good reason for burning it. It was crude and I didn't want anyone else to see it, but of course I told Charley. I described the way it was written. A cut-and-paste job from magazines and newspapers. I'm sure he knew what I was going to do."

"Do you know who else received one?"

"Do you?" Millicent parried.

"Yes," Faith advanced.

"All right, then, let's try to figure it out. If the two of us can't, I don't know who can." It was a major victory, and before Faith could let it go to her head, she told herself to remain steady and took out a pad and pen.

"When did yours arrive?"

"This morning—and it was mailed in Post Office Square on Thursday afternoon, like the others I know about."

Before she could go off on the tirade against the U.S. mail that Faith had heard lo these many times before—"My dear, we used to have two deliveries a day! You could mail a letter in Aleford at night and it would arrive at its destination at breakfast. Now you're lucky if it makes it in a week. Far simpler to hand-deliver."—Faith quickly interjected, "What about the others? Who's gotten them?"

"Brad has received one. He read it to me on the phone before taking it to the police. Also the Batcheldors and the Scotts. Who do you know?"

"Pix got one, also this morning. It alluded to the whole Cindy Shepherd affair and suggested that Sam had not stopped philandering." Being with Millicent tended to make Faith use words she had hitherto seen only in print.

"Brad's was about that Deane girl he'd been seeing several months ago, and it was rather graphic about what they may have been up to. He seemed to think the whole thing was funny, especially since they've parted company."

"And the Batcheldors?"

"That was more circumspect. It just said they shouldn't go out in the woods if they wanted to stay healthy. It was a threat. But the one the Scotts got was particularly vicious, mentioning her father."

"Her father?"

"He was an alcoholic and hit a little girl when he was driving while intoxicated. She survived but was paralyzed from the waist down. Shortly after, he took his own life."

"That's terrible!"

"Yes, especially since it was so many years ago. And to lay it at the Scotts' doorstep! It had nothing to do with them. Louise was a girl herself at the time. I remember it well."

And you were how old? Faith was tempted to ask, but she did not want to mar the precarious alliance. Millicent was notoriously sensitive about her age, admitting to no more than a vague reference to sixtysomething.

"Pix's was signed 'A friend.' How was yours signed?"

"The same, as was everyone else's except Brad's. Brad's wasn't signed. But that might simply mean whoever it was ran out of letters, got careless, or was in a rush."

Faith made a note of the omission and the possible reasons.

"Such a cowardly thing to do." Millicent's cheeks were flushed. She preferred to meet her enemies head-on. "And I always resent it when you read that anonymous letters are a 'woman's crime.' As if a man can't cut letters out just as well."

Faith agreed. "I don't think we should assume it's one or the other. And the recipients are mixed. Let's think about that. What do you all have in common?"

Millicent looked at her with pity. "Didn't you read last week's *Chronicle?*"

Faith had to admit the weekly *Aleford Chronicle* was still in a stack of papers in a basket in the kitchen. She knew that two children, husband, house, and career were no excuse for not keeping up with local issues, at least not to Millicent.

Millicent got up and went over to the decorative wooden canterbury next to an armchair. She plucked the newspaper from past issues of *Early American Life, American Heritage,* and other favored reading matter. Wordlessly, she turned the pages and pointed at one of the letters to the editor. Faith skimmed the lengthy plea to save Beecher's Bog, which ended with the words, "First the bog, then the green!" But it was not the letter itself that drew Faith's attention. It was the signers: Millicent, Pix, the Batcheldors, the Scotts, and Brad Hallowell.

"We wanted to create some interest for Friday night's meeting," Millicent explained. "You'd be amazed to know how many people aren't aware of what Joey Madsen is trying to do."

"Does Charley know about the letter?"

"Of course. I told him right away. Obviously, we were targets for our activity on behalf of the bog. And it's also obvious who's most interested in stopping us—Joseph Madsen and company."

It certainly seemed that way.

Faith left Millicent's full of information, yet feeling curiously hollow. She knew who had received the other letters and how, but the idea that Joey Madsen would be spending his time with scissors and Super Glue to intimidate his opposition just didn't fit. He, like Millicent, confronted people head-on—sometimes literally.

She walked slowly by the green and almost bumped into Pix, who was striding along with two of the dogs.

"Oops, sorry, Faith, we almost got you. After I dropped the kids off, I decided I needed to get out. Artie and Dusty always love walkies, too. What are you doing?"

"Not much. I've been talking to Millicent. . . ."

"Oh, that explains the downtrodden look. Come on, walk with us. It will do you good."

Pix was one of those believers in the efficacy of fresh air for all the ills of body and soul. Faith was not.

"Tom's taken the kids over to Drumlin Farm, so I think I'll go to work for a while and make up some cookie dough for the freezer. We're going to need every spare minute soon, so I'd like to get ahead."

"Then I'll come with you, but just to keep you company."

Faith laughed. "That would be great."

As they drove to Have Faith together, Pix told Faith that Charley had canceled their meeting. All the people who had signed the *Chronicle* letter had received the other kind. So far, no one else had reported getting one, so he believed he'd established the link. Sam had also called and was getting the first available flight. Pix was feeling much, much better.

"Millicent wanted the bog letter to go into this week's issue, so Sam wasn't here to sign it. I did speak to him about it on the phone, but he said he had to investigate a little further before he'd sign anything sponsored by a group called POW! It's that legalistic mind of his."

And years of living in Aleford, Faith was sure.

"If he had, the letter would have been addressed to both of us, I suppose," Pix continued.

It was an interesting point. The letter did sound as if it had been intended for both of them. Perhaps the writer had assumed Sam would join in with his wife's views. Then when the paper came out and his name wasn't there, the address was changed. The Scotts' letter was addressed to the couple, but concerned only Louise.

At the catering kitchen, Faith swiftly assembled her ingredients and started to work. Pix sat on a high stool and wrapped her long legs around it.

"Knowing that everyone else got one cheered me up, which is awful, but I suppose normal," she told Faith.

"Absolutely normal. Safety in numbers. I'm relieved, too. It's probably someone disgruntled with the idea of limiting development, and yes, that could be Joey Madsen. But a couple of things still bother me."

"Something's always bothering you, boss," came a cheerful voice from the doorway.

It was Niki Constantine, Faith's assistant. When she had reopened the catering business, Faith had advertised in the greater Boston area and interviewed dozens of applicants. Niki presented the perfect combination of impressive credentials, dedication—"Food is my life," she often intoned, only half-jokingly—and a sense of humor. This last was essential in an operation like Have Faith. Niki had assumed more responsibility as time had gone on. Faith knew the young woman would leave to start a firm or a restaurant of her own one day, but she hoped that day would be a long way off.

Niki had grown up in a large Greek family in Watertown. Although food might be her life, she was thin and wiry, never eating much, but tasting constantly. Her short black curls were wiry, too, and sprang out from her head in disarray—a little like one of the metal pot scrubbers they used.

Faith had not been expecting her. "What brings you here? I thought you had a hot and heavy date with the guy from Harvard Law. Weren't you going off with him this weekend?"

"I was, but I got cold feet. He's so respectable and perfect I know he must be wrong for me. For one thing, my parents are dying to meet him."

"And that's a no-no?" Pix asked worriedly. She'd wanted to

meet every one of her children's acquaintances since sandbox days. Evidently this was not the thing to do.

"Chill, Pix. You're different. If Samantha brings someone home when she's my age, you won't start making a seating chart for the wedding."

They all laughed.

Niki grew serious again. "The worst thing about it is he's so understanding. He wasn't even mad at me. Told me he knows I need my space. What are you going to do with a man like that?"

"Probably marry him," Faith said.

Niki frowned at her. "Anyway, we're going dancing tonight. He's a good dancer. Usually these preppy types look like Pinocchio, too humiliating. Now I'm going to make stock. I've been carrying these veal bones on the subway and bus in fear the bags would break and I'd be arrested for trying to dispose of my lover, conveniently chopped up in little pieces. Which takes care of all about me—what's going on here?"

They filled her in and she gave Pix a big hug. "How horrible for you. We had an obscene caller when I was in college and we had to change the number. I remember the first time it happened. It was such a shock, because you're expecting something so different. Somebody selling carpet cleaning or wanting to be your broker, and then these other words come out. Of course, you've solved it already, right, Faith?"

"Not really. The most obvious suspect is Joey, but the letters don't seem his style. If anything, he'd write back in the paper for all the world to see." Joey Madsen was noted for his letters to the editor. They pulled few punches and named names.

"What about his wife?" Niki suggested. "Standing by her man?"

Faith had considered Bonnie, then eliminated her for the same reasons. Bonnie didn't sneak around. If she was upset about something, Aleford knew it.

"But," Pix pointed out, "Joey is trying to get his plans approved. He can't very well attack POW! in public without making himself look bad. He's got to keep everything legal and aboveboard. Maybe the letters are his way of trying to frighten us into abandoning our cause."

Faith was kneading the rich shortbread that formed the base for her chocolate crunch cookies (see recipe on page 273). There was another reason to believe Joey was behind the letters. It had struck her as soon as she'd heard it in Millicent's parlor. The wording. Could it possibly be a coincidence that both Lora Deane and the Batcheldors were being told to do something if they "wanted to stay healthy"—one on the phone; one in writing?

She thought about the other letters as she wrapped the dough for freezing. Why wasn't Brad's signed? Could Joey, in some twisted way, actually consider himself a friend of the others? He'd known them all long enough. Brad was a newcomer. Maybe Joey didn't want to presume. It was laughable in the face of the act.

"Whoever it is, Joey, Bonnie, Mr. or Ms. X, it's someone who's really rather rude." Pix's emphatic voice cut into Faith's thoughts.

"We could all agree with that," Niki said dryly.

"What I mean is everything in the letters is common knowledge in Aleford. He or she hasn't revealed something that most people don't already know. So it's simply plain bad taste to mention it. None of *us* would."

It made sense. "Not blackmail material, just reminders of hurtful times. Except for the Batcheldors. What about them?" Faith asked.

"Think about it. What could you bring up? Margaret has spent her life looking at the world through rose-colored binoculars and

Nelson, when he's not trekking along behind her, has his nose buried in a book. But they signed the letter, so they had to be included."

Faith thought about mentioning her close encounter of the weird kind with the Batcheldors, then decided not to. She wanted to mull this over some more. Did the letter writer know what the Batcheldors were up to in the woods? She resolved to take another stroll there herself, avoiding the bog and definitely not taking the kids. Amy was well on the way to developing ski maskaphobia.

Pix left to get ready for her husband's late-night return, although Faith was not sure what this entailed. With kids in residence, it didn't mean a black lace nightie or, in Pix's case, a fatted calf of any sort. Most likely, it involved making sure they had a bottle of Laphroaig, his favorite scotch, that Danny wouldn't have a friend sleeping over, and that Samantha honored her curfew. Peace and calm in the wee hours of the morning—with no mail delivery.

Faith and Niki worked a bit longer and then closed up shop. Niki changed into a tiny silver satin dress before she left. Faith loved it on her. A much more intriguing look than the girl in black about Niki's age whom Faith had seen on the subway recently with a broken wineglass wired to her bodice.

"Definitely not the corporate-wife image," she commented as Niki stuffed her work clothes into a bag.

"Maybe what she has on underneath," Niki said. "Don't tell Mom, but this dress is a slip."

Monday morning always comes, and Faith was rushing around tidying up, all the while reflecting on the absurdity of the effort. The toddlers weren't going to notice whether the parsonage was dusty—or even if it was standing, so long as there was plenty of juice and crackers. Yet their mothers, even in their usual blink-of-an-eye drop-off, would. But play group was a blessing. Normally, the children all went to a lovely woman who had been providing day care for

Aleford's little ones for years. One of the reasons she was able to remain so lovely, and in business, was that she very sensibly took a week off every once in a while, and then the mothers took the children in turn. One's own turn came infrequently enough to be only a minor inconvenience. Faith had discovered with Ben, however, that some of the mothers went slightly over the edge when it was their morning to shine. One day he'd come home with an enormous cookie shaped like little Ben and decorated in exquisite detail right down to the exact colors of his rainbow sneaker laces. Faith stuck to play dough, two colors, and, weather permitting, a walk across the street to the green, where the children could roll around on the hallowed turf to their heart's content. This was the plan for this morning, as well.

Hastily buffing some brass candlesticks while Amy occupied herself in picking out all the raisins from her bran muffin, Faith hoped Charley could get Joey to admit that he'd authored, if that was the correct word for the method employed, the "friendly" letters. Madsen was the most obvious suspect.

As they sat in church the day before, it was apparent that the word had been spread—and not the word Tom was preaching. The pleasant buzz of conversation and greetings before the service was missing. It seemed as if everyone had waited until the last minute and then hastily filed in just before the stroke of eleven. What talk there was tended to be furtive and hushed. It was the same at coffee hour. The Millers and the Batcheldors were there, but people were avoiding them, giving them a sympathetic nod in passing, yet unsure of what to say. It wasn't a death—or a birth. It was perhaps something they weren't even supposed to know about.

Faith wondered if the letters had stopped. She'd call Charley later and tell him what Pix had said—that whoever it was was writing about things everybody knew, indicating it had to be someone living in town, but maybe somebody who didn't know its deepest, darkest secrets—or was too polite to mention them. Not that the letters showed an excess of good manners. In exchange, Charley might tell her what he'd been doing.

Had Millicent read Charley her letter? She'd been vague about it. Faith couldn't think of anything about Millicent that you'd bother cutting up a magazine for. Overweening pride? Ancestor worship? Maybe she really wasn't a descendant of the midnight rider through his fourth cousin once removed and her whole life was a sham. But Millicent lectured all over the state on virtually every aspect of the Revere family, from what they ate to what they wrought. She was the pillar of the DAR, Historical Society; anything remotely connected with the glorious past, as her parents had been and so forth. Faith wondered why Millicent had never married. Surely she would have considered it her obligation to carry on the line. Maybe there was something there. Millicent left at the altar—but who would dare? Or maybe Millicent wasn't the end of the line—but again, who would dare? Besides, wed or unwed, if Millicent had produced any progeny, she'd have raised her child herself and done the job thoroughly. Goodness knows, she had opinions enough on the way others raised theirs. Millicent may not have literally taken to the rod, but she would definitely not have spoiled the child.

Faith looked over to see how her own child was doing. She had managed to cover herself with a layer of fine crumbs and there was a raisin pasted to her cheek with spit. Faith grabbed a cloth. Romper Room would be starting any minute. Everything was ready. The only thing Faith had to remember was to keep on eye on little Jeffrey, who ate the play dough, yucky as it was. He ate paste, too.

She scrubbed at Amy's sticky cheeks and brushed some of the crumbs from her fine blond hair. She wished she could tell Charley about Lora Deane's calls and see if he thought there was any connection to the letters. The next selectmen's meeting was Wednesday night. It hadn't even been a week since Faith had walked in on Tom and the nursery school teacher. All weekend, she and Tom had taken turns calling Lora to find out what her sister, Bonnie, had said. Contrary to the advice of the police, and common sense, Lora had left a cheery message on her machine informing callers that she was out of town, presumably having fun, and to please leave a message. They did, but Lora hadn't called back.

"At least we haven't had to worry about her. If we'd been getting no answer all weekend, I'd have had to go over there and check up on her," Tom had said at breakfast. He was leaving early in hopes of getting a word with her when he dropped Ben off.

"True, but it is pretty silly to advertise the fact that your place is empty."

"I doubt she has much, honey. What do stuffed animals bring on the street these days?"

Faith hadn't heard from Tom this morning and assumed this meant he hadn't been able to get the teacher alone. She resolved to pin Miss Lora down herself after school and bring her back to the parsonage for lunch.

The morning went by with blessed speed. The toddlers had left the place relatively intact, although it was going to be a job getting the play dough from behind the kitchen radiator.

Everything was going according to plan. Lora accepted the invitation eagerly—maybe she was getting tired of peanut butter and jelly—and Faith was able to get her alone after lunch. Amy had nodded off into her tapioca pudding and Ben was sequestered with Tin-Tin on Nickelodeon, Lora having promised to take him for a walk afterward all by himself. He could hardly contain his excitement and after interrupting them for the third time, asking, "Is it time yet?" Faith had snapped at him, "No, and it isn't going to be if you come in once more," thereby revealing in front of her child's teacher what a bad mother she truly was. Miss Lora did, in fact, look a bit sorrowful. Faith couldn't wait for her to have kids of her own—kids in residence.

Over a second helping of tapioca, which Lora seemed to enjoy as much as the Fairchild children, she confided that Bonnie had not responded exactly as Lora had hoped. Faith was annoyed with herself for not having predicted the outcome, or at the least its strong "kill the messenger" possibility.

"She was ripping," Lora said. "Now she won't even talk to me. Everyone in the family's going to find out, if they haven't already, and it's going to be all my fault."

"Did she come right out and deny it, or didn't you get that far?" Faith asked.

Lora obediently started from the beginning. "I called her up and asked if I could go over there to see the baby. He really is the sweetest thing, little pudgy cheeks, the kind you just have to nibble."

Faith added Cabbage Patch dolls to what she already knew to be a sizable collection of teddy bears. Miss Lora told the kids stories about them.

"We spent time with little Joey; then she put him down for a nap, so I figured it was a good time to talk. I told her about the calls and she was very sympathetic at first. I was kind of embarrassed to bring it up, but I said straight out, 'You know, Bonnie, Joey has been pretty upset because I wouldn't lend him the money for the Estates. You don't think he's doing this to kind of get back at me, do you?' "

Faith could picture the scene. She'd been in Bonnie's kitchen once, dropping off some large containers of Have Faith eggplant lasagna Bonnie had ordered for a luncheon her women's club was having. The room was so clean, you wondered if it had ever been used, but Faith could see plates of cookies and brownies that surely had not come from boxes. The house was only a few years old and still looked like a model home. There wasn't any clutter, not even the kind Faith tolerated—out of the way in baskets or behind closed cabinets. No sign of a morning paper, no pictures except one that perfectly picked out the color of the tile floor and matching curtains. It was of a large fish surrounded by either offspring or prey, depending on one's point of view. There wasn't even a Post-It next to the phone or on the gleaming fridge. Bonnie kept her life in absolute order without reminders. Faith knew instinctively this was a woman who used leaf polish on her houseplants.

"I didn't know how mad she was at first, because she didn't say anything. Just sat there. I started to tell her I was sure I was wrong. I mean, she was beginning to scare me. Staring off into space, with her hands folded on the table. Then she stood up and told me to get out of her house. I couldn't believe it. Bonnie, my own sister—well, half sister. So I tried to tell her that this was all crazy—to forget I'd said anything and let bygones be bygones."

"What did she do?"

"She wasn't even listening to me, kept kind of moving me to the door. She grabbed my jacket and pushed it at me. 'Just leave, Lora,' she said. So I did."

But, Faith said to herself, she didn't deny it. Out loud, she asked, "This was on Thursday. Have you heard from her or anyone else in the family since?"

"Not directly. I was gone over the weekend. Normally, I have Sunday dinner at my grandparents. We all do. My grandmother knew I wasn't going to be there, but she called Friday afternoon late and asked me if I could change my plans. So maybe Bonnie told her. I never got a call before when I haven't been able to make it. At that point, even if I could have gone, I wouldn't have. You don't know how they can get. Everyone would be on Joey's side, and I just couldn't take it."

"What about your brothers?"

"Well, maybe they'd be better, especially Eddie. But as I told you, family is family and I was wrong to accuse Joey, especially to his wife. I see that now."

Faith didn't. Lora was trying to get help and it was unfortunate that her sister had reacted the way she had.

"Lora, I really think you ought to tell Charley. I've found out a little more about Brad, and he does seem to be capable of violence—at least to his bedroom wall."

"I heard about that." Lora sounded contemptuous. "But he'd never hit me. He knows I wouldn't stand for it, nor would my family. And, as I told you, I am not telling the police. Especially not now." There was pride in her voice. Lora might not be the most popular member at the moment, yet she knew their priorities. She might have broken the Deane code, but they would come to her defense if she needed it.

Faith played to her family feeling. "Then if you still won't go to the police, tell your grandparents. I'm sure you've heard about the letters people have been getting, and there may be some connection with the calls."

She'd forgotten that Lora had been away and so wouldn't have heard about the letters. She filled her in, and the teacher was definitely alarmed, although not, it seemed, about herself.

"What is going on in this town? I can't believe it. It sounds like some kind of nut is on the loose! Though why he would be calling me and writing to these POW! people doesn't make any sense. I don't care about the bog."

She'd put her finger on the main thing that was missing in Faith's logic. The wording of the call and the letter was the same, but the targets were completely dissimilar.

Faith had one last question. Ben would soon cross the line between anticipation and frustration. The last thing his mother wanted Miss Lora to witness was a full-blown Fairchild fit.

"And the other calls? They've stopped? I know you weren't there, but was there anything on your machine?"

"Nothing, except a lot of hang-ups. But people don't like to leave messages. My mother is the worst. You know, clears her throat several times, then whispers, 'I'll call you back. It's Mother'—like it's a deep secret—and hangs up fast. That's if she leaves anything. I'll call her tonight. Maybe she's been trying to reach me."

Faith nodded. The parsonage machine offered a sample of virtually every message-leaving style.

"Mom?" a little voice called out tentatively. "I'm getting overwaited."

"It's time, Ben," she called back, and sat well out of the way. If she'd had a stopwatch handy, he might have made the record books.

Play-group days always left Faith fatigued, and she'd gone straight to sleep, despite all the thinking she'd planned to do. Those minutes between head touching the pillow and oblivion tended to be her most productive time of day and she kept a pad and pencil next to the bed to scribble notes for recipes or other projects that every once in a while seemed just as brilliant in the morning. So when she was awakened by the scream of the sirens, she was more than usually cranky. From the sound of them, they were converging in the Fairchilds' driveway.

Closing her eyes tightly, she tried to summon sleep again. Tom, who only woke if one of the children sneezed or whimpered, had not moved a muscle. She hitched the comforter over her ear and then sat up. She wasn't in Manhattan. She was in Aleford. Sirens in the night, especially this many—the noise was continuing unabated—were not a common occurrence. Now, in her old apartment, a night *without* sirens would have been the exception.

She went over to the window and looked across at the green. No activity there and nothing seemed amiss. She walked down the hall and crept into Ben's room, which was at the rear of the house. She could hear shouts from a bullhorn, but not the words. And she could see bright orange light at the end of the block. The whole sky appeared to be in flames. Two figures were in the Millers' backyard, and as she watched, they ran toward the street. Obviously Pix and Sam. She ran, too, back to her room, where she threw on some clothes.

"Darling," she whispered in her husband's ear. Getting no response, she shook him slightly, then harder. "Darling!" she repeated, and Tom woke up all at once. "What is it? What's happened?" He reached to turn on the light and the glare flooded the room. He rubbed his eyes. "Faith, what's all that noise?"

"There seems to be a huge fire at the end of the block. You can see it from Ben's room. I'm going to find out where it is."

"Wait, I'll come with you. No, the kids. But be careful."

Tom was in a slight state of confusion and had pulled out one of his black clerical jackets instead of his bathrobe from the closet. Faith took it from his hands and effected the change. She left him sitting on the bed, looking at his slippers.

"Go to sleep. I'll come back and tell you what's going on as soon as I can."

It was cold, yet the color of the sky gave an illusion of warmth as she walked rapidly down the block, joining others similarly awakened from their beds. There was an air of excitement. She had started smelling the smoke as soon as she stepped out the door. Cold was no longer a problem as she got closer. The heat was intense and companies from all the surrounding towns were fighting the blaze. The new wood crackled and went up like the proverbial matchsticks. But no need to be concerned about life or property. This house had never been lived in, and never would be. It was the new spec house the Deanes had almost finished—the house on Whipple Hill Road that the neighbors had often wished would disappear. And now it was—right before their startled eyes.

Faith looked around at the faces in the flickering light. A fire, especially a large fire, has a peculiar effect on people—mesmerizing, fascinating, beguiling. It brings out the pyromaniac in everyone. The flames were magnificent, beautiful. They shot high up into the night sky; torrents of sparks cascaded to the ground. Faith found herself almost enjoying the spectacle—that is, until Fire Chief O'Halloran's voice shouting instructions to Aleford's Ancient Order of Hook and Ladder Volunteers reminded her that this was real and not *Backdraft* at Universal Studios. The firefighters were struggling desperately to keep the blaze from spreading to the surrounding houses; the street was a river of water as the hoses drenched trees, walls, and chimneys.

How had it started?

Faith knew there would be no answers tonight. The smoke was filling her lungs. She had to leave. The house would be a total loss. But the Deanes would be insured. Insured. Insurance. How much and to whom?

She turned to go home. She could see some of her neighbors gathered in small groups, but she didn't feel like talking to anyone, even the Millers. Fortunate or unfortunate—which was it? The neighborhood would be happy, although the Deanes still owned the land. The Deanes couldn't be, even with insurance. All that work. She looked around to see if any members of the family were here. They would have to be. And they were. Gus and his grandsons were standing with Charley MacIsaac by one of the trucks. They were watching in silence, their faces grim.

How had it started?

A few steps toward home, she was stopped by a loud shout. It was one of the firemen from Byford. He was directing his hose into one of the windows on the first floor. Faith paused. He shouted again.

"Jesus Christ! There's somebody in here!"

Chapter 4

Nelson Batcheldor did not find out he was a widower until 4:30 A.M. It had taken that long for the fire to be extinguished enough to recover the body. There had never been any hope of survival. And the only reason a positive identification was made so quickly was that Margaret had died as she'd lived—binoculars in place.

Chief MacIsaac appeared at the parsonage, where the Fairchilds were waiting. As soon as Faith heard that someone had been trapped inside, she'd hurried home and the two of them sat together, waiting to hear who the victim was. At one point, Tom had walked down to the fire, but soon returned. There was little he could do there, he'd told Faith, except get in the way. She remembered her own first moments of fascination at the sight of the fire and felt sick.

Charley was wearing a heavy firemen's raincoat and his face was streaked with grime. He refused Faith's offer of coffee. He'd been drinking it for hours.

"It was Margaret Batcheldor, and we have to tell Nelson."

Charley seemed to break down for a moment. He cleared his throat, swallowed hard, and went on. "Damn nice woman, even though she did go overboard with the birds. What the hell could she have been doing in the house? No birds there. Unless she thought one was trapped or something. . . ." He sounded utterly defeated.

Tom and Faith were listening intently, but it took a moment for them to register.

"Margaret? Margaret's body?" Tom asked.

Charley nodded and Faith started to cry. "Poor Nelson. What's he going to do without her?" It was impossible to think of one without the other.

"I thought you ought to be there when I tell him, Tom. He's going to need you."

Faith gave her husband a fierce hug. He and Charley left immediately and she wandered about the house, unable to settle down to anything, certainly not sleep. She had a fleeting impulse to call the Millers, but then decided not to. She didn't feel like spreading this kind of news. Aleford would know soon enough.

Margaret Batcheldor trapped in a fire in the house the Deanes built. Margaret and Nelson, the recipients of a poison-pen letter. Margaret and Nelson, pillars of POW! Finally, Margaret and Nelson in ski masks and out of mufti, emerging from Beecher's Bog. Aleford had had its ups and downs, serious tragedies, a feud or two, but nothing like this. The smoke from the fire seemed to have seeped in through the walls of the house. It was as if some noxious gas were permeating their lives, carrying distrust and now death throughout the village.

She began to long for the children to wake up. Her thoughts were beginning to terrify her. She picked up a book, a new Barbara Kingsolver, but the words swam in front of her eyes.

"Momeee!" a frightened voice called out, "Where are you?

Where's Dad? You're not in your bed? I want to know. Where are you?" It was Ben, and she rushed upstairs to reassure him. Holding him close, reassuring herself.

Nelson answered the door. He was in rumpled striped pajamas and had obviously been sound asleep. He seemed extremely surprised to see the two of them and his mouth dropped open at the sight of Charley in his raincoat and Tom clad in dog collar and jacket at such an ungodly hour.

"I'm afraid we have bad news," Charley said. "Can we come in?"

"Of course, of course," Nelson said, bewildered. "I'll get Margaret."

Tom and Charley looked at each other. This was not going to be easy.

"Why don't we sit down over here," Tom suggested, and led the way to the couch and chairs comfortably arranged in front of a large fieldstone hearth. Bird plates and bird pictures adorned the walls. Carved birds and porcelain birds perched on every surface. Needlepoint bird pillows were carefully arranged wherever one might think to sit.

Charley came straight to the point. "Margaret's had an accident. I'm afraid she's dead, Nelson."

"Dead! Margaret! That's impossible!" Nelson's voice rose to a high-pitched screech and he jumped up. "She's asleep in her bed. Nothing's happened to Margaret!" When he ran out of the room, they followed. Could he possibly be right?

He wasn't. They found him in a small bedroom crammed with more bird artifacts and shelves of guides and photographic essays. There was a single bed beneath the window, its spread stretched taut. A bed that no one had slept in.

"But I don't understand. Where is she?" He grabbed Charley

by the shoulders, and although Nelson was much the weaker man, Tom had all he could do to pry him away. Then Charley took one side, Tom the other, and they forced Nelson to sit on the bed between them.

"When did you last see her?" Charley asked.

"When I went to bed last night. I was tired and went up first. She was going to sleep in here." For a moment, he seemed embarrassed. "I guess I snore sometimes, and anyway, she was getting up early to go birding and didn't want to disturb me." He began to sob. "Why didn't I go with her? What was it? Her heart? The doctor said she would be fine if she took her medication. Outlive us all." He put his face in his hands and let go. Tom and Charley waited a while.

"Is there anyone you want us to call? A relative or neighbor?" Tom asked.

Nelson shook his head. "We're the only family we have, except for some cousins we haven't seen for years. But friends. Everybody was her friend." His voice broke.

Charley put his hand on Nelson's shoulder. "Want some coffee? Or maybe a shot of something?"

Nelson shook his head again. Charley took a deep breath. "She didn't have a heart attack, or at least we don't know that yet. There's been a fire at the new house the Deanes have put up over on Whipple Hill. Margaret was inside."

"You mean she burned to death!"

Charley kept his hand on Nelson's shoulder. "There was nothing anybody could have done. By the time she was discovered, it was too late. It was a very bad fire. The whole house is just about gone."

"But what was she doing there?" Nelson was truly dazed now.

"We were hoping you might have an idea."

Nelson shook his head. "She was going to leave early and she did say she was meeting someone. But that was normal. I can't imagine why she would have gone into that house. It's not even near any of her spots." Tears were running out of his puffy red eyes and dripping off his nose. He made an ineffectual wipe at them with his pajama sleeve.

"Did she say who she was meeting?" Tom asked.

"No, but it was probably one of our usual group. They all want to go with Margaret. She's so knowledgeable."

Tom noticed Nelson was still speaking in the present. For a moment, the three men sat in a row in Margaret's room. Nobody said anything. Charley stood up.

"I have to get down to the station and file a report. Believe me, I realize how painful this is for you, but you'll have to wait for the body to be released before you can have a service. There has to be an autopsy."

Nelson winced.

"As soon as you feel up to it, we'll talk about plans for the funeral," Tom said. "Meanwhile, I'm going to go downstairs and get us some coffee, maybe a little breakfast. Come and show me where things are."

Nelson shuffled off obediently, a pathetic figure in his nightclothes.

"I'll be in touch," Charley said quietly to Tom. "Let me know if he thinks of any reason at all, however far-fetched, why she could have been there, and get him to give you a list of the names of the people who went birding with her."

"Okay. One question, though. Is an autopsy really necessary? I would have thought he could have been spared that when the cause of death is obvious."

"We all know it's Margaret because of the binoculars, but the state doesn't, and there could be other things."

"Like what?"

"I'd rather not say unless I have to," Charley replied in an uncharacteristically cryptic manner, and Tom had to be satisfied with that.

By dawn, word of Margaret's death had spread as rapidly as the fire had through the fresh lumber the night before. It wasn't long before friends and neighbors were appearing at Nelson's door with food and words of comfort. He'd changed out of his pajamas, and Tom left him sitting in the kitchen with the Scotts, the Batcheldors' closest friends. Nelson continued to have no idea why Margaret had been roaming about the Deanes' house in the wee hours of the morning. He did give Tom a list of the names of habitual birders, though. He was obviously still in shock, breaking down when each new arrival offered condolences. Tom left, secure in the knowledge that Nelson would be as fine as circumstances permitted now that the well-oiled machinery of care in a small place like Aleford had slipped into gear. By sundown, Nelson Batcheldor would have enough food in his freezer for the rest of the year.

The town had just started to react to the shock of Margaret's death and the fire when word leaked out that in addition to Margaret's remains, the police had found remnants of a sizable container of gas by the body.

Margaret Batcheldor, an arsonist!

Tom called Faith from the church office with the news. A parishioner had called him with the rumor and he'd checked it out with the police. Faith was stunned, yet as she hung up the phone, she couldn't help but remember Margaret's odd attire in the woods, as well as her obvious militancy at Friday's POW! meeting. Fighting fire with fire? Could she have intended to destroy one of the Deane properties as a warning against further development? Margaret always made it absolutely clear that she thought birds, and the other inhabitants of Aleford's woods, pastures, and ponds, were just as, if not more, important than people. She certainly thought them more valuable than property. But if so, the gesture had gone wrong—very, very wrong. Faith imagined Margaret, perhaps in her ski mask again, dousing the beams with gas and then igniting them. Unaccustomed to an activity of this sort—it was not like rubbing two sticks together—she must have been terrified by the ferocity of the blaze, then overcome by it. It was too tragic. Faith suddenly felt angry. Why hadn't Margaret's husband or her friends realized how close to the edge she was? Surely Millicent, of all people, must have known.

Millicent. All this business of taking a stand, the constant invocation of the sacred past. Faith had heard that after she and Tom had slipped out of the POW! meeting, there had been a lengthy discussion about possible courses of action, including not-so-subtle allusions to the stores of powder and guns Colonial inhabitants had hidden in these very woods in the weeks preceding that famous April morning. Presumably this was all in reference to the historic nature of Beecher's Bog, but maybe Margaret hadn't seen it that way. Maybe she took it as a call to action. What were the Batcheldors up to? Or Margaret on her own? Faith had heard that Margaret ruled the roost at the Batcheldor house. It was entirely possible this very determined woman had decided to act solo.

Faith strode to the phone. The kids were not due home for another hour. She wanted to hear what Millicent had to say. Before she could get to it, it rang. Tom's voice sounded weary—more weary than simply from losing last night's sleep. Sleep deprivation was something parents actually began to get used to, or at least pretended to.

"Somebody threw a brick and shattered Lora Deane's living room window last night. She came home about midnight and found it. She's pretty hysterical and has told her grandparents what's been going on. She went there immediately."

"I was afraid of this. It was only a matter of time before whoever's been calling her would get tired of phone games and move on to more exciting stuff. So, she's going to the police after all."

"Her grandfather has taken charge and was trying to reach Charley when he got called out to the fire. This morning, they've all been so upset about the house that the brick hasn't seemed as important, but apparently Gus did tell the police. She said her grandfather was mad as hell that she hadn't come to her own family right away."

"Well, at least she'll be safe with them."

"I hope so," Tom said glumly, and hung up.

Tuesday morning had dawned gray and gloomy. A fine rain was falling, which observers were sure would soon change to the kind of steady downpour that meant mud season. By midmorning, the few spring bulbs in bloom hardy enough to venture forth had been squashed back to the earth. Aleford was drenched. It was also scared. Rumors were flying faster than a speeding musket ball. Much faster. Not only theories about the fire and Margaret, but also word about the poison-pen letters. By the time Faith heard about them in the post office, the original seven recipients had grown to fifty and the relatively mild language had become Howard Stern material. She did what she could to correct the story, but no one believed her. No one wanted to believe her. They were battening down the hatches in the face of a storm and they didn't want someone coming along telling them not to worry—especially an outsider, and a New Yorker at that. Probably didn't seem like much to her, New York being the hellhole it was, but Aleford knew better.

They weren't right about the letters—there were only five in all: Scotts, Batcheldors, Millicent, Brad Hallowell, and Pix—but they were right about the depth of the crisis. By evening, there wasn't a house that had not both literally and figuratively set out the emergency candles and flashlights, and cooked up plenty of food—prepared for the worst. The thunderstorm had moved up the coast and more news had spread. Margaret Batcheldor might be a charred corpse, but she hadn't burned to death. A ferocious series of blows on the back of the head had killed her, not the fire.

Margaret had been murdered.

Faith sat in the parsonage watching the lights flicker and listening to the hum of the refrigerator go on and off. She was alone with the kids, who had greeted the wind and rain with delight. Ben had been sorry that the power had managed to stay on through his bedtime. She knew he was upstairs trying to keep himself awake. She pointed out that going to sleep was just like a power outage. Dark was dark. But he failed to see her logic. In her heart, she agreed with him. As a child, it had always been thrilling to lose power during a storm. As an adult she only had visions of spoiled food. And at the moment, not too many of those. There were too many other concerns. Tom was at Nelson Batcheldor's with Charley again, as he had been since late afternoon when the report of how Margaret had died came from the medical examiner's office.

Faith realized she was feeling a little annoyed. Tom, by virtue of his profession, was getting in on all the action. And Charley was probably revealing far more to him than he ever told her. Male bonding or whatever. At least she'd be able to hear about it when Tom came home. Meanwhile, she was stuck with the threat of no electricity and a mind she couldn't shut off.

Fortunately, they had gas heat. Still, she felt chilled. But it wasn't the kind of cold another layer of clothing would help. Margaret, sweet, dotty Margaret. Had she come upon the arsonist and been killed to prevent her from talking? Or was she setting the house on fire, and killed by whom? The only suspects who made sense were the Deanes. But why wouldn't they put the fire out or at least call the fire department before the house was a total wreck?

Because Margaret was dead. It all came back to that. Maybe the blow was intended to stun her, stop her. Yet it had been more than one, Charley told Tom. Someone had been extremely vicious.

Who had called the fire department? she wondered. It hadn't been important to know before; now it was. The new house was wedged between two older houses. Someone must have seen something. Margaret would have had a flashlight. But then, this was a town that ate at six o'clock and was in bed no later than ten. No night owl looking out a window, no late-night dog walkers.

She heard the car in the driveway and rushed to the kitchen door. Tom came in and folded her in his arms.

"Kids asleep?"

"That or a good imitation on Ben's part. Are you hungry?"

"Starving. You can't imagine how much food there is at Nelson's, but somehow you don't like to interrupt a man's grief and ask for some lasagna or a bowl of pea soup."

These were Aleford's standard funereal offerings, along with platters of small, triangular, spongy white-bread sandwiches spread with minuscule amounts of fillings Faith didn't even like to think about—anchovy paste for one.

She started by slicing a large wedge of rosemary focaccia in half, then drizzled it liberally with extra virgin olive oil, sprinkling a combination of ground Romano and Parmesan cheese on top. She quickly layered thin slices of green and red peppers with cappicola and added more cheese. The whole thing went into the oven to warm while she heated up some soup—cream of broccoli with a dash of curry powder. She placed the food in front of her husband and was rewarded with a big grin.

"Boy, did I marry the right woman."

Faith loved to feed people, especially her family. She sat close to him at the big round table that was the gravitational center of the house—the place where they ate most meals, the kids drew pictures, and friends automatically headed. Faith had religiously avoided anything suggesting either Colonial New England or neo-country in her kitchen, opting instead for the sunny colors of the south of France and bright Souleido cotton prints on the chairs and at the windows, with nary a cow or pewter charger in sight.

"Now tell me everything," she demanded.

Tom's mouth was full and she waited impatiently. Maybe she should have grilled him before the sandwich.

"There's not a lot to tell," he said finally, and seeing the look on her face, he put the sandwich down for a moment. "Person or persons unknown killed her and left her in the fire. There's no way of finding out whether she was setting the fire or whether the fire was set to cover up the murder."

"And nobody heard or saw anything?"

"Ed Ferguson, who lives next door, thinks he heard a car around eleven. He'd gotten up to pee, but he's not too sure about the time. It couldn't have been Margaret's car, because she didn't take it. She was on foot."

"Which seems to eliminate her as the arsonist. Surely she couldn't walk all the way from her house to Whipple Hill Road lugging a can of gas without attracting some notice. Plus, it's quite a distance."

"Not if you cut through the woods, which of course she probably did. And even if she walked down Main Street at that time of night, nobody would have been around to notice."

This was true. The woman could have been naked and on horseback without a single observer. And if she came through the woods, might she have hidden the gas in some thicket on one of her previous maneuvers?

Tom munched away.

"Who reported the fire?"

"The Fergusons again. I guess Ed gets up frequently. He saw the flames and by the time O'Halloran got there, it was the inferno you saw. The Deanes had planned to put in the insulation this week, so the place was filled with that, plus wallboard. It made for great fuel. Any more soup?"

Faith went to get the pot and ladled more into Tom's cup, then decided to have some herself.

"What about the brick? Was there a note wrapped around it? Why throw it, unless you had a message to deliver?"

"Nope, nothing. Just a plain old brick. Gus went to the state police headquarters today. Told them about the calls, too, and is demanding police protection for his granddaughter. Charley says Gus seems to think it's Millicent and her group."

"Calling Lora?"

"Yes, Gus thinks they're too cowardly to confront him or his grandsons, so they're going after Lora."

Faith was thinking about the brick. Brad Hallowell had thrown a punch at his wall. A fist. A brick. She frowned. "The last time we walked by the construction site, there were a lot of bricks lying around. They'd finished the chimney ages ago, but maybe they planned to use them for the steps or walk."

"So whoever killed Margaret decided to pick up a brick and heave it through Lora's window for the hell of it on his or her way home?"

"It's not impossible. It's certainly complicated things, and if I were a murderer, that's what I would want to do."

"Any victims in mind?" her husband asked, scraping the last of the soup from his bowl.

"Well, you know what they say," Faith replied.

"What *do* they say?"

"You're much more likely to be done in by your spouse than by a random stranger."

"I've already been done in by mine. Now let's go to bed. The dishes can wait."

The decision was made even easier. Outside, there was a sharp crack of thunder and the wind howled. All the lights went out and the parsonage fell silent. Hand in hand, they groped their way out of the kitchen, up the stairs, and didn't even bother with the flashlight prudently placed by the side of the bed.

There was no question that Wednesday night's selectmen's meeting would make history as the highest-rated television show in Aleford's history, and as the most heavily attended. People stood several rows deep in the hall, craning their necks for a view. Faith and Pix had arrived early and had managed to snare seats.

The meeting room looked like the partners' conference room at an old established law firm: dark wood paneling and a gleaming semicircular mahogany table facing the audience. The selectmen sat in dark red leather wing chairs, the backs of which tended to rise thronelike above the members' heads. Faith noted that Bea Hoffman's feet didn't touch the floor, but dangled, even though the small woman was perched as far forward as possible. The audience sat on folding chairs and whiled away the time before the meeting started by studying several framed prints celebrating Aleford's glorious past and one photo enlargement of President Ford's Bicentennial visit. Though there were bookcases filled with bound copies of town annual reports, they looked untouched.

Flanked by the state and American flags, Penny called the meeting to order sternly. Pix had heard that Penny had phoned Millicent earlier in the day and told her in no uncertain terms that the board would not tolerate a circus atmosphere. Millicent had been extremely offended, and it would probably be a while before the two friends shared mugs and muffins at the Minuteman Café.

"The first order of business is the presentation of an"—Penny paused searching for the right word—"alternative view of the proposal Mr. Madsen has submitted to the board for the development of the area known as Beecher's Bog. I understand that Miss McKinley will represent her group."

Millicent was sitting in the front row, flanked not by flags but by Brad Hallowell and Louise Scott. She was wearing her red suit again. Faith gave a thought to the appropriateness of the color with Patriots' Day almost upon them. It did make one stand out—just as it had the British officers, whose coats were more scarlet than the foot soldiers' and made excellent targets for the militia who sensibly aimed at them first. But Millicent wasn't a target, not tonight, anyway. She was the projectile. Brad followed her to the front of the room, carrying a number of oaktag sheets that appeared to be POW!'s visual aids. He sat down and Millicent began to speak.

It was a repetition of Friday night's meeting, except she had brought examples of all the places Aleford had lost. It was pretty impressive. She'd put up a picture of an old farm, a house in the center, woodlands, or some other open space, then show a picture of what was there today. The small strip mall at the Byford border. A housing development. With a flourish, she produced a map of Aleford from 1960 with all the open space colored green, then set a current one next to it. The audience gasped. The green spaces had shrunk by at least two thirds.

"We were a milk town, a farming community. There's precious little left of that, but we must preserve *some* of the character of this bygone era for future generations. Unless we act now, I foresee a time in the not-so-distant future when our children won't hear songbirds or be able to go on nature walks. The only plants they'll know will be the ones cultivated in their own backyards. The only wildlife they'll see will be in sanctuaries and they'll have no idea that Aleford was once a green and pleasant land."

Faith thought the reference to Blake stretching things a bit, although his "dark Satanic mills" might be invoked. But she agreed with the rest and hoped the board would. Millicent was building up steam.

"They'll think the only old houses Aleford ever had are the ones surrounding the green, protected by the Historic Commission," Millicent continued, emphasizing the word "*protected*." "What of Civil War Aleford? What of Victorian Aleford? What of—"

"This is all very interesting, Miss McKinley," Sanborn Harrington interrupted, "But what exactly would you have the board do? Mr. Madsen owns Beecher's Bog and as an owner it is his right to do with it as he pleases if he meets the town's requirements for development, which he has."

Someone hissed. Faith thought it might be Brad. Millicent did not appear perturbed—of course.

"I'm glad you asked that question, Sanborn. POW!—Preserve Our Wetlands!—which organized around this issue, has collected almost enough signatures to reconvene Town Meeting, where we intend to place two motions on the floor. Rather than take up the board's valuable time, I've made copies for everyone of the motions involved and would respectfully refer members to the cited precedents, available at the library and in town hall."

Millicent handed each board member a sheet of paper. She was smart enough to know that any proposal involving turning a page already had one strike against it.

Several members scanned the motions and looked up stunned. Sanborn looked angry. "I repeat, Miss McKinley, your research is an admirable foray into the town's past, but as for the present—what is it you are proposing to the board?"

"What we are asking the board to do is"—She paused, and Faith thought what the stage had lost when Millicent had opted for lanterns instead of footlights—"nothing."

"Nothing?" Penny asked.

"Nothing," Millicent replied firmly. "We'd like you to postpone your decision on Mr. Madsen's proposal until Town Meeting has considered the motions I've described. I do not think this slight delay places an undue hardship on the petitioner in question." Her voice dripped with scorn. "The bog isn't going to vanish overnight."

That did it. Whether it was the reference to one of the Deane properties vanishing overnight, as in houses burning down, or Millicent's apparently successful blocking of a member of his family's plans, Gus Deane had had quite enough. He came marching down the center of the room, pushing his way through the crowded seating like Moses parting the Red Sea. He shook his fist at Millicent.

"I've had just about enough of you and the rest of your group. You may think you can destroy property and threaten innocent girls without anyone stopping you, but not while there's a breath in my body."

Gus was not a tall man, yet there was clearly a great deal of breath in his massive body. His hair was completely white and the thick curls created a halo effect. He did indeed look biblical—if not Moses, then one of the more wrathful prophets.

Penny was banging the gavel for all she was worth. The room was going wild.

"Mr. Deane! Mr. Deane! I must ask you to resume your seat!"

"No, I will not. I have something to say. We've listened to her. Now you'll have to listen to me."

Charley MacIsaac moved from the back of the room and stood to one side of the selectmen. Penny gulped down an entire glass of water and glanced from side to side at her fellow board members. Morris Phyfe broke the silence. "Let the man speak. Everyone else has had a say, and I expect we'll be throwing out *Robert's Rules* quite a bit in the next few hours."

Penny nodded at Gus and he stood and faced the room.

"Some of you are my friends. Some of you don't know me at all. And some of you are my enemies. Not that I give a damn." This last word was bleeped to those watching breathlessly at home but he might as well have said "read my lips," so clear was the word.

"I want to clear the air; then we can get back to business—namely, approving a perfectly reasonable construction plan that will bring new taxpayers to town, to say nothing of jobs.

"Number one." Gus held up his hand. Like Joey's, they were huge—calloused, with fingers like knockwurst. The room waited. He raised his index finger. "Number one. Don't think we haven't been hearing all day that we set the fire ourselves for the insurance money and that Mrs. Batcheldor got herself killed when she wandered in on us. Now this is bullshit"—another bleep—"and you all know it. There's no way the insurance is going to cover our loss. And as for the poor woman, why not ask what in God's name she was doing there? And who put her up to it? So, number one, I don't want to hear any more about the Deanes setting fires or knocking people off. If the police were doing their job, they'd have figured out the facts by now. I have."

Charley's expression didn't change a bit as the camera panned slowly over his face.

"Number two." Gus raised his index and middle fingers. Somehow it seemed as if only one was up. "Whatever scum is bothering my granddaughter—and you know who you are—is going to answer to me, and I *will* find you." No one watching doubted otherwise. "Until I do, I am holding the Aleford Police Department and the Massachusetts State Police responsible for her safety and for the safety of her property.

"Now." He seemed to be winding up for a big finish. His broad forehead was so furrowed that the white bristles of his eyebrows jutted out toward the group in one defiant straight line. "None of these things happened until the formation of this cockamamy POW!

group. It seems to me"—he turned to address Charley—"this is no coincidence. They've got it in for us and we're not going to turn tail. We have as much right to be here as they do, even if we didn't step onto Plymouth Rock or whatever."

Brad Hallowell jumped up from the front row. Millicent, to her credit, futilely grabbed at the back of his sweatshirt. "But you don't have the right to rape the land! You don't have the right to destroy the earth for a few bucks! You don't—"

It wasn't clear what Gus roared out. Some said it was "You little swine"; others opted for a more colorful expression. What was clear was that Gus lunged at Brad, who met him, fists raised. Charley moved rapidly toward the pair, surprising those who thought Chief MacIsaac was less nimble than he used to be. Nimble or not, it was all over before he reached them. Millicent placed her skinny but resilient frame between the two men and Penny pounded the gavel so hard, the handle broke and went flying across the room, missing Cheryl Hardy by a few inches. Cheryl looked stunned, got up, and left, vowing to watch the meetings on TV in the future—at home, where she would be safe and might even finish the elaborate argyle sweater she had started for her husband when they were courting ten years earlier.

"This meeting is adjourned. Please clear the room," Penny shouted above the din. "Clear the room immediately!"

Several people had come to Charley and Millicent's aid. Gus was being pushed out one door, still yelling at Brad. Brad was being detained in his seat.

"I guess he's blown any chance he might have had with Lora," Pix commented to Faith. They were staying put.

"I think those chances went out the window long ago, but if I were he, I'd make that visit to Nepal or somewhere farther away about now."

"He can't. Millicent's got him so busy doing things for Patriots' Day that it would take more than Gus Deane to convince her to let Brad leave town. And he's the only one the Minutemen have at the moment who can drum the call to arms."

"But Gus Deane plays Captain Sewall! And isn't he the current company commander?"

"Yes, but don't worry. They really do become the figures they play. And Captain Sewall has no quarrel with young Tom Havers. It's 1775 for a brief moment. You'll see. Nothing will happen."

Looking at the glowering youth sitting with his arms stiff at his sides, clenching the chair, eyes straight ahead, apparently oblivious to Millicent's soothing words, Faith sincerely hoped Pix was right. Patriots' Day was less than a week away. Not much time to cool off.

Margaret's funeral was held Friday morning. Nelson had spent time with Tom the day before going over the service. It was surprising, he told Faith, how many references to birds there were in the Bible. They had settled on Psalm 104, some appropriate hymns, and Margaret's favorite poem, Shelley's "To a Skylark," to be read at the graveside. This had been the only request her husband remembered that she'd ever made about her funeral.

Faith took out her funeral dress, a black Ralph Lauren wool knit she'd bought when she'd first arrived in Aleford and assumed the duties of a ministerial spouse. Before they were married, Tom had been insistent that she would be able to go her own way. "It's my job, not yours," he'd told her. So sweet, so naïve. She'd kissed him and gone out to buy the dress. It had since witnessed so many obsequies that she could never wear it anyplace else without instinctively looking about for a casket.

She slipped the dress over her head and stood by the window. It was pouring—not a drizzle, not a sun shower, but a steady curtain of solid precipitation that obliterated the landscape, turning the early spring into a monochrome. There had been so much rain this year after a curiously snowless winter. So much rain, but not on Monday night. Not on the fire.

Ben was at school and Amy was at a friend's house. There would be the funeral, the interment, then back to the house for thimbles of sherry and lots and lots of those triangle sandwiches.

Was this what Margaret would have liked? It was going to be pretty sedate, although not without tears. What would Faith herself want? Faith pictured her own funeral and wished for some serious wailing and gnashing of teeth. Tom had promised to go at the same time, so presumably the kids, elderly people themselves by then, would be pretty broken up. Faith wanted a funeral where people would feel free to throw themselves on the thin red carpet that went up the center aisle of the church. Maybe roll around a little. She wanted hymns that could be belted out. She wanted "Amazing Grace" the way it ought to be sung.

It wasn't very likely, particularly if her sister, Hope, outlived her, as she no doubt planned. Hope would not be scandalized by such a display of raw emotion; she would simply say it wouldn't do, and that would be that. At least Faith could leave instructions about the food. Maybe champagne and caviar. We die as we live. Or was it the other way around?

As she searched for some dark hose, she realized she hadn't known Margaret very well. Such different interests. Such different schedules. Margaret, a murder victim. So unlikely. This friend of feathered friends. Tom had mentioned that neither Nelson nor Margaret had any family to speak of. She wondered why they hadn't had children. Margaret had spoken of her mother with obvious affection, a mother who set those feet, so sensibly clad in sturdy brown Oxfords, on the path through hill and dale in search of birdsongs. A pretty picture. Wouldn't Margaret have liked to perform the same role? She remembered seeing Nelson installing some shelves at the preschool one morning. Miss Lora and the children were at his side. Faith had never seen the man so animated, so obviously happy.

There was always something a bit wistful about the Batcheldors. Margaret had not had a career, but she'd been born in that sliver of time between the assumption that a woman's place was in the home and the exodus into the workforce. She would have had a foot in each era, and that must have been confusing, as indeed such a picture presented. Faith tried to think about what Margaret actually had done. Nelson was more active in the church than she'd been, although she was a member of the Alliance. She'd done some volunteer work and was prominent in the Aleford Conservation Commission. She'd definitely had organizational skills, but seemed content with her life outdoors, field guide in hand. Tom had told Faith that a signed photo of Roger Tory Peterson was hanging on the wall in Margaret's room. Maybe Nelson didn't want her to work. Fortunately, Faith wasn't married to someone with this problem.

She was going to the funeral with Pix. Pix would have a hat. So would Millicent and most of the other women. Faith looked in her closet. A large Virginia Woolf straw was certainly not suitable, nor a floppy velvet beret, even though it was black. Besides, it was raining. She got out her umbrella, raincoat, and a pair of gloves. Pix would appreciate the effort and Aleford would have to lump the hat.

"Poor Margaret! Such a terrible day," Pix remarked after they had shaken the water from their coats like spaniels and assumed their seats in one of the First Parish pews.

Faith knew what her friend meant. It was bad enough to have died the way she did; the least God could have done was to make the sun shineth upon her.

"Not too many people. Maybe the weather has kept some of their older friends away," Pix commented, turning around to scan the mourners. She had the uncanny ability to estimate a crowd, and Faith pictured embedded in Pix's frontal lobe one of those little devices the Museum of Fine Arts had at the entrance to count people. "I'd say there can't be more than twenty-three people, maybe twenty-four."

Faith looked, too. She would have thought more would have come, if only out of ghoulish curiosity. There were people she didn't recognize, but some of them were probably from the library where Nelson worked.

"Her world was pretty small—the bird-watchers, the members of the Conservation Commission. I've never even been inside their house," Pix said. Now this *was* a surprise. Pix under the aegis of one organization or another, or simply for pleasure, had been in and out of most of the homes in Aleford. Her tone of voice indicated she was mildly surprised herself.

"Well, you didn't miss anything." Faith had been there with Tom on parish calls. "Lots of knotty pine, bird things, of course, and that's about it. We had Triscuits and tomato juice." Faith tended to remember what she had been served even more clearly than where.

The organist began to play the first hymn. Everyone stood up. Tom mounted the pulpit and they began to sing, "Where ancient forests widely spread." By the time they got to "Till death the gates of heaven unfold," Faith knew she was depressed. Dear God, how she hated funerals.

It got better when Tom began to speak and there *was* comfort in the familiar words of the service. He was reading from John, "In my Father's house are many mansions." To comfort the bereaved—that was the whole point of the service.

Nelson had pulled himself together and was sitting dry-eyed in the front pew, close to the casket. There was a large basket of flowers on top with a few small artificial birds perched on the sprays of inevitable gladioli. Nelson was flanked by the Scotts. Louise's nose was bright red and she seemed closer to breaking down than the next of kin. Nelson squeezed her hand, which only served to start the tears again. Faith thought of Amy's reaction to Nelson in the woods. The poor man seemed to be better at provoking tears than stanching them lately.

They read Psalm 104 responsively. Tom had done a good job, and it was filled with birds. Some ancient progenitor of Margaret's, with a life list in hand, may well have authored it—at the very least, a kindred spirit:

The trees of the Lord are full of sap;
the cedars of Lebanon, which he planted.
In them the birds make their nests;
as for the stork, the fir trees are her house.

Faith began to feel uneasy. She was having trouble concentrating. Church sometimes had this effect on her. What was Margaret doing in the new house? What was Margaret doing in the woods?

Let the sinners be consumed from the earth,
and let the wicked be no more.
Bless the Lord, O my soul!
Praise the Lord!

She was jolted from her thoughts but not her anxiety. Tom's voice, as he read the last verse, had assumed a totally different quality. He was not just stern but angry. Suddenly, every one in the church was reminded of the way Margaret died. And the sinner still walked among them.

Tom's homily touched upon Margaret's love of nature and service to the community. He spoke of the deep sorrow that inevitably follows when a life is cut off before its time and the test this presents for one's faith. Faith, his wife, heard him and took the words literally—as a challenge.

The last hymn was one of those that changed key frequently, making it difficult to sing, and by the third verse only Tom and a few other diehards were trying. Everyone else came in for the "Amen" and then trooped out into the rain to the cemetery.

The cemetery next to the church had long since filled up and now it was mostly visited by those interested in Aleford history and earnest souls who found delight in hanging rubbings with pithy epitaphs such as "Death is a debt, to Nature due,/I've paid the debt, and so must you" on their walls. The new cemetery, dedicated shortly after the Civil War, was across town. As need arose, the grounds had been extended, and it was like a large park, a park with headstones. The heavy carpet of moss and abundance of willows lent a suitably doleful air to the surroundings. On most days it was a pleasant walk from First Parish, but not today. Faith got into Pix's car and they joined the cortege. It wasn't a very long one.

There were even fewer people than had been at the church and they clustered together, umbrellas overlapping, trying to keep dry. The tree trunks were streaked with black and beneath the leafless branches the ground was a sea of mud. The wind was picking up. The people from the funeral home had quickly gotten back into the hearse after depositing the casket. Tom struggled to hold both his prayer book and umbrella until Faith came to his rescue, shielding him from the elements with her large umbrella.

Giving her a grateful look, he started the service with Shelley's poem, and never had "Hail to thee, blithe spirit!" seemed more inappropriate. Tom persevered. Faith had forgotten how long the ode was. By the time he got to:

Teach me half the gladness
That thy brain must know;

Such harmonious madness
From my lips would flow,
The world should listen then, as I am listening now.

Faith's feet were soaked and the arm holding the umbrella had gone to sleep.

"Earth to earth, ashes to ashes, dust to dust . . ." Tom dropped a handful of dirt on top of the casket as his deep voice, so well suited to his calling, repeated the familiar words. Familiar words, yet however often Faith heard them, they always produced the same effect on her. A door was being shut. Another one might be opening, but this life was over. When were you ready? Sixty, eighty, a hundred? Never? Margaret hadn't been ready. Margaret had been denied all thought at the end. It was horrible.

Faith heard the mourners start, "Our Father," and she joined in. Margaret Batcheldor's funeral was over.

Pix dropped her off at one o'clock and Faith immediately called Lora to tell her she was on her way over to pick up Ben. Lora ran an extended day program twice a week and this had fortunately been one of the days. As Faith hurried down the stairs into the church basement, where the nursery school was located, she realized that of course no one from the Deane family, nor any of their friends, had attended Margaret's funeral. Faith had half-expected Gus to show up. It was the kind of thing he did. Lest anyone have any doubts. What kind of murderer would go to the victim's funeral? she could almost hear him say. But perhaps his wife had encouraged him to stay home. Lillian didn't like the spotlight. Perhaps he hadn't thought to go at all. And it wasn't true, Faith thought. About murderers. They often did go to their victim's funerals—out of bravado, or to make sure the deed was well and truly done. Maybe remorse?

It had been a small group back at the Batcheldors' house. The rain was still coming down hard, and even with all the lights turned on, the atmosphere was gloomy. They lived in a small stone Arts and Crafts–style cottage that had been built in the twenties. Today the stone walls and small-paned windows did not seem cozy. The Scotts were there, acting as hosts, keeping everyone supplied with sherry and, yes, those sandwiches. Millicent grabbed Pix and, as Pix reported later, filled her in on what would be presented at tonight's POW! meeting. Charley MacIsaac sat morosely in a bare wood Stickley-type chair next to Nelson. Charley was not drinking sherry; he had managed to find something quite a different color that filled half a tumbler. He was avoiding the sandwiches, too.

Conversation tended toward the repetitive: "I can't believe she's gone." "She was a very special person." No one mentioned the fire. No one mentioned the time of night.

"Mom, hey, Mom, look what I made!" Ben tackled her, effectively pulling her into the present tense.

"He is so talented, Faith. I think you may have a real artist here," Miss Lora said seriously. "He is unusually gifted." She was holding a dripping-wet painting. It looked like a rainbow done by a nearly five-year-old child. Faith took a chance.

"What a beautiful rainbow, sweetheart. When it dries, we can take it home and put it up on the fridge."

"Oh, Mom, it's not a rainbow. See the legs? It's a zebra from Magic Land and here's the boy who rides him in the sky and here's . . ."

Swearing for the ninety-ninth time that she would never guess what a child had drawn until given either an extremely obvious hint or the answer, Faith managed to get Ben away without the painting by explaining the rain might damage it. This made sense to both Ben and Miss Lora, who was as insistent that the masterpiece grace the Fairchild home as soon as possible as Ben had been.

Lora did not look like someone who was resting easy in the

comfort and security of her grandparents' home. She had deep circles under her eyes. Faith asked her how things were going as Ben left to get his raincoat and froggy boots.

"Oh, everything's fine. Well, I mean it's not great living at Grandma and Grandpa's, but at least no one's throwing stuff through my windows."

"Do you have any idea who it could have been?" Tom had already reported that she did not. He and Charley had been spending quite a lot of time together lately and evidently, as Faith had suspected, covered much ground. Still, maybe Miss Lora would spill the beans to Faith, a sympathetic woman, far removed from an official capacity.

No such luck.

"I can't imagine who would do such a thing." It sounded as if she'd said this phrase before—and more than once.

"You don't think it could have been Brad? You did think he could have made the calls? Or Joey?"

"Definitely not Joey!" Lora's cheeks flushed in annoyance. "I told you, I was wrong to accuse him."

Ben came back and the conversation ended, but Faith knew it wouldn't have gone anyplace. Whatever Lora knew or suspected, she was keeping to herself. No show-and-tell, no sharing circle.

Tom came back around three. He looked wrecked and Faith knew he still had his sermon to finish. She sometimes wished he were a bit less honorable and would either repeat an earlier one or use one of those sermon books—at least as a starting point. But someone in the congregation would be bound to point out the repetition even while vigorously shaking Tom's hand at the church door at the close of the service. And Tom scorned all aids, the ecclesiastical equivalent of Cliffs Notes, even the computerized Bible, complete with subject search, on CD-ROM, that was being touted by some of his colleagues. Faith thought it sounded great and wondered who did the readings—Charlton Heston? But Tom steadfastly refused, surrounding himself with stacks of books and papers. Whether it was the divinity ordering one's life or pure chance, somehow he managed to make sense of the chaos, plucking the sources he needed and turning out sermon after sermon each week—intelligent, inspirational, occasionally truly memorable. And never too long.

The kids were making sugar cookies with their mother in the kitchen. She was tired, too, but after Amy woke up from her nap, Faith had felt a need to do something with family and food for comfort. Margaret's funeral had continued to stay with her like the cold, soaking rain that had worked its way down the back of her coat collar at the cemetery.

"Why don't you lie down before you start working? I'll keep the kids in here with me and maybe you can get a quick nap."

"It sounds great, but I know I won't be able to sleep with this hanging over my head. Maybe I'll work a little, then take a break."

"We're going to have dinner early. POW!—remember? Samantha is baby-sitting, but if you want to stay home, I'll call her."

"No, I want to go. Who knows what may happen?" Tom attempted a light tone, yet the words were strained.

Faith agreed. She wasn't offering to stay home.

Everything had started with the formation of POW! Gus had thundered the other night. And he was right—the letters, the attack on Lora's apartment, the fire, the murder. The calls had come before, but the calls might be unrelated.

She grabbed the flour canister just before Amy sent it toppling over the edge of the table, and got out a rolling pin for Ben. She set Amy on the floor with the tin of cookie cutters and let her play with the shapes.

"At least let me make you a cup of coffee, or some tea? And I hope you didn't eat any of those sandwiches, did you? You must need something."

Tom had, in fact, mindlessly consumed quite a few of the bite-sized sandwiches before he realized how foul they tasted. He'd avoided the sherry and had been drinking coffee all afternoon. It was the last thing he wanted now.

"How about a big glass of milk and whatever cookies you guys make?"

"I'm making rainbow zebra cookies, Daddy. Just for you," Ben said.

Faith eyed him warily. He was getting dangerously close to cute. She'd have to read *Where the Wild Things Are* to him again—soon.

"When they're ready, I'll bring you some. The first batch is going in now." Faith gave Tom a big hug.

It was upon this scene of slightly boring domestic tranquillity that the doorbell intruded. Faith wiped her hands on her apron and went to answer it. When she opened the door, she gasped.

Detective Lieutenant John Dunne of the Massachusetts State Police stood without.

Chapter 5

Familiarity had not diminished the impact of John Dunne's presence. As Dunne stepped into the hall, Faith marveled anew at the sheer bulk of the man: six foot seven with an ample frame to match, his head grazed the parsonage's authentically quaint low ceilings. In his late forties, the salt was beginning to overpower the pepper on his head. Otherwise, he was unchanged from Faith's first encounter—or, as she liked to think of it, partnership—with him five years earlier. He still dressed more like a CEO than a cop, and as she took his Burberry—had to be special order—she noted the well-cut suit he was wearing. Her private theory was that Dunne dressed so impeccably, even down to the French cuffs he favored, to draw attention away from the rest of him—especially his face. It was, in a word, homely. When he was growing up, his mother had probably told him it showed character. It got worse when he smiled, which fortunately was not often. He was not smiling now.

"I wonder if I could have a word with you and Tom?"

Detective Lieutenant Dunne had grown up in the Bronx, but

his wife was from Maine, and Massachusetts was as far south as she'd go. Fourteen years in New England had not altered his accent. If anything, it had thickened. It was a not-so-subtle statement of regional pride—of egg creams, the Zoo, and Manhattan, a short subway ride away. Faith, who had resisted "paahking her carr in Hahvad Yaad" herself had been drawn to Dunne immediately—and ever since. In turn, she was growing on him, but how, specifically, varied from time to time, depending on the mood he was in. At the moment, he wished he could tell her to stay in the kitchen and keep baking the cookies he smelled. It had as much chance of working as the possibility of his acquiring a rent-controlled West Side apartment with a view of the park as a pied-à-terre.

"Of course. Tom's in his study. Go on in and I'll join you as soon as I get the kids settled. Coffee? Something to eat?"

"No thanks." Faith expected as much. Dunne seldom accepted refreshment while on the job. For once, she was glad sustenance had been rejected. She didn't want to miss anything.

Having quickly opted for that mother's standby, a video—in this case *Winnie the Pooh*—Faith walked into the study only a few minutes later.

"I've assumed the whole thing was Millicent's idea," Tom was saying.

"What whole thing?" Faith asked. With Millicent, Tom could be referring to anything from temperance to changing Aleford's name back to what Millicent believed was its original one, Haleford.

John Dunne sighed. The papers on Tom's desk fluttered. She was back. There was no way he was going to get a private chat with the reverend. Once again, he faced the prospect that Faith would get overly involved, get in the way, get in his hair, get . . . He could go on, and did—to his wife.

Yet, he reminded himself, Faith did know more about what

was going on in town than Tom, who the detective presumed was busy concentrating on loftier matters.

"I want to know about the POW! group," Dunne explained. "Who started it, anything that comes to mind."

Faith thought it more judicious to answer his questions before asking her own.

"Tom is right. Millicent started Preserve Our Wetlands! and the core group formed around a letter sent to the *Chronicle* protesting Joey Madsen's plans to develop Beecher's Bog."

Dunne nodded.

"The people who signed the letter were Pix Miller, Louise and Ted Scott, Margaret and Nelson Batcheldor, Brad Hallowell, and Millicent herself. You know about the poison-pen letters they got afterward?"

"Yes," Dunne said. "Charley told me. He also described the meeting of POW! that he attended and I understand there's another one tonight. But what I want to know is whether there have been others you know about, smaller meetings."

"I'm sure there have been, although I haven't been invited to any. They would have had to have met to talk about the big meeting and compose the flyer. Although, I suppose Millicent and Brad could have done that themselves. I can find out from Pix if she's been at any meetings." Having offered help, Faith felt she could slip in a question.

"Do you think Margaret's active membership in POW! had something to do with her murder?" Dunne hadn't rung their doorbell to sell raffle tickets for PAL. The state police would have been called in right away in a town with a police force the size of Aleford's. The detective might be asking about POW!, but he was definitely investigating Margaret's death.

He frowned. It was marginally more grotesque than his smile.

"I didn't say anything about the Batcheldor case," he spoke sternly. "Back off, Faith. All I want to know about is POW!"

Outwardly chastened, Faith told him everything she knew and described the selectmen's meetings, as well. She had been prepared to tell him about meeting the Batcheldors in the bog, but he'd said stick to POW!, so she did.

At the end, he nodded again and addressed Tom. "It would be useful if we had someone who could report what goes on at these meetings. Charley's there, but some extra eyes and ears would help. Obviously we can't go."

"I suppose so," Tom said. He wasn't altogether easy with the role of infiltrator, but if Dunne thought there could be a connection between the group and the murder, they had to try to find it.

Faith was not miffed. She was used to John and knew that even though he was specifically asking Tom, he meant her, too—however much it pained him.

"You want us to be moles. No problem. Now, if we could disguise ourselves in Carhartt jackets and get jobs with Deane Properties, we'd be all set."

It was exactly what Dunne had been afraid of—Faith was already on the case, at least in her mind.

"I just want to know about the conservation group. Period."

If he had known Faith was taking this to mean that she didn't have to share whatever else she uncovered, he might have phrased it differently. He might not even have walked in the parsonage door in the first place.

He snapped shut the Filofax in which he'd been making notes and stood up, narrowly missing a beam. The study was in the oldest part of the house.

"I'll hear from you tomorrow, then." It was not a question. Tom showed him out and Faith raced to make sure the tape had not finished. Tigger was about to take Roo's medicine and Ben had not taken Amy out of the playpen. She was in time.

Resisting the impulse to dress up as either Boris Badenov or Natasha—she seemed to have an impulse for disguise lately—Faith arrived at POW!'s second meeting early enough to get a place up front. She draped her jacket on the seat beside her to save it for Tom, who was waiting for Samantha. Softball practice had run late. Samantha had still not heard from her last two colleges and was no closer to a decision about the others than she had been a week ago. The whole episode of the poison-pen letter had been overshadowed by where Samantha was going to go to school, the main topic of conversation at the Miller house once again. Samantha herself seemed quite calm when Faith had spoken to her about her choices. It was Pix who was going off the deep end. "I don't even know what time zone she's going to be in or how much of a phone bill to expect!" she'd told Faith. The real issue was Samantha's leaving. Pix was going to miss her terribly, and without a daughter in residence, the whole family constellation would change. "I'll be outnumbered," she'd told Faith. "All the blouses in the wash will be mine." Faith had commiserated without totally understanding. Granted, it was many years away, but she thought it might not be so bad getting back to just the two of them—with lots of visits home, of course. Pix viewed the gradual reduction in size as the loss of limbs from one kind of family tree.

Millicent strode up onstage just as Tom slid into the seat next to his wife. "No envelopes thick or thin today, and she's sick of talking about it. So don't say anything about the *C* word when we get home," he told her quickly before Millicent began.

"Poor Samantha! It's horrible to be the center of attention sometimes."

Millicent didn't have a gavel. She didn't need one. The room, which was even more crowded than last time, instantly grew quiet.

"Before we begin, I'd like to have a moment of silence for our member, Margaret Batcheldor, who died so tragically this week. Most of you knew her and of her devotion to our cause. I would like to dedicate all our future efforts in memory of Margaret."

Millicent bowed her head and the only sound was the ticking of the large clock mounted on the wall next to the stage. Sixty seconds later, Millicent's head snapped up and she was on to the first order of business.

"We'll start the meeting with a report from the head of the signature drive, Brad Hallowell. Brad, stand up."

Brad stood.

"We have submitted more than the required number of signatures to the town clerk and after verification, which should be completed by Tuesday, since Monday is a holiday, a special Town Meeting will be called for the following week." Someone gave a cheer and everyone clapped. Brad sat down.

Faith tried to think of a way she could question him. They still didn't know who'd made the calls—or thrown the brick. Lora was at her grandparents, but she'd have to go back to her own place sometime. Brad was basking in success at the moment, smiling and happy. He didn't look threatening, but his scuffle with Gus at the selectmen's meeting suggested otherwise.

"Wonderful work! Everyone is to be congratulated, and special thanks to you, Brad, for doing such a fine job coordinating things. I may just have to get one of those computers myself someday!" The audience laughed at the pleasantry. Until they came out with Chippendale or Sheraton models, it was unlikely that high tech would invade Miss McKinley's parlor.

"I'm pleased to report that our treasury is in fine shape due to your generous contributions, and we have more than enough for a town-wide mailing to explain what is going to happen at Town Meeting and ask people to call their members to express support for the articles. Pix Miller and Louise Scott have agreed to head up this committee, and they'll need volunteers to stuff all those envelopes. You can sign up after the meeting. I've written an informal environmental-impact statement that we'll include."

"When does the woman sleep?" Faith whispered to Tom. She leaned back in the wooden chair like the kind that used to be in movie theaters, the kind that demanded you sit down quickly and stay seated or it would jackknife on you. It was almost as uncomfortable as the pews at First Parish. So far, there was precious little to report back to headquarters, she thought. Signature collection and a hefty treasury. Possibly there was something there. She could ask Pix who the big donors were. Everyone had been asked to kick in at least ten dollars initially to cover the cost of the flyers. But a town-wide mailing was expensive. Millicent herself lived on a very fixed income—or so she said, frequently. Brad certainly made good money, but was he committed to the point where he was assuming the bulk of the cost? Faith wished she could make a note, but she didn't want to look conspicuous.

Faith was getting bored. Maybe it was too much to hope for a repeat of the fireworks at the last selectmen's meeting.

Millicent was discussing tactics for Town Meeting. Someone suggested that all the Town Meeting members in POW! meet separately to talk about how best to present the articles. Millicent thought that was a pretty good idea. Faith didn't. It meant Tom would find out what was going on before she did. Town Meeting was something the Fairchilds had always done wherever they found themselves, running for election before the boxes were unpacked, although in Tom's family's case, this normally meant years. The Fairchilds were savers and everything went with them. On one visit, Faith had been startled to discover some Allied Van cartons in her in-law's attic marked, "Children's Misc. Schoolwork and Odd Curtains."

"Now to be blunt . . ." Faith heard through her thoughts. Millicent might be getting to something interesting at last, she hoped. "We have to be very careful not to tread on any toes between now and the meeting. A certain family in town has come in for a great deal of criticism and mudslinging is not the way we do things in Aleford. They will have their day in court, just as we will. Town Meeting will decide."

This was pretty decent of Millicent—to call off the hounds and leave the Deanes in peace. But, Faith reflected, it was also very smart. There was nothing to be gained by going after them. It made POW! look bad. Millicent was a great believer in the power of moral superiority.

Suddenly, Faith began to feel sorry for the Deanes and was glad Millicent wasn't a mind reader—close to it though she was. What about the Deanes' rights? Faith didn't want the land developed, but Joey did own it. It belonged to him, and those opposing him would be equally furious if, for instance, Joey told them they couldn't paint their houses a certain color or add on a bedroom because of some sainted "quality of life in Aleford" article.

"I'm getting mixed up about which side I'm on," Faith said in a low voice to her husband.

"Me, too," he responded, speaking into her ear. "I don't like the bedfellows on one side; don't like the bed on the other."

Millicent was asking for someone to help draft the cover letter for the mailing. Faith, finally seeing an opportunity, shot her hand up like an eager "pick me, pick me!" third grader.

"Why, Faith," Millicent said, the words tumbling out before she could help herself.

"Thank you, I'd love to work on this," she said in acceptance, even though she well knew Millicent was merely voicing surprise.

Faith never volunteered for anything. She'd learned from watching Pix that one thing did not lead to another, but to fifty or sixty.

Tom raised his eyebrows. It gave him an endearing look. Faith smiled. "I simply want to be of service, darling."

"Sure you do," he said, the eyebrows approaching his hairline.

At the close of the meeting, Ted Scott read a few passages from Thoreau to keep everyone in the mood and Millicent told them they would gather again, same time, same place, the following Wednesday. POW! was gaining momentum and they would need to meet more often.

Faith was waiting for her at the side of the stage.

"When do you want to meet?" she asked.

"Meet?" Millicent made it sound like an indecent suggestion.

"Yes, to draft the letter."

"Oh, that. Well, I can't think about another thing until Patriots' Day is over. I have a million things to do before Monday."

Faith was sure this was not an exaggeration. Apart from organizing the reenactment, Millicent was also in charge of the DAR's pancake breakfast served afterward to some of the hundreds of spectators who flocked to the green. Then there was the morning youth parade and the big parade later in the day. Millicent had received the Bronze Musket, the town's highest civic award, twice—the only person in history to do so. In Aleford, this particular plaque was so prized it fell into the category of what-to-save-first-in-the-event-of-disaster. For a couple of the recipients, it might be a hard choice between musket and, say, spouse.

"How about Tuesday?" Faith was persistent. "The mailing should be well in advance of Town Meeting, and we could read it to the members the next night."

"All right, Tuesday. Ten o'clock at my house. I'll see if Brad can make it. He's working at home for these two weeks."

Just as Faith had hoped. Brad Hallowell. At last a chance to get to know this tempestuous young man, a young man Millicent obviously did know well, even down to his work schedule.

She left Millicent and went in search of Tom, who was talking to Pix. Faith suggested they walk home together. Sam Miller, while opposing Alefordiana Estates, told his wife he could not belong to any organization that had an exclamation point. He'd taken his son to the movies.

It wasn't difficult to find out what Pix knew about POW!'s funding. All Faith had to do was ask.

"I assume you're talking about amounts over a hundred, right?"

"Yes," Faith answered, this being the rough equivalent of *benefactor* in New York City, your name to be chiseled in marble or over an archway.

"The Scotts gave a hundred and fifty and so did the Batcheldors. Brad gave two hundred. The largest donation was five hundred from anonymous."

"Anonymous? Come on, you must have some idea of who it is, or Millicent does. The check had to be signed."

"Nope." They were approaching the parsonage and Pix slowed her steps. "The money was in cash. Millicent found it in her mailbox with the donation slip from the flyer inside."

"Well, what did that say?"

"Nothing. Just 'anonymous' printed next to 'Name'—and no other information."

"Not too many people in town have that kind of money, or rather, they do, but they don't give it away. Take a guess, Pix. Who do you think it is?"

"I have given it some thought," Pix admitted, "and we did talk about it when we met to plan last week's meeting. It could be Bea Hoffman or one of the other selectmen—someone who can't publicly support us."

"Does Bea have that much money?" Faith asked. Bea had never struck her as a lady with much in the way of disposable income. Same coat since Faith had been in Aleford. Same pocketbook, too. Although this frugality should have alerted her.

"Oh yes, Bea is very wealthy. Her mother's family."

They were at the gate to the parsonage.

"I'll come in and get Samantha," Pix offered. "No sense in having her walk home alone."

"I'm happy to walk her home, but she always laughs at me," Tom protested.

"Since it's only a few steps, I can see why," her mother said, contradicting herself. But Faith knew Pix wasn't concerned for Samantha's safety. She just wanted to store up as much time as possible with her daughter.

Samantha was curled up in one of the wing chairs, reading. She yawned and stretched.

"They were perfect," she told Faith, who believed her. One's children always were for other people. "How was POW! tonight?" She laughed.

"Fine. And we have enough signatures to reconvene Town Meeting. Poor Joey Madsen better give up now," Pix said. "By the way, did you see that his lawyer was there again tonight? I think Joey should come himself instead of sending a spy!"

The tops of Tom's ears turned pink. "Maybe he has his reasons. Such as not wanting to cause a riot."

Faith looked at her husband. "I agree with Pix. Spies, the very idea."

At two o'clock the next afternoon, Faith was looking out the kitchen window, trying to predict the weather. They were about to take the kids to the Boston Children's Museum. Should it be raincoats or not? Pix seemed to have acquired this meteorological knack at about the same time as she had learned to walk, and Faith had noted other Aleford residents who would touch their tongues to index fingers, test the air with great deliberation, then matter-of-factly tell you the temperature, barometric pressure, and the precipitation for the next several days, with an occasional reference to what was rolling in from Canada.

"Raincoats?" she asked Ben and Amy. Maybe they'd picked it up, too. Ben was already adding *r*'s to the end of certain words where none existed.

"It's not going to rain, Mom. It's warm. I don't need a jacket," Ben said firmly. So firmly, Faith was tempted to believe him, except he never wanted to wear a jacket.

"We'll throw them in the car. I wonder what's keeping Daddy." Tom had been at the church office since early morning, taking a sandwich with him.

After her husband had left, she'd reported in to Detective Lieutenant Dunne. It had been a brief conversation and the only item that really seemed to interest him was the anonymous five-hundred-dollar donation. It was the only thing that had interested her the night before, too. She told him that she had volunteered to be on a committee, and he told her to keep in touch, but she could tell his heart wasn't really in it.

She returned to peer out the window like Sister Anne, but it wasn't her brothers she saw. It was Miss Lora. Miss Lora was getting out of a very new, very jazzy bright red Miata convertible—a car Faith herself coveted. Miss Lora? Sports cars? She was carrying a carton and called something back over her shoulder to the driver. Faith strained to see who it was, but he was too far away and the top was up. She quickly grabbed her purse, got out the keys to the extremely practical familial Honda, and prayed for Tom to return quickly. Maybe not prayed as such, but wished hard. It worked. As soon as he was in earshot, halfway across the cemetery, she opened the door and called out, "Tom, could you hurry up? The kids are really eager to get going." It was true. It was also true that so was she—eager to follow Miss Lora and see who was behind the wheel of the car.

Reverend Fairchild walked through the door, expecting a hug and a kiss. Instead, Faith pulled him to one side. "Did you see Lora?"

"Lora? No. Why? Was I supposed to?"

"No, no," Faith said impatiently. "But she just got out of that sports car in the church driveway and went inside. Did you recognize who was driving the car?"

Tom had finished his sermon. While not a cloudless blue sky, it was a washed-out watercolor approximation. He was on his way home to spend a pleasant afternoon with his wife and children. There was a spring in his step. He'd had a good run that morning. He hadn't, in short, seen the driver—or the car.

"Car?"

"Look out the window! That red sports car—you didn't notice it?"

"Not really. Is this important?" He loved his wife, yet there were definitely times when their worldviews diverged, and this was one of them.

"Lora got out of the car, carrying a cardboard box, said something I couldn't hear, and went into the church."

"So long as she wasn't taking things out of the church in a box, I'd say there's nothing here to be concerned about. Why don't we get going? I just need to go—"

"She's back! Tom, come on, we've got to find out whose car it is. She seemed so edgy yesterday when I picked Ben up, and she looked terrible. You haven't forgotten how frightened she was that night in the study? I just want to know what's going on."

Tom hadn't forgotten how terrified the young woman was and he became infected with Faith's sense of urgency.

"You're right. Let's go."

They strapped the kids in their car seats. Tom backed out of the garage and drove down the street to a spot with a clear view of the church.

"Why are we stopping? I thought we were going to the museum? I want to climb on that big phone and make bubbles. Why—" Ben was puzzled.

"Hush, sweetie. We need to stay here for a minute and think. Maybe you could think of some other things you want to do in the museum."

"I want to play with that computer and—"

"Think, Ben. Think. Quietly," Faith said, then patted his sleek blond head affectionately. She was trying very hard to save him a fortune in future therapists' fees. Amy was taking her shoes and socks off. No problems there.

Tom started the car.

"She's coming out. Good girl. She's locking up."

The Miata pulled out of the church driveway and turned right along the north side of the green, then left onto Main Street. Tom followed. The Honda was a silver-gray one and he hoped it would be inconspicuous. He'd never done anything like this before, but he'd seen enough movies. He let two cars get between him and the very conspicuous sports car as they passed the library. The Miata was traveling at an overly respectable twenty miles an hour.

"Not speeding through town. Think that means it's someone who knows Charley usually has a car on Parker Place?" Chief MacIsaac was proud of this extremely lucrative source of revenue for the town, revenue from nonresidents, of course. Everyone local slowed to a crawl.

"Lora's with him, so we can't assume anything."

"True."

As soon as the posted speed limit went to 40 mph, the Miata

jumped forward. With one car between them, Tom followed suit. They were heading straight down Main Street, away from Aleford and toward Arlington, Cambridge, and Boston.

"I'll bet he turns toward Route Two."

"Too easy." Faith only bet when she knew she would win. "Lora lives in the opposite direction, so they're not going to her place. Why would they be going to Arlington? The car has bright lights, big city written all over it, and the fastest way to get there is on the highway."

At the small, treacherous traffic circle down by the Woodrows' farm stand—a family operation that had mushroomed from bins of tomatoes, lettuce, and corn in season to arugula and jicama—the small red car made a sharp right. The Fairchilds were slowed down by their attempt to enter the circle, something akin to Russian roulette, except with cars, when all the Saturday shoppers were leaving the stand.

"Don't worry. We won't lose them. We were right. They have to be going to Route Two."

Tom turned down the ramp and they spotted the car farther along the highway, not too far ahead of them. He speeded up.

"Hey, Dad, this is fun. Go faster!" Ben called out. Tom grinned. He had no idea anymore why he was doing this, but it *was* fun.

The highway stopped and they followed the car around two more traffic circles, less lethal because of the perpetual construction occurring outside the Alewife Transit Station and Fresh Pond Parkway. It slowed everyone to a crawl. Finally, at the Charles River, the road divided definitively. The left would take them down Memorial Drive past Harvard; the right led to Storrow Drive and Boston.

"Don't lose them. Don't lose them!" Faith cried.

"Don't lose them, Daddy!" Ben echoed.

Tom could just see a patch of red that he assumed was their

quarry. Traffic was heavy on this Saturday afternoon and there was no way to stay closer to the car. He tried pulling into the next lane and was rewarded with both an obscene gesture and the blast of a horn. He wished he'd worn his work clothes.

The light changed and he pulled forward. It was no good. He couldn't see which way they'd turned.

"We have a fifty-fifty chance. Quick, tell me what to do," he said to Faith.

"Take Storrow. We're going that way, anyway."

The red car was stopped at the next light. Tom grinned triumphantly and pulled up behind them. There were so many cars now that looked like the Fairchilds' that he felt safe. Besides, he didn't want to lose them again. Faith put on her dark glasses. She wished she had a scarf to tie around her hair like Garbo or Madonna, but Faith wasn't the type to tie scarves around her hair. The sunglasses would have to do.

The light changed and Tom trailed the car to Copley Square.

"It's a clear day. Maybe we should take the kids to the top of the John Hancock Building," Tom suggested as they passed the tallest building in the city, sheer glass jutting up to the sky, and now that the windows had stopped popping out, perfectly safe. He liked going up there. You got a great view of the city, and while you couldn't see as far down the South Shore as Norwell, where he grew up, he could point in the right direction for the kids.

South Shore childhood memories receded rapidly, replaced by Boston's South End. They drove down Clarendon, across Columbus, and then the Miata turned left and pulled into a parking place on Chandler Street, a legal one—something of a minor miracle.

"Over there! Across the street!" Faith gestured in front of Tom's nose, causing him to step on the brakes.

"Honey, there's a hydrant. We can't—"

"We're not getting out. If we see a—" She had started to say the word *cop*, then recalled Ben had unhappily reached that age where you could say virtually nothing in front of him—had reached it a long time ago.

"If we see a person with a notebook in hand, we'll leave. We're not getting out of the car. At least not all of us."

"This isn't the museum." Ben offered the observation as a flat statement of fact.

"We know that, but we need some more thinking time. You do that, too, sweetheart, and we'll be at the museum soon." Amy was attempting to remove her sweater and overalls.

"Are they waiting for someone, do you think?" Tom asked. No one had moved from the Miata.

"Possibly."

They sat in silence for a few minutes more. A young man dressed in black jeans with an A/X T-shirt, spotlessly white except for the logo, came strolling down the block. He paused at the car. Faith rolled her window down. He looked at his watch, glanced at the sports car, and moved on.

"Some kind of code?" Tom asked.

Faith reminded herself that Tom read a great many more mysteries than she did. She'd like to humor him, but years of sleuthing, amateur though she was, told her the guy was probably merely stopping to check the time.

She shook her head, then put her hand on Tom's arm. The door was opening. She turned around to face the backseat and put her finger to her lips. "It's a game," she whispered. "Quiet as mice."

The driver got out, closed his door, and walked around the front of the car to put money in the meter. He was a total stranger. She looked over at Tom. He shook his head.

Whoever it was matched the car well. The look was Louis, not Brooks. This was someone who paid attention to labels. Someone who thought clothes were important and a reflection of self. Someone not unlike Faith herself. For this spring Saturday afternoon, he was wearing a soft cream-colored silk shirt, light brown cotton slacks, tight, but not too tight in the rear—enough to show, not show off—and a cotton sweater the color of perfectly poached salmon, flung casually around his shoulders. No gold chains or an earring, just a simple watch that Faith was pretty sure even at this distance was a Piaget and tasseled loafers for decoration. He was fairly tall, lean, and his blond hair was at a length about halfway between Fabio and Macaulay Culkin.

Miss Lora with this guy? Faith and Tom didn't have to speak. Each face mirrored the other's surprise.

Then Lora got out, on her own steam. Whoever he was, he was either too conscious of women's rights to open the door for her or did not have any manners. Faith reminded herself that Lora had struggled with her carton unaided.

She wasn't carrying anything now, except one of those funny little knapsacks made of clear vinyl. Faith focused on the bag. It confused her. The whole thing confused her. Where *was* Lora Deane? Whoever had gotten out of the car did not look anything like the person who had gotten in. Had some sort of switch been made? During the brief time they had lost track of the Miata? But why? And with whom?

Tom was quicker, although apparently equally stunned. "Just like Betty Grable." He was smiling. "You know, 'Why, Miss Jones!' "

And Faith did know. The old "take off your glasses, remove the bobby pins, shake out your hair, perch on the desk, and cross your shapely legs" number.

Like Miss Jones, Lora had ditched her glasses—contacts? She'd also pulled her hair from its habitual ponytail, applied makeup—skillfully—and taken off the loose-fitting jacket she'd had on earlier. Underneath it, she'd been wearing a very short plum-colored jersey dress that showed what the jumpers and overalls had been hiding all this time. Miss Lora had a great body. She was wearing fishnet stockings, and Faith would have been happy to take the bet that they weren't panty hose. *Respect* might be the watchword at school, but today's word was more like *garter belt*.

Faith quickly turned around, ready to clamp her hand over Ben's mouth, yet he very obviously did not recognize the woman who had taught him to make macaroni necklaces and sing "John Jacob Jingleheimer Schmidt." It appeared to Faith that as far as Ben was concerned, the Miss Lora across the street had nothing to do with his beloved teacher. This other Miss Lora might just as well be from another planet.

The second Miss Lora, the faux Miss Lora—or was it the real Lora?—had looped her arm through the driver of the car's and the two of them walked down the block, turning into one of the old redbrick apartment buildings that lined the street. This part of the South End had gentrified early, so the neighborhoods looked much as they had originally. Trees and other plantings had grown up. The renovations weren't sparkling with newness. There was a slight patina of age.

"I'm going to see where they went," Faith told Tom as she slipped out of the car.

She walked past the building to make sure they weren't lingering in the vestibule, but they had apparently gone straight in. It must be where the Miata owner lived. Faith dug in her purse, a large Longchamp drawstring bag whose French styling masked its contents. These ranged from small toys, boxes of raisins, crayons, Handi Wipes, and other necessities for child rearing to blush and lip gloss. She pulled out a pen and her own Filofax—John Dunne's was a little less scratched, but he wasn't packing granola bars—then walked purposefully down the short walk to the entrance of the apartment building.

The outer door was unlocked. It wasn't a large building. There were only five mailboxes and five buzzers. She started to write down the names: Carlson, Macomber, Smith/Pearson, Bridey Murphy—Bridey Murphy? Obviously, someone with an interesting sense of humor and a desire not to be found. Deane. Deane!

Was the man with Lora one of her half brothers? One to whom she was very close? Very, very close. Or maybe the outfit was meant for someone else, someone who was meeting them here? Brothers and sisters did sometimes walk arm in arm, though this seemed unlikely.

Deane. But which Deane? She was tempted to ring the buzzer, or another one, to try to figure out which apartment it was, but if Lora saw her, even Faith could think of no plausible excuse for being there.

Reluctantly, she returned to the car and told Tom.

"I don't know where the other Deanes live. I guess I assumed it was Aleford, since Bonnie lives there, Lora herself, and, of course, Gus. It's possible one or more of the brothers isn't married and could well live in town. I'll have to ask Pix." Faith was thinking out loud. To herself, she added, Before I come back here to check things out. Lora Deane's transformation from country mouse to city vixen had been amazing. It was one thing to whip together a batch of play dough with numbers of children trying to help; quite another to put on make up in a moving vehicle. What other tricks did the young woman have up her sleeve?

The noise level at the Children's Museum always left Faith with a headache, and her own kids were so wired when they emerged that all she could think of was home, food, and bed. After enough time had passed, she'd be eager to take them again. The place was wonderful, but all those cries of delight . . .

Back at the house, Faith was preparing dinner while Tom was

giving Amy hers. As soon as Faith's headache had disappeared, on Storrow Drive somewhere around the Harvard Business School, she'd gotten hungry and told Tom they needed a good supper. Nourishment to try to make sense out of the day, out of all the days recently. They'd stopped at Bread and Circus in Fresh Pond for some striped bass. Not that she particularly subscribed to the theory that fish was brain food. All food was brain food.

Now Faith was quickly making polenta, which she poured into a pan to stiffen. When it did, she'd cut it into wedges and fry it in olive oil. She had a pan of sliced onions, garlic, tomatoes, and red and yellow peppers sautéing on a low flame. She gave it a quick stir before checking the fish she was poaching in some stock and a little vermouth. Ben had been trained to eat anything and did—so long as Faith remembered to call rabbit *lapin* and mushrooms *champignons*.

"Pour us a glass of the Puligny-Montrachet that's in the fridge, would you, honey, and slice some bread. There's a baguette on the counter," she called to Tom, who was enjoying the sight of his daughter's attempts to feed herself string beans. They kept slipping from her fingers. He popped the last one in Amy's mouth and went to the fridge. Soon they were sitting down to the fish that Faith had placed on top of the polenta, the sauce covering both.

"Aaah." Tom rubbed his hands together, noting there was plenty more. There was always plenty more.

The phone rang.

"Damn—I mean darn." He corrected himself for the benefit of his children and to avoid the annoyance of being imitated—something that always managed to occur in the presence of one or more of his parishioners.

Faith was up. She hated it when people had to eat her food cold. "You start. I'll get it." She shoved her plate in the oven and picked up the kitchen phone.

It was Pix. But from the sound of her voice, Faith knew immediately it wasn't about where Samantha was going to college.

"What's happened?" Faith asked. The phone had a long cord and she walked as far away as she could.

"More of those letters. Only this time, they're all the same." Pix stopped. Faith was tempted to run next door. This could take forever. But she waited.

"What did they say?"

"We all got them again." Pix was answering another question. "Same post office. Today's mail. Millicent called me to see if I had one. She'd already talked to the others."

"And they said . . ." Faith prodded.

"They said, 'Be careful on Patriots' Day.' "

"That's all, nothing about place or time?"

"That's all, just 'Be careful on Patriots' Day.' And not signed 'A friend' like the last one. I'm frightened, Faith—and mad. Who could be doing this!"

"I wish I knew."

Faith hung up and went back into the kitchen. Tom looked at her quizzically.

"More of those letters. I'm going next door."

He nodded. "I'll put the kids to bed. You can tell me about it later."

She completely forgot her dinner was still in the oven.

Pix and her husband, Sam, were sitting in the kitchen when Faith arrived. Pix had a baby quilt in her lap she was not working on, although there was a threaded needle in her hand. The door had been open, as was the custom in Aleford, and Faith had come straight in. She locked it behind her.

"I suppose we'll have to start doing this sort of thing now," Pix said mournfully.

"For the time being." Sam was trying very hard to resist the impulse to move his entire family to a new, undisclosed location.

"Why don't I make some coffee?" Faith offered, and hearing no refusals, she went ahead. She'd grabbed a tin of the cookies she'd made with the kids as she was leaving the parsonage. Even if they didn't want them now, they would later.

"I can't believe it's Joey Madsen—or any of the Deanes. He's mad about what we're doing, but he'd be more apt to lose his temper the way Gus did and let us have it at one of the meetings," Pix said.

Faith agreed—in part. The fact that Joey had not been heard from had been troubling her. It *was* his habit to rant and rave. So why wasn't he doing it now? With so much money at stake, maybe Joey was trying another tactic and keeping his natural impulses in check. Or, to be fair, his lawyer could be advising him that flying off the handle wouldn't move the project along and could have the opposite effect.

"Were they written the same way? Cutout letters, ballpoint block letters on the envelope?"

"Exactly the same. The police have mine, otherwise, you could see for yourself."

So much for a possible copycat theory, Faith thought. But that wouldn't have made much sense, anyway. It was difficult enough to believe that someone had sent one set. That there would be another poison pen aimed at these same people was beyond all imagining. The only difference was in the omission of the signature, and it was an omission that alarmed her. If the others were ostensibly sent in a friendly manner, dropping it underscored the seriousness of the threat. She took a cookie, bit into it, and realized she was hungry.

Sam was proposing that they leave town on Patriots' Day and go someplace safe—Faith suggested Manhattan—when there was a noise at the back door. All three of them jumped.

"Get down on the floor and don't move," Sam ordered. "I'll call the police."

But it was the police. Seeing Chief MacIsaac's puzzled face through the glass, Sam immediately opened the door.

"Forgot you'd be bolting things up and thought it was open as usual," Charley said.

Pix stood up and dusted herself off.

"This is getting ridiculous. I refuse to be a prisoner in my own house or scared to walk around in my own town. I haven't missed Patriots' Day once. Mother says they started taking us as soon as we were born, and I'm not going to miss this one."

Pix also had her Sunday school pin with a cascade of bars for perfect attendance hanging from it. Faith had seen it. Pix's family, the Rowes, were known for showing up.

Faith handed Charley a mug of coffee.

"I understand how you feel and I'd probably do the same, but wouldn't it be more sensible to skip the celebrations just this once? Or you could go to Concord for theirs."

"Concord!" From the tone of Pix's voice, Faith might have been suggesting London, England, for Patriots' Day.

"I agree with Faith," Sam said firmly.

"No." Pix folded her arms across her chest. She could be very stubborn, and the set of her mouth and the gesture told the assembled company that this was going to be one of those times. "Our forefathers and foremothers didn't run on April nineteenth and neither will I."

Charley had been silent. He'd already heard the same basic speech from Millicent Revere McKinley and Louise Scott. Ted wasn't home. He hadn't talked to Nelson or Brad yet, but he expected more repetition. Both men were members of the minutemen and participants in the reenactment. As for Millicent, there was no question that she believed Patriots' Day would be canceled if she wasn't there.

"The state police have been notified. We're taking this very seriously. They'll provide extra coverage and someone will be with you at all times. Now, don't say anything." He held up his hand as Pix began to protest. "No choice here. Nothing's going to happen and we want to make sure it doesn't."

Faith was relieved by the illogic of the statement. She planned to be at her friend's side every waking minute of the day, too—no matter how early that minute was.

"What about the kids? I haven't told them. I don't want them upset." Having given in on one thing, Pix was taking a stand on another.

She was going to lose this one, too.

"We don't know anything, so we have to assume all of you are targets. If you don't tell your children, they're not going to be able to look after themselves—or accept our looking after them."

Faith remembered that Samantha, a class officer, would be riding in one of the classic convertibles. Charley had used the word and it had stuck in Faith's mind: *Target*. Sitting duck.

"Can we move the senior class officers to a closed car?" she suggested.

Pix winced. They were right. These were her kids.

Charley nodded and took out his scruffy spiral memo pad. "Okay, let's get it all down. They're in the youth parade and the big parade, right? And what about Danny, is he marching with anything?"

"DARE, but that's just the big parade. He'll want to ring the bell at the belfry in the morning, though. He always does. And we all go to Millicent's pancake breakfast. I'm in the kitchen and Sam passes out the food. The kids help clear and set up." The Millers' Patriots' Day routine was unvarying—and exhausting.

"Well, at least when he's marching with the DARE group, he'll be surrounded by cops," Faith observed. DARE was the drug education program the police ran for the upper elementary and middle school kids.

Charley took some more notes. Pix appeared to feel better. She was quilting. Chief MacIsaac stood up to leave and Pix had a sudden thought.

"I can see how you'll be able to cover us, but how on earth are you going to keep track of Millicent?"

It was just what Charley had been thinking, too.

Faith sat in church the next morning wondering if they would ever get back to normal. Once again, the peace of the sanctuary was gone, replaced instead by a tension so palpable, you could taste it. A kind of a morning mouth taste, a taste even a good toothbrushing couldn't entirely dissolve. Last Sunday, it had been the first letters. Today, Margaret's death—and more letters. Plus the undercurrents—Lora's calls, the brick through her window, and Lora herself. Faith tried to find a spot on the pew cushion that still had some stuffing.

She planned to spend the afternoon with Pix. They were going to take all the kids up to Crane Beach in Ipswich to fly kites. Tom had calls to make, but Sam was coming. Faith had already packed a picnic. They needed to get away, and the idea of sitting and watching a large expanse of water appealed to her. Pix had agreed.

Faith stood up for the last hymn. Yes, it would be good to spend the day outside—and away from Aleford. Aleford—overnight it had become a place of danger. They'd be away, but they'd be marking time. As they sang "Amen," the bells rang in the steeple. It was noon.

In twelve more hours, Patriots' Day would begin.

Chapter 6

The sky was pitch-dark when Faith woke. Unlike other Patriots' Days, this morning she had no trouble getting out of bed. The trouble had been getting to sleep at all. She felt muzzy. She needed some coffee, a lot of coffee.

"Tom, Tom, wake up." She leaned over her husband. He smiled and reached for her, then remembered the day and what it might bring. The smile faded and he kissed Faith hurriedly.

"I'll get Ben dressed while you get ready. Mrs. Hart should be here soon," Tom said.

Amy was at the age where any change in routine produced disastrous results. Eloise Hart was a parishioner who'd agreed to stay with the toddler until a more reasonable hour.

When Faith returned from brushing her teeth, she found a gleeful Ben bouncing on their bed in his Minutechild garb.

"Did you remember his thermal underwear—and yours?" she asked Tom. "It's freezing out, as usual." Faith most enjoyed Patriots' Day after the sun rose and her toes thawed.

Tom was struggling into his homespun frock coat and Faith

took his mumbled reply as a yes. She looked at her own costume and pitied those poor women who had had to struggle through their onerous chores weighted down by layers of heavy petticoats and coarse woolen hose. Normally, Tom delighted in his role as the Reverend Samuel Pennypacker. Aleford tradition more or less demanded that whoever Samuel's modern-day counterpart was at First Parish join the Aleford Minutemen Company and participate in the reenactment. Star of several college productions and George in Norwell High's staging of *Our Town,* Tom hadn't needed any urging, and he read Samuel's diaries in the Aleford Room at the library each year to get into the role.

Faith played his wife, Patience. Patience didn't leave any diaries, nor did she figure in her husband's except for an occasional reference, "Patience with child again." Faith had seen both their headstones in the cemetery and noted that Mistress Pennypacker had outlived her husband by fifteen years. Maybe Patience *was* a virtue. Patience didn't have to do much at the reenactment except rush onto the green when the smoke cleared and tend the wounded. Faith didn't do anything to prepare. This was Ben's first reenactment. He was little Elijah Pennypacker. Faith reminded him that children in those days were extremely obedient and that he must stay by her side at all times.

The bell rang and Faith went to answer the door, nearly tumbling down the stairs, encumbered by skirts as she was. It was Mrs. Hart. As Faith let her in, the lights in the Millers' kitchen went on. None of the Millers were participants in the reenactment, but they all took turns ringing the alarm bell in the old belfry and would join the spectators lining the green. Faith wondered if they had company for breakfast, company who might be packing something more modern than a musket. Charley had promised protection, and if there wasn't anyone there yet, Faith herself resolved to stay by Pix's side. Patience might miss the battle this year.

Each year, the Aleford Minutemen met for breakfast before the event, gathering at the parish hall of the Catholic church. This third Monday in April was always a very ecumenical day. Besides the DAR pancake breakfast, the Baptists and the Episcopalians hosted them. Faith made coffee for Mrs. Hart and put out some apple crumb cake, bagels, cream cheese, and lox. Let her choose from these all-American favorites. Hastily drinking some coffee herself, Faith went into the living room and called softly up the stairs, "Tom, Ben, we have to be going." They came immediately, Tom's heavy boots clumping noisily.

"Sssh, you'll wake Amy!"

Ben was so excited, he was hopping from foot to foot.

"Go pee, Ben. One more time," Tom instructed.

"I don't have to," he protested—one more time.

Faith was anxious to get over to the Millers'. She needed to see Pix.

"Come on. They have bathrooms at the church. And it's getting late."

They said good-bye to Mrs. Hart and put on their woolen cloaks. Tom draped a plaid blanket over his shoulders. He'd seen a print of a New England minister of the time so attired and had adopted the garb himself. It meant he was the warmest person on the Common, too.

They stepped outside. The moon, full two days earlier, was still large and bright. The cold early-morning air seeped through their clothes. Faith was chilled. It was 4:15.

The Millers were ready to leave, too. You had to get in line early if you wanted a turn at pulling the bell rope. Faith was relieved to see Patrolman Dale Warren was with them. As she did every year, Pix was urging her family to pretend that they actually *were* on their way to sound the alarm.

"It was cool, maybe not as cool as today, but definitely not warm. Everyone who lived close to the green, the way we do, would have been gathering at the tavern, waiting for information about the British troops. Keyed up—something was finally happening—but scared, too."

Faith had heard it all before, yet this year she thought Pix's voice held real fear. They left them at the bottom of Belfry Hill and walked briskly toward St. Theresa's. It was still pitch-dark, but Aleford was filled with activity. Cars were parked on the side streets; Main Street was blocked off. Figures, some in period dress, passed by, flashlights illuminating them for an instant. Despite the numbers of people about, the town was quiet—lying in wait, as Pix had said. Inside St. Theresa's hall, the contrast was immediate. All the lights were on. It was warm and noisy. The Minutemen kept up a steady stream of conversation as they ate. Faith blinked at the sudden change and grabbed at Ben's cloak as he started to race off.

The Aleford Militia had been founded in 1773 and was still going strong, an uninterrupted history documented by their meeting records. It was open to any U.S. citizen over the age of eighteen and, unlike other Aleford institutions, a number of its members actually lived out of town. Just as there had been several generations from the same family on the green over two hundred years ago, there were several generations of various families represented in the Minutemen. In 1775, Aleford had, strictly speaking, not organized a company of Minutemen, members of the militia who would be ready to fight at a moment's notice, but it kept the militia as such. The mists of time and prejudices encouraged by myth had obscured this fact long ago and Minutemen they were.

The first person Faith saw was Gus Deane devouring a large mound of scrambled eggs and sausage, using his toast to help. It looked delicious. Faith got her own plate, parked Ben and his at a table with some other children, then went over to chat with Gus, who was Capt. Ebenezer Sewall, the head of the militia today. He was regaling a small group with reminiscences of Patriots' Days past.

"Remember the year George came round the bend at the tavern during the rehearsal, riding his daughter's little hobbyhorse instead of a real one? I thought I'd die laughing. Don't know how we made it through the actual thing without cracking up. When he came riding up to the tavern shouting, 'The Regulars are coming!' everyone kept picturing him on the damned toy!"

Faith looked at the men around her, who had joined in Gus's merriment. The room was at a fever pitch of excitement, as if they really *were* preparing to defend their rights, their village. Besides the talk, there was a continuous bustle in the adjoining rooms. The women and older children were managing the breakfast things. Miss Lora, dressed as a servant girl, a long checkered kerchief crisscrossed over her bodice, came by with a platter of piping-hot sausages, the steam curling up to her face. She paused to say hello. Ben was in heaven. Others were putting the finishing touches to their costumes, adjusting hats, garments. One man was handing out the muskets from the small stage at one end of the hall.

"The British are coming!" Bonnie Madsen called from the door, and the company from Boston that assumed this role each year filed in. They were impressive. Bright silver buttons gleamed on their red coats, silver gorgets at their throats. Their wigs were elaborately coiffed. Anything that was supposed to shine did. Tom had told her each outfit cost upward of a thousand dollars, all made by hand. In contrast, the farmers and artisans who made up Aleford's force got away cheap—fringed homespun shirts, rough jackets and vests. Some wore the tricorne hat. The only gleaming metals aside from a buckle were a few pewter flasks slung from their shoulders on leather thongs. Others had canteens, homemade wooden ones. Many of the men had full beards. Faith's own son was sporting a red mustache from the fruit punch put out with the orange juice. She went over to the table to get a napkin.

Ben's eyes grew wide as he watched one British major pour himself some coffee and select a doughnut. The drummer boy came up next to him and grabbed two. "Don't sneeze on the doughnuts, Nathan," the major bellowed as the young man reached for a pocket handkerchief. Ben ducked behind his mother's voluminous skirts.

"Is it time?"

"Almost," she answered, and looked about the room for Tom.

He was talking to Nelson, who was dressed like the others, except he wore a black armband. Millicent, already at the green, might fuss that it wasn't authentic, but even she wouldn't say he couldn't wear it. Last year, Margaret had been here, too, helping with serving. A man Faith didn't recognize stood beside Nelson. Though he was dressed for the reenactment, she was willing to bet this would be his first and only one. His chest, with a noticeable bulge, was covered with straps; he was carrying a powder horn and shot pouch. Tom's pouch held his Bible and a hunk of bread—he'd read that was what Samuel had carried—in addition to his ammunition. Faith thought it more likely this Minuteman was toting some kind of cellular phone. Nelson left the room, his flask clanking against his powder horn, and the unknown Minuteman followed him out.

As dawn approached, tension mounted. Her first year, Faith had been amused to note that the British and Colonial troops did not fraternize. Tom said it was because they didn't know one another, since they only got together for rare events like today's. She'd watched every year—the same people, the same place—and decided he was wrong. It might be a reenactment, but soon these men would be facing one another on the field of battle. Captain Sewall hadn't taken a cup of tea, or noggin of rum, with his British counterpart that morning and he didn't now. There were nods and greetings, yet that was all.

"It's almost five, time to get to the tavern, and those of you who are on the green better hurry," Gus commanded. Joey Madsen came into the room and grabbed his musket.

"Ramrods out!" shouted Gus. "Ramrods out!" This reminder was made each time a group left. There had been a reenactment, not in Aleford, of course, where one of the participants had forgotten to remove the ramrod from his gun; when he fired, it shot into the crowd with deadly force. Miraculously, no one had been injured.

"Let's go, Mom. Everyone's leaving." Ben was pulling on Faith's hand. She had been postponing the moment—the hall was so nice and warm.

"Go to the bathroom first," she bargained. He ran off and she decided she'd better do the same. They'd be on the green for a long time.

Outside the kitchen, she found Brad Hallowell, next to his drum, wolfing down his breakfast.

"Overslept," he said between bites. "Damn alarm didn't go off and my mother didn't want to wake me up. Thought I needed my sleep."

Faith reminded herself that Mrs. Hallowell was a relative newcomer to Aleford and Patriots' Day activities. In some households, her behavior would have caused her to be labeled a Tory spy. She certainly doted on her son, her only child, Faith thought as she waited to get into the bathroom. Several of her homespun sisters had had the same idea. Mrs. Hallowell had been extremely put out with Lora Deane for breaking up with her darling boy. Put out enough to make the calls? Lora had said it was a man's voice, but it wouldn't be hard to imitate one for those few words. Some mothers would do anything for their sons.

Her own was approaching, annoyance shadowing his little face. "Aren't you done yet?"

"Ladies take longer, and I don't care for the way you're speaking to me."

"Sorry, Mom."

She gave him a quick hug. It was her turn. "I'll hurry. We won't miss anything. I promise."

Anything for their sons.

It was twenty after five. There was a glow at the horizon and the dark sky was now deep purple. Here and there, a lighted window shone. Faith watched the silhouettes of the leafless trees surrounding the green become more distinct, until she could see the swelling buds on the branches. The steeple at First Parish pierced the sky. She looked around for her husband. Samuel Pennypacker had been one of the first to muster on the green. She spotted the blanket. He stood next to a lantern with a flickering candle inside. Faith took Ben's hand and went over.

"Be careful, Tom." She was filled with foreboding. Patience must have felt the same way. Faith was having no trouble getting into the mood this April morning.

"I will." He squeezed her hand and gave Ben a kiss. "Now you'd better get off to the side." As he spoke, the alarm began to toll. Steady, loud, the sound quieted the crowd of spectators. Tom blew out the candle in the lantern. It was daybreak. Two geese flew silently overhead.

He looked about for Nelson. He planned to stay as close as possible to the man.

Faith joined the other women and children at the far end of the Common. The spectators were kept from the field by ropes. Some had brought stepladders for a better view. Small children were hoisted on their parents' shoulders. The bell kept ringing. Faith pictured the Millers grabbing the rope in turn and pulling hard. She remembered the time she had rung the bell herself. She'd had to use her whole weight to get it started.

At six o'clock, they heard hoofbeats. Soon the rider appeared calling for Captain Sewall, who emerged from the tavern, followed by a stream of men. "The Regulars are coming!" Faith had been surprised the first year. No one said, "The British are coming." Her fourth-grade teacher had been wrong.

Two shots were fired in the air—the alarm guns. The alarm bell fell silent. Gus turned to Brad Hallowell and ordered him to start drumming. "Men, we are going to muster on the green," the captain called out.

Although she had seen it before, Faith was caught up in the drama, and the crowd pressing against the ropes a few feet away seemed not to exist. Ben's hand was in hers, warm and warming. She was vaguely aware how cold she was, her breath a cloud. She wished she knew where the Millers were. The shots had startled her.

"Watch closely," she told her son. "Everything happens very fast." All these spectators, some from far away—and it would be over in a flash. A flash and puffs of smoke. But at the moment, Gus was calling the roll—slowly, dramatically, drawing out each name. He stood before the rude band and one by one they answered.

The British drums could now be heard, approaching from farther down Battle Road, its name later changed to Main Street. Inexorable. The drums were terrifying. Gus ordered his men to march to the far end of the green and form two lines. "Load and stand ready," he ordered. He was born to lead, Faith thought. Standing straight as a ramrod himself, he was not wearing the rough clothes of the farmer he'd been, but Captain Sewall's bright blue militia uniform. Sewall and Deane, centuries apart, yet with this curious link. Faith had a sense that they were both men you'd want on your side.

Now the sky was pale yellow at the horizon, the color of a good Chablis, and faintly blue above. The Minutemen were saying their lines, all documented.

"There's so few of us, it's folly to stand here."

"Easy. Stand your ground."

The British appeared, transformed from the doughnut-eating crew of an hour ago into an efficient war machine. Their bayonets glittered. They reached the green. Their red coats—bloodred coats—were a splash of color against the grass, glistening with dew. Marching all night through unfamiliar terrain in 1775, the Regulars had been fatigued, wet, hungry—and frightened. Numbers of the size of the forces on both sides had been greatly inflated.

"Disperse, you damn rebels! Disperse!"

"Go back to Boston!"

The Minutemen stood their ground. A rude band, but not untrained, Faith had learned. Many had fought in the French and Indian Wars. They were dressed as the farmers and artisans they were, but they kept their weapons cleaned and knew how to shoot. The drums kept beating. For a moment, time stood still. There was indecision on both sides. Then the shot rang out.

No one knows who fired first. It may not even have been someone on the green. One recent theory attributes it to a restless Aleford teenager crouched behind one of the nearby stone walls. An accident? Deliberate? Whatever the motive, it caused the green to explode in a barrage of noise and smoke. Ben put his hands over his ears. The smell of black powder filled the air.

"Disperse! Disperse!" Gus ordered, and the men fled, leaving two fallen from their line. The British pursued relentlessly. Faith closed her eyes as the all-too-realistic reenactment of the use of a bayonet occurred in front of her. The smoke was so thick, it was hard to pick out anyone. Men were screaming in pain and terror. The British commander frantically ordered his troops to stop, but, out of control, they continued to attack the damned rebels. Finally, the drum sounded. They had been trained to obey it instantly: the carnage was arrested. Slowly, they marched off the Common and down the road to Concord, accompanied by the drums. It would be a long day, and when they returned, they would face double the number who had gathered on the green, a force that would exact its price, shooting at the easy red targets from the woods, behind stone walls, their houses.

Now it was Patience's turn, and she rushed onto the green with the others. At first she couldn't see through the thick smoke; then as it began to lift, carried by the breeze, she located Tom. He was bending down next to Nelson. Faith ran faster.

The man Nelson Batcheldor played wasn't supposed to be injured.

"Get the EMTs over here," Tom screamed. "We need help! Someone's been hurt!" He had rolled Nelson on his back and was starting mouth-to-mouth.

The unknown Minuteman was speaking into his phone. Sirens abruptly dragged the scene into the twentieth century and real panic set in.

"Someone's been shot for real!" Faith heard a spectator shout. "A ramrod, it was a ramrod!" People began to run away. She knelt next to Tom. There was no blood. Nelson hadn't been wounded. His eyes were closed and his skin had a deathly pallor.

Charley MacIsaac got on the public-address system, which normally would have been used at this point to talk about the day's upcoming events.

"One of our company has been taken ill. There is no cause for alarm. Please, everyone stay where you are so we can provide medical attention. The program will proceed in a few minutes."

"Taken ill"? Nelson wasn't ill. He was scarcely breathing. It appeared that, like his wife, Nelson had been murdered.

"I'm going with him. Go home and stay there. I'll call you." Tom sounded frantic.

"How could this have happened? No one has left his side!" Faith suddenly remembered Ben next to her and pulled him close. "Sweetie, Mr. Batcheldor is sick and Daddy's going with him to the hospital. We're going to go home, but first I want to find the Millers and ask them to have breakfast with us." She willed herself to stay calm. Her voice sounded like someone else's—someone who spoke very deliberately. Charley was still instructing the crowd to stay put, but people continued to press forward to leave.

"What about the pancake breakfast. I thought there was a pancake breakfast." Ben's lower lip quivered. Patriots' Day wasn't turning out the way he expected.

"We'll have our own pancake breakfast. Now help me find them. See if you can spot Samantha." Ben adored Samantha and brightened at the thought of breakfast with her.

Faith turned away as the EMTs rushed Nelson off the green, Tom close behind. Nelson—was he the intended victim, or did the poison-pen writer plan to pick them all off, one by one? She had to find Pix.

The Millers were by the large oak near the Centennial Monument, obeying Charley's request. Dale Warren was saying something into his two-way radio.

Pix ran toward her. "What's happened, Faith? What did Charley mean? Who's sick? Dale doesn't seem to know anything."

"It's Nelson." Faith fumbled for words. What could she say? She didn't want to alarm her friend, but she wanted her to get the hell out of here. "He may be gravely injured, and it may be the letter writer, although I don't see how. You've got to leave here immediately. Tom went with Nelson in the ambulance and he's going to call when he knows what's happened. Please"—she reached for Pix's arm—"I think you should come to my house, all of you, and stay there for a while."

Sam agreed, but Pix protested, "We said we would help at the breakfast."

"These are unusual circumstances. People will understand."

Dale Warren decided things. He'd put the radio back in his

belt. "Chief MacIsaac says you're to go home and stay there. The Fairchilds' will be all right, too, I guess. Anyways, he wants you off the green."

Pix gave in. Her face had grown pale. Samantha held one of her hands; Sam grasped the other. "This can't be real," Pix said to no one in particular.

Danny and Ben were running ahead. Faith lost sight of them in the crowd and rushed the others forward.

"You must stay where I can see you!" she said to the two boys angrily, driven by fear.

They looked sheepish and slowed down. Danny was wearing a tricorne hat, as was Ben. Both carried flags. Patriots' Day. This modern-day reenactment was fast becoming the nightmare it had actually been in 1775.

Back at the parsonage, Amy was still asleep. So was Mrs. Hart.

"Was it a good one?" she asked, sitting up at the sound of their entrance. "A big turnout? No surprises, I expect. We still lost this round, eh?" She laughed.

"Yes, we lost," Faith said soberly.

"Never a peep out of the little angel, and unless you need me, I'll go over to help my sister at the DAR breakfast."

Faith thanked her and headed into the kitchen to make her own pancakes. Sam, Pix, and Dale Warren were sitting silently at the Fairchild's large round table. Samantha, Danny, and Ben were in a small room off the kitchen, watching an instant replay on the local cable channel. Faith went in, drawn by the noise of the battle.

Reaching into his pocket, Danny gave Ben one of the pieces of paper that held the powder charges. At the end of the battle, children always rushed onto the grass to pick these up. Ben smelled it. "I didn't like the guns," he said. "They made too much noise. But I wasn't scared. My sister would be scared, but I wasn't."

Faith looked at the screen. The whole thing had been filmed.

Would they have captured the moment when Nelson fell and how? She came out and told Dale, who immediately called the police station to have someone get a copy of the tape.

Soon the house was filled with the smell of pancakes on the griddle. The mood lightened. The kids joined them around the table.

"These are delicious! What kind are they?" Sam asked, starting in on a stack.

"I don't know exactly," Faith said. "I just threw some things together, but I'll call them Patriots' Day Pancakes (see recipe on page 272). They've got sour cream in them and that's white, the blueberries are blue, of course, and the raspberries, red." She had mixed the two berries together since she didn't have enough of each. She took a bite, although she didn't have much of an appetite. Thoughts of whether Nelson was still alive had dulled it—plus, she'd already had one breakfast. The pancakes were good. She ate some more.

Then they waited. Pix was uncharacteristically restless.

"Couldn't we call the hospital?"

"I doubt they'd give us any information. Especially considering the circumstances."

"Can't you call, Dale?" Pix had been his sister's room mother in fifth grade and she thought the young man ought to be able to find something out, given his position.

He shook his head. "I couldn't tell you anyway, unless the chief said so. The last thing he told me was he'd be in touch and only to call if there was an emergency."

A grim reminder, and everyone in the room felt it.

From upstairs, Amy started crying. She was awake and hungry.

It was seven o'clock.

Faith felt as if it should be at least the afternoon and Amy rising from her nap. The hours since they'd first left the house were moving as slowly as the thick maple syrup that the kids coaxed from the jug for their pancakes.

At nine, the phone rang. Faith picked up before the second ring.

"Tom? Is he alive? What's happened?"

But it wasn't Tom; it was Millicent.

"And how are you, Faith? I understand Pix is at your house and I'd like a word with her, if it's not too much trouble." Her tone clearly indicated she did not think much of Faith's telephone manners.

"Of course, I'll get her right away." Faith was tempted to explain, yet it wouldn't make any difference. Yes, this was a crisis, but that was no excuse for letting standards slip.

Pix went to the phone. "Probably wants to yell at me for not being at the breakfast," she whispered to Faith.

"She'd better not," Faith replied. At the moment, she deeply wished Millicent had never asked Pix—or any of the rest of them—to sign that letter. Had never started POW! So what if Joey Madsen wanted to put up a bunch of big houses?

She went into the living room. Dale was reading the latest issue of *New York* magazine with the appearance of someone who's bought one of the periodicals Patriot Drug kept behind the counter. Sam was giving a good performance of reading today's paper, but he was still on the page he'd been on when Faith left the room. He put the paper down. Faith had stopped offering food or coffee an hour ago. Nobody wanted anything—except for the day to be over. Samantha had taken charge of Amy and Ben. She was one of those teenagers who actually liked small children, moving straight from her horse phase to babies. They were in the kitchen, drawing on large sheets of shelf paper. Danny was watching the Boston Marathon on TV.

"What do you think our friend Millicent wants with my wife?"

"And badly enough to track her down here, although that would be child's play for Millicent. But I have no idea. The two are involved in just about every activity in town, so it could be POW! business or the Garden Club plant sale. Or Pix could be right and Millicent is calling her on the carpet because you didn't show up to help at the breakfast."

"They couldn't have had much of a turnout. People were leaving town as fast as they could," Sam commented.

Their speculation was stopped by Pix's return. She was laughing.

"She's under house arrest, too, or whatever you call this. Charley won't let her do anything in public today and she's furious. She wanted my support to complain to the police. I think she's planning to call the Middlesex County DA's office to register a formal complaint."

"Protective custody," Dale piped up, "That's what I'd call it." He returned to his magazine.

"In a way, I don't blame her," Pix continued. "Not that I'm leaving the premises, but Millicent works all year on this day. I think they should at least let her review the parade. That's her favorite part."

Every year, Millicent, town officials, and other favored individuals—the closest egalitarian Aleford got to royalty—sat on a specially constructed platform near the green and watched the parade pass by, awarding the prizes for best float, best band, and so forth. Sat high up, out in the open. With hundreds of people strolling around below, cotton candy and fried dough in hand. But there might be a hand holding something else. Faith shivered. She was with Charley. She didn't want Millicent to put one foot out of her clapboard house. She fleetingly wondered what Millicent's bodyguard was doing. Probably helping her wind wool.

"Did you tell her that?" she asked Pix.

"Not exactly. I certainly wouldn't advise the woman to defy the police. I told her what I was doing, but of course said I could not presume to make up her mind."

"What did she say?"

"Thanked me and said it was exactly what she wanted to hear."

"Great," Faith said. Now she'd have to worry about Millicent, who was probably tying bedsheets together at this very moment while the police officer was trapped downstairs, his hands bound by the skein of wool.

She had an idea. "What about the Scotts? Maybe they could wait together? They're such sane people."

"The Scotts, very sane people, have left town. Ted told Charley they'd check in with him to find out when it's safe to come back," Sam told her. "I tried to get my wife to do the same, but obviously it was no use." He shot a somewhat-sour look at Pix.

They settled down to wait again. The kids were in the backyard on the swing set. The yard was fenced, but Dale moved over by the window anyway. He'd finished the magazine. Another half hour passed.

Unaccustomed to inactivity of any sort, Pix was clearly getting restless.

"How about cards? Bridge?" she suggested.

Faith only knew how to play poker and Go Fish and was about to say so when Dale muttered something about being on duty, which immediately limited the choices.

"Double solitaire?" Pix said. Clearly the woman was getting close to the end of her tether.

"Sure," Sam said. He knew his wife. "Have you got two decks of cards, Faith?"

Looking for cards proved a welcome time killer. Pix went with Faith as she searched through various junk drawers and boxes of games that Tom was wont to buy at garage sales and auctions. The

Fairchild clan were inveterate board game players, and when Tom came across a vintage set of Monopoly or Clue, he acted as if he'd found the Grail.

Triumphantly, Faith held two decks aloft. "I remember these because of the labels." One was from the *Queen Mary*, and the other from Caesar's Palace. "A widely traveled family with broad tastes and maybe a sense of humor."

Sam and Pix started to play. Faith, odd woman out, went into the kitchen to think. She sat by the window, idly watching Samantha swinging with Amy on her lap. The toddler laughed uproariously every time they swung gently forward. Faith stopped focusing on the scene outside and tried to sort through the thoughts elbowing one another for space in her mind.

Someone in Aleford wrote those letters. No one else would have known the poison involved. But whoever it was wouldn't necessarily have had to have lived in town too long. It was only five years ago that Sam had had the affair with Cindy. Brad's letter had been obscene, referring to certain sexual acts he may or may not have performed with Lora Deane, although given Lora's transformation on Saturday, anything was possible. Their relationship was even more recent. Louise Scott's alcoholic father and his accident dated further back, but it was something that might have come up in a certain kind of conversation about either drinking problems or car crashes. And the Batcheldors'. Faith searched her memory for the exact wording. Their letter had been the least specific—although no one, with the possible exception of Chief MacIsaac, knew what was in Millicent's. The Batcheldors' said they should stay out of the woods if they wanted to stay healthy. Almost the same words used on the phone to Lora. It was the only one that contained a direct threat. And now Margaret was dead; Nelson might be. What was in the woods? Why the Batcheldors?

All the POW! letter signers had received both letters, except

Margaret, of course. Were there other recipients—too frightened to go to the police? And why the pointed omission of the signature—on Brad's both times, the others only the second time. It suggested a precise person, someone who said only what he or she meant. A friend the first go-round, now a foe. But enmity toward Brad from the beginning. That could mean one of the Deanes, especially Lora's grandfather or brothers, but they hadn't known about the calls when the first letters were received.

The Deanes. Who lived in the apartment on Chandler Street? The letters and Lora seemed to be unconnected, but she kept popping up.

Faith tore a piece of paper from a pad on the counter and wrote: "apartment," "signature," "other letters?" and then "Brad." She paused and after a moment jotted down "Margaret—meeting whom?" This last was a reminder to find out whether the police had located Margaret's birding companion. Nelson had said she was going to meet someone. Who? She tucked the paper in her pocket. She knew she wouldn't forget it.

Faith looked at the phone hanging on the wall and willed it to ring. It was one of the ones they hadn't replaced. A dial phone. Ben viewed it as a priceless antique. So did Tom.

She gazed, unseeing, out the window again. The same names kept coming up over and over. A couple of these people were turning up on both her suspect and victim list: Lora Deane, Brad Hallowell. Lora's family. And they had all been together this morning at the breakfast and on the green.

The phone rang at eleven. Faith was cleaning out the pantry by now and Sam owed Pix two thousand dollars. Dale and the kids were watching the Marathon.

This time it *was* Tom. He started speaking right away.

"He's alive. He's still in danger, but there's hope."

"Oh, Tom, thank God! What was it?" All morning she'd held

on to the slim possibility that Nelson had had a heart attack or something else natural, however unwelcome. Then the whole affair could be a ghastly coincidence.

It wasn't.

"He was poisoned. They've pumped his stomach and are analyzing the contents."

"Poison!" A crystal clear picture of her husband giving the victim mouth-to-mouth flashed into Faith's mind. "Tom, is there any possibility that you . . ."

Tom had had his own uneasy moments. "I'm fine. They won't even tell me what they think it is, not yet anyway, but the doctor said he didn't believe I was in any danger. Whatever it was, you had to have had a lot of it."

"But how could he have been poisoned right before our eyes?"

"Exactly," Tom said grimly.

"His flask. He was carrying one of those pewter flasks!"

"I'm sure the police are checking it. I've been out in the waiting room. I haven't even seen Charley since we came in. Dunne arrived a couple of hours ago and then left. There have been cops in and out ever since. They took everything Nelson was wearing or carrying away, including his musket."

"Maybe Charley will tell you more when you do see him."

"Possibly. I'm going to stay a bit longer. Nelson's still unconscious, but he could come around in the next few hours, and I want to be here." Tom had been feeling a bit incongruous sitting in the hospital in his Minuteman garb, but he didn't want to take the time to go home to change. It wasn't important enough for Faith to bring him his clothes, either. They'd been listening to the Marathon at the nurses' station near the waiting room too. Everyone knew it was Patriots' Day. He prayed for it to pass swiftly and safely.

Faith hung up the phone and went to tell the others. How were they ever going to get through this long, long day? Waiting for the call had given them some focus. Now there were only empty hours ahead.

"Poisoned?" Pix said, shocked. "When would someone have had the opportunity? Unless it was extremely long-acting. But he would have been showing *some* symptoms. Did he look any different to you, Faith?"

Faith thought for a moment. "He looked tired, but not really any different from how he's looked since Margaret died. I can't imagine that he's been sleeping well. Yet he was definitely moving more slowly." Nelson, and Margaret, too, walked with brisk, purposeful strides—the strides of people who have feeders to fill, bookshelves to build. She remembered watching him leave the hall at St. Theresa's, and while not exactly dragging his feet, he wasn't rushing off to battle as were some of his fellow militiamen. She hadn't been feeling especially perky herself at that hour in the morning, so she'd taken no notice of it until now.

"But he didn't seem to be in pain, particularly gastric pain?"

"No, I would have noticed that."

"Did you see him eat anything?"

Faith started to answer, then stopped herself. Who was supposed to be asking the questions here, anyway? After solving two murders, Pix had returned from Sanpere Island last summer ready to tackle anything from the case of Judge Crater to what happened to Jimmy Hoffa. Faith loved her friend dearly, but she wasn't about to hand over her magnifying glass.

Fortunately, Samantha came into the room, effectively stopping her mother's persistent line of inquiry. Faith half-listened to the teenager while thinking about Pix's question. She had not, in fact, seen Nelson eat or drink anything, but there were several rooms off the main hall and she had been in and out of them. It was possible he'd taken a doughnut, some coffee, or juice, all of which were in the main hall. He wasn't at St. Theresa's when she'd arrived and she never saw him with eggs and sausage later, so if the flask wasn't poisoned, it was most probably one of those three. Pretty hard to poison a doughnut, particularly one fresh from a box from a national chain. Coffee or juice, but again how, with a cop next to him and Nelson himself presumably keeping a close watch?

"It will be perfectly safe! Anyway, they're after you, Mom, not me," Samantha's voice penetrated Faith's speculations. Whoever said children were honest was right. Ruthlessly honest.

"I just called Jan and the car will pick me up here or at home. No one will even open a window, and the driver's an auxiliary policeman anyway," Samantha was pleading. She turned to her father. "Please, Dad, this is the last parade I'll ever be in."

"I certainly hope not," he said dryly.

"You know what I mean!"

Pix sighed. "The whole thing is so crazy. I can't imagine that anyone could want to harm us, but we—or, as you aptly point out, sweetheart, I—did get the letter. I'd like to assume Nelson was his or her intended victim and get on with my life, and my family's, but my correspondent does not strike me as a particularly honorable or trustworthy person. What's to prevent him from striking tomorrow or the next day or the next? Can we keep living like this—in hiding?"

The Scotts could be out of town for quite a while, Faith reflected, because of course Pix was right. Murderers did not follow rules. *Honorable, trustworthy*—no, these were not words that sprang to mind.

"So you're saying I can go, right?" Samantha was surprised. She'd expected a lot more opposition, especially from her mother. For a moment, adolescent that she was, she wondered if she ought to go if her mother thought it was okay.

"Sam?" Pix walked over to her husband and took his hand.

"Closed car, comes here, brings her back. A cop at the wheel.

Probably as safe as the yard," he answered. "But no getting out of the car. Anybody. Go to the bathroom before you leave."

"Daddy!" Patrolman Dale Warren was in the room again and Samantha was mortified.

Danny came running into the room. "You're letting Samantha be in the parade and not me! It's not fair! You let her do everything!"

It was Sam's turn to dig his heels in. A closed car was one thing. A three-mile march straight up Main Street, even in the DARE contingent, was another.

Help came from an unexpected source. "Couldn't he come with me? There's plenty of room, and one of our class projects was peer counseling with kids at his school. He could even wear his DARE T-shirt."

Everyone looked at Danny to see if he'd accept the compromise. Faith was getting a glimpse of a future she'd just as soon learn about when she got there—many years from now.

"Okay," he said. "Those cars are cool. Wait till I tell Mark. He's gonna wish he was here, too."

" 'Going to,' dear," Pix said automatically, thanking God her oldest son was safely in New Haven.

"This solves one problem, anyway," Sam commented as the kids left the room for the phone.

"What?" Pix asked curiously. Something his lawyer's mind had picked up on that she'd missed?

"Now we have something to do this afternoon. We'll be glued to the TV, watching the parade to make sure the kids are all right. Can we stay for lunch, Faith? I think we're going to need nourishment.

The parade started from East Aleford at about two o'clock and usually reached the green about three. Promptly at 1:30, a gleaming turquoise-and-white 1955 Chevy Bel Air picked Samantha and

Danny up. Amy had gone for her nap and Ben was complaining about missing the parade. They usually watched from the front steps of the church.

"I'll take you out when the clowns come," Faith promised.

"And I want to see Samantha and Danny. I want to be in the parade. Why can't I be in the parade?"

"You can when your legs get a little longer," Faith answered. The Aleford Minutemen marched, all in their proper uniforms for the parade, wives and children behind them.

Tom had called again to report that there was nothing to report and said he'd be home soon. That had been an hour ago.

Faith looked in the refrigerator and decided on big overstuffed sandwiches. She had some dark rye and piled thick slices of smoky Virginia ham, sharp cheddar cheese, lettuce, with some spicy chutney on the bread. She set the table, putting out bowls of cherry tomatoes and Cape Cod potato chips—an indoor picnic.

Sam was starting his second sandwich and finishing his first beer—Sam Adams lager, in honor of the day—when Tom walked in the back door. They all started talking at once.

"I'll tell you everything; just give me a minute. If I don't get out of these clothes, I'm going to develop a serious rash. Even with my long underwear, this wool itches like crazy. Now I know why our ancestors all have such pained expressions in their portraits. I thought it was ill-fitting teeth, but they were merely waiting for a break to scratch."

From the way Tom was speaking, Nelson must be out of danger, Faith thought.

"Do you want a sandwich?" she asked.

"At least two," he called back over his shoulder.

When he returned, the first person to demand his attention was Ben, who had been doing Legos in a corner of the kitchen.

"Mom says we can't watch the parade from the church," he told his father woefully.

Tom and Faith looked at each other over the little tyrant's head. Guilt, guilt, guilt.

"I told him I would take him to see the clowns—and Samantha and Danny, if the senior-class car isn't too far away from the clown contingent," Faith explained.

"That's going to have to be it for this year, Ben. You know Mr. Batcheldor is sick and we have a lot of grown-up worries right now."

This plus a promise of cotton candy appeased the boy enough to send him back to his construction. Faith set Tom's food on the table and all of them looked at him expectantly.

"Chloral hydrate. But that's not to leave this room." Everyone nodded solemnly.

"A Mickey Finn," Sam said. "Of lethal proportions." He liked to read mysteries from the thirties and forties.

"Exactly. Nelson was regaining consciousness and I went in to see him. Charley and Dunne were both there asking him questions, which is how I found out. It must have been put in something he ate at the breakfast, because it acts quickly and there was no trace of it in his flask. They were trying to get him to remember what he'd had, but he was pretty out of it."

"It is still used to help people sleep, though," Pix said. "My mother had some in the medicine cabinet from my father's last illness, until I made her throw it out. It was in a brown bottle, a red liquid. Father used to complain about the cherry taste. That would be pretty easy to put into Nelson's juice."

Faith thought of Ben's bright red mustache. The cloyingly sweet juice would have masked the flavor of just about anything.

"But pretty hard to top up the man's drink in a crowded room without attracting some attention," Sam said.

"It also came in capsules, but those were too hard for father to swallow at that point," Pix remembered. She also remembered her children and jumped to her feet. "It's after two o'clock; maybe the cable company will be televising the beginning of the parade."

They all crowded into the small room with the TV to watch. At first, all Faith could see were fezzes. The Shriners made up a good fourth of the parade—Shriners dressed as Minutemen, Shriners in tiny Model T Fords, Shriners playing bagpipes, Shriners on floats, Shriners on motorcycles, and her own favorite—Shriners playing snake charmer's flutes dressed in *Arabian Nights* costumes with gold leather shoes that curled high in the air at the toe. A huge model of the Shriners' Burn Institute adorned yet another float. The fezzes were mingling with huge bunches of balloons carried by vendors, banners, musical instruments, and flags—so many that at times the screen was filled with nothing but red, white, and blue.

"There they are!" Pix cried. They had a fleeting glimpse of the car, now decorated with blue and gold streamers and other Aleford High insignia. Danny and Samantha were just visible, wedged in the midst of the other occupants. Everyone was smiling. The camera panned to the Aleford High Drum and Bugle Corps behind them and a group of pint-sized twirlers. Two of them dropped their batons. The Patriots' Day Parade had started. The screen went blank for an instant and then the morning's reenactment appeared.

"They won't show any more until they reach the center," Faith said, staying to watch the reenactment, as she hadn't earlier. She'd been too eager to tell the police to get a tape. Everyone else stayed, too.

It was like watching something that had occurred months or even years ago, Faith thought. Just as it had been that morning, the figures on the green were scarcely visible in the darkness; then as the day dawned and the action started, the players appeared. Nelson had answered in the roll call, but the camera was on Gus Deane, so it was impossible to see how Nelson looked. His voice sounded a bit reedy and weak, but the sound quality was not the best. Faith saw him take his place in the line; then the musket fire started and it was impossible to see anyone. She wished she had thought to tape it herself. She wanted to go back over it.

Nelson didn't look well when the smoke cleared and seemed to stumble as he obeyed Captain Sewall's commands.

She left the room to call the cable company to find out when it would be broadcast again. She had a feeling it would be replayed often today.

Ben was sitting in the corner. With Tom home, she could take her son out to the celebration for a while. Not that she felt like celebrating, but she definitely felt like getting out.

They walked across the green toward the reviewing stand, stopping to get Ben his cotton candy. He pulled gauzy pink pieces of it away from the cardboard tube it was wound around. Some was already in his hair. Faith pulled a piece off, too, and for a moment the grainy sweetness on her tongue tasted good, a reminder of family outings—carnivals, the Jersey shore. She swallowed. It was enough.

"Come over here by the curb. We'll be able to see them and wave when they go by," Faith told Ben. They hadn't missed the clowns, more Shriners. They hadn't missed something else, too.

Millicent Revere McKinley, flag in hand, waving the other with practiced, stately mien, was standing on top of the reviewing platform. She was flanked by two state policemen and there was no mistaking the look of triumph in her eyes.

Chapter 7

It had been a long day and it was a long night. The Millers and escort went back home after the parade, only to return for supper at Faith's insistence. She would have liked to have stayed by Pix's side until midnight, but Pix had declared that doing nothing was exhausting and she wanted to go to bed early. Devoted friend that she was, Faith could not see herself lying across the bottom of the Millers' connubial four-poster. In any case, one or more of the dogs usually occupied that position. Dale was relieved by someone from the state police, and Faith tossed and turned all night, afraid the phone would ring.

Somehow, she got everyone off to work and school the next morning, then presented herself at Millicent's for the meeting to compose the letter for POW!'s town-wide mailing. She felt even more bedraggled when Millicent opened the door, starched, every hair in place. The exultant look Faith had seen on her face the day before had, if anything, intensified. And she not only had energy; she was raring to go. Faith considered leaving, pleading a sudden indisposition. Then Brad appeared at the end of Millicent's walk and

Faith felt a sudden rush of adrenaline. She had work to do.

Brad had his laptop. They were all sitting around Millicent's dining-room table. She'd pointedly got out the table pads when she'd seen the computer.

"Don't want to mar the surface. Mahogany, you know."

Faith looked at the highly polished surface. Millicent's whole house reeked of beeswax. Mahogany veneer, maybe.

After this operation, Millicent sat at the head of the table and opened a bulging folder.

"Now, we want to be forceful, but we don't want to alienate people."

"Before we get to the letter, how did you convince the police to let you onto the reviewing stand yesterday?" Faith couldn't help herself. She knew she was playing right into Millicent's crafty little hands, but she had to ask.

Millicent gave Brad a slight smile. There was a trace of pity in it. She'd arranged for him to be on the platform, too, in recognition of all the work he'd done on the parade and other events. Unfortunately, Brad had had to contend not only with the police but his mother. He'd been lucky to go to the bathroom unescorted and he'd had to sneak out the back door this morning for the meeting.

Yet mostly, Millicent's smile conveyed superiority. Assuming her rightful place on the platform in the face of all obstacles was one of her more minor accomplishments—a piece of cake.

"I called the state police and talked to that nice Detective Dunne. He understood completely. I also mentioned I was leaving the house and the young man they'd sent would have to forcibly restrain me to keep me here."

Faith could imagine the scene. Millicent could match wits but not muscle. She was thin and had those angular bones that looked as if they would snap in a strong wind. And she would have put up a fight. No doubt about it. Dunne had obviously pictured the ill-matched pair rolling about the well-worn Oriental, dodging furniture and knickknacks, the poor officer trying not to do any damage to them or their owner.

"So you just left?"

"No, I didn't have to. John very nicely sent a car for me, which was ridiculous. It was only across the green, but he insisted. He also sent another policeman. I promised him I would return home immediately afterward and that seemed to satisfy him. 'Millie,' he said, 'we just don't want anything to happen to you.' So thoughtful."

John Dunne was also in the select group that was permitted to shorten Millicent's name.

Having cleared this up, Millicent got back to business.

"Now, as I was saying, we need to find the right approach. Our original broadside was effective, but this occasion calls for greater subtlety."

After several tries, they came up with an acceptable letter. It was straightforward, avoided inflammatory statements, but was strong, ending with the warning: "If we do not act now on behalf of Aleford's future inhabitants, they may not have an Aleford to inhabit."

Brad had thought of the phrase and he was enjoying the sound. He repeated the words several times like a mantra.

Faith had been struck by two things about Brad during the meeting. First, he was clearly very bright. The other feeling she had about him was harder to define. He had mentioned that he spent a great deal of time playing certain Dungeons and Dragons–type games with fellow enthusiasts on the Internet. He seemed to regard POW! as another kind of game, talking about strategies for winning, tactical maneuvers, and referring to those not in agreement as opponents. He cautioned Faith not to talk about what was in the letter. It would lessen the impact, he'd said, but she felt that was a ploy. Secrecy added drama. Millicent played right along.

"I certainly wouldn't want Joey Madsen and his people to find out what's in our mailing. They'd be certain to send out one of their own contradicting everything and getting everyone all muddled about the facts." She gave Faith a piercing look.

Faith had every intention of telling Dunne and maybe Tom, yet kept quiet. Word wouldn't get to Joey from them.

"I'm sure Joey will be sending out a mailing, or at least will write to the *Chronicle.* And since he's a Town Meeting member, we can expect a good floor fight." Brad was relishing the moment.

He's immature, Faith thought suddenly. That's his biggest problem. It *is* all a game to him. He likes to pit the grown-ups against one another and watch. She didn't doubt his sincere commitment to the environment, but something else was going on—intrigue, danger, real threats. The monitor screen come to life. He'd spoken of the letters with the same enthusiasm he'd reserved for his computer games.

"If whoever it is had used e-mail, I could have cracked this thing by now. The person may not have it, or may have known what I would do." He seemed to think the first possibility absurd, despite sitting in the same room with two people who still licked stamps.

Faith was getting a little tired of him. He was so single-minded. Maybe Miss Lora was a better judge of character than Faith had previously given her credit for—judging her primarily on the depth of her relationships with preschool children. Maybe his boyishness had attracted her, besides his obvious good looks, then she'd gotten bored. Certainly the looks were here, though. His dark hair curled damply obviously fresh from a shower and he smelled like Ivory soap. His shirtsleeves were rolled up. Those muscles didn't come from keyboarding.

"I think we all deserve a good hot cup of tea after this work," Millicent offered. Faith accepted. She wanted the caffeine and she wanted some time alone with Brad.

He sat fooling with his laptop. He didn't appear to be in need of conversation. Faith plunged right in.

"My son, Benjamin, is in Lora Deane's preschool class. She's a wonderful teacher. I understand your anonymous letter referred to her." Faith watched his expression closely and saw his surprise. Whatever he had expected her to introduce as a topic of conversation, it was not Miss Lora.

"Yeah, well," he stammered, and looked about the room. There was no help forthcoming from the breakfront or the row of extra chairs, each at exactly the same distance from the wall. "I mean, we went out for a while, that's all. The letter was pretty crude." He grinned, then re-collected himself. Faith was a minister's wife. "Filthy lies, all of it."

Faith waited. Sometimes this worked. It did now. He started talking again, filling the empty air between them. His fingers were still hovering over the keyboard.

"She's the one who broke it off. Just left word on the machine that she didn't want to go out anymore. No discussion. Nothing." His anger was evident. "I pity the next guy who gets involved with that—I mean with her."

He remembered Faith's original remark and added, "Oh, she's good with kids." It was not something he seemed to feel was especially noteworthy. He began to drum his fingers on the table. He was a nail-biter. Lora would have cured him of that, Faith thought. A few applications of some nasty-tasting stuff—but her mind was wandering.

"So you wouldn't want to get back with her?"

"Did she ask you to speak to me?" His eyes narrowed in suspicion. "Anyway, it's too late. Way too late."

Before Faith could ask him why, Millicent appeared with the tea tray. For three meager cups, she was as loaded down as for a banquet. There was a pitcher of hot water, a smaller one of milk, a plate of thinly sliced lemons, a strainer and stand, two sugar bowls—one for white, one for unrefined—tongs, cups, saucers, linen napkins, a cozy, and the pot itself.

"Now," she said brightly, "how do you take it?"

Faith wasn't altogether sure.

She had hoped to get some more time alone with Brad Hallowell, so Faith had consumed more tea than she wanted. But finally she had to leave to pick up the kids. Brad showed no intention of following her example. It had been foolish to think they would discuss the inner workings of POW! in front of her, if there were any. Keeping Brad by her side was more likely Millicent showing off and a reluctance to return home on his part.

She stood up to leave and Millicent's phone rang. When Miss McKinley excused herself to answer it, Faith sat back down, hoping for a long conversation. Picking up where they had left off, she had just started to explain to Brad that no, Lora had not sent her and to ask why he'd said it was too late to get back together with such finality, when Millicent came through the doorway. Brad looked relieved. Millicent stood behind her chair, her hands clenched around the back. There was a grim set to her mouth.

"This is not good news, I'm afraid. Not good for POW! at all."

"Nelson! Is he dead!" Faith cried.

"No, nothing like that." Millicent waved her hand dismissively. "Apparently, over the weekend one of the Deanes' pieces of heavy equipment was vandalized—an excavator. Someone cut the hydraulic hoses on the boom. I gather it's a very expensive repair. They're blaming us, of course." Millicent seemed extremely conversant with the technical jargon relating to construction work, Faith thought. She did get the idea, though. Person or persons unknown had sliced the things that made the steam shovel lift its load.

Brad leaned forward and pounded the table so hard his computer shook. Millicent looked askance. "And you know the bastards did it themselves! Probably was one that didn't work anyway and they're out to collect more insurance money!"

Faith doubted this. Gus Deane did not strike her as the type of man who would cripple the way in which he earned his living. If a machine was broken, he'd fix it. She'd often heard him extol the virtues of owning your own machinery, being your own boss.

But it was getting late. She had to get Ben and Amy.

As she walked back along Main Street, she tried to think what connection this new piece of the puzzle had to the others. Tampering with the steam shovel was an indirect attack on POW!—which would, it was true, be suspected immediately. The letter writer was also attacking the group in writing and for real. Did this mean the same person? At least the latest attack was on an inanimate object.

She'd left Millicent and Brad earnestly discussing POW!'s response—ignore it or issue a statement? Neither of these two anonymous-letter recipients seemed in the least bit nervous about their own well-being, or perhaps they assumed since Patriots' Day was over, the threat was gone, too.

Millicent had told them Nelson wasn't being allowed any visitors. She had called the hospital and she reported, "He's out of danger and should be at tomorrow night's meeting." Faith didn't let on that Tom had seen him yesterday. Millicent liked to be the bearer of tidings, not the recipient.

Faith crossed the green, avoiding the spot where Nelson had fallen. How did this attack fit into the puzzle? And Margaret, the first death. Had Nelson discovered something about the identity of her killer? But if he had, he wouldn't have kept it to himself, would he? Unless it was someone he knew, knew well. Faith felt depressed. Things seemed to be turning out like one of those bargains you picked up at a yard sale—a gorgeous, expensive jigsaw of the cathedral at Chartres that, after many hours of hard work, you'd find was missing the last few pieces of the rose window.

The sky was gray and it looked like rain was on the way again. She'd hoped to check out the bog today, maybe taking Pix and the dogs along with the kids. The weather would make it impossible. Nor could she return to the Chandler Street apartment and make discreet inquiries. Children did not know the meaning of the word *discreet* and tended to get in the way. She'd try to go into town tomorrow morning.

Any question of whether Miss Lora had heard about the latest attack on her family was answered by the teacher's first words to Faith, whispered furiously after the precaution "Little pitchers have big ears." And what did that mean, anyway? Faith wondered. "I know you weren't involved or Reverend Fairchild, but you have *got* to tell your group to leave us alone. I don't know what my grandfather's going to do, and Joey is ready to kill somebody!"

Faith didn't doubt it. "I was just with Millicent McKinley and Brad Hallowell. They are as shocked and upset as I am. I'm sure POW! didn't have anything to do with this. Does the construction company have any enemies you can think of? Another company that wanted a particular contract? Or maybe it was kids, too many beers on Patriots' Day weekend?"

Lora stared at Faith in disbelief and forgot to whisper. "Give me a break! POW! is the only enemy we have and the only group nutty enough to do all this. Besides, a bunch of loaded teenagers would try to start the thing for kicks or spray-paint it."

Faith quickly bundled Ben away, picked Amy up, and tried to reach Tom. He wasn't in his office and she assumed he must have gone to the hospital to see Nelson.

It wasn't a day for a walk in the bog, but it was a good day for work. She was not going to be at POW!'s meeting tomorrow, Wednesday night—a meeting that had assumed dramatic proportions. Have Faith was catering dessert and coffee for a library-endowment-fund function. Besides that, there was the *real* Patriots' Day dinner party they were preparing for on Friday night—April nineteenth.

When she opened the door at the company kitchen, she found Niki busy making pastry cream for the following evening. It would fill small tarts topped with raspberries. The former premises of Yankee Doodle Kitchens that Faith had taken over was large and well equipped. She'd added a play area for the kids at one end and had managed to convince Ben that coming to work with Mommy was an extraordinary treat. There were toys and books here he didn't have at home; plus, he might sometimes get to lick a spoon. Niki held out one to him now.

"Pretty sucky weather," she commented glancing out the window at the sheets of rain pouring down. "Oops, forgot the kids were here. Should say, Pretty inclement today, what ho."

"What ho," Faith said. She thought it was pretty sucky weather, too, and wondered if she was one of those people who suffered from light deprivation. There hadn't been much sunshine so far this spring. But then, there were plenty of other things to account for her mood. She took Ben and Amy to their corner, depositing her daughter in the playpen for a nap and settling Ben with his Lincoln Logs. She looked at the two of them and tried to remember what Ben had been like at Amy's age. Same, silken flax-colored hair and same sweet baby smell. It went so fast, too fast. She gave them each a kiss.

"Is Pix coming?" Niki asked when Faith returned.

"No, she has a conference with Danny's English teacher. It seems he's adopted the role of class clown and the teacher doesn't find it amusing. Pix doesn't, either, but she also thinks he's bored. If anyone can handle this, Pix can—simultaneous curriculum revamping and humble-pie consumption."

"Speaking of which, what are we serving for dessert Friday night? Have you decided?"

"Yes. A plate of three sorbets: cranberry, apple, and blueberry—New England fruits, garnished with fresh fruit. And since people want something decadent for dessert, even here, those chocolate crunch cookies. We can do half with white chocolate."

"Yum," Niki said. "They're toothsome, and speaking of toothsome morsels, I saw your Miss Lora at Avalon Saturday night. And she wasn't wearing a smock."

A week ago, Faith would have dismissed Niki's observation, yet now she knew it was entirely possible that Miss Lora was spending her free time dancing at this Boston hot spot and not doing the loopty-loo at home.

"You're sure?"

"Of course I am." Niki was always sure. "At first, I didn't recognize her without her glasses and those Mr. Green Jeans outfits she usually wears, but it was her, or she, whatever. Cool dress, ended just below her ass, Mylar or something shiny. Definitely spandex."

Faith was going to Chandler Street even if she did have to tote her offspring.

Early the next morning, as soon as the kitchen door closed behind Tom and her brood, Faith grabbed a light jacket and got in the car. She followed the same route they had taken on Saturday, slowed now by morning commuters. She turned down Clarendon and started searching the side streets for a parking place. Every empty space was either resident permit only or a tow zone. Finally, she spotted one on Tremont by the Boston Center for the Arts, pulled in seconds before the car behind her could cut her off, and got out.

Niki had described the man Lora Deane had been with at Avalon and it sounded like the same person she'd been with earlier on

Saturday. When Faith had asked Niki if he could possibly be Lora's brother, Niki had had a hard time stopping laughing. "If it was her brother, they're giving new meaning to 'incest is best,' " she'd told Faith wickedly. Hiring Niki had been one of the smartest things she'd ever done, Faith thought as she walked back toward Chandler. Work was never dull.

She did have a plan for this morning, and to that end, she had brought her clipboard. Today she'd be a graduate student doing research on feelings of community in Boston's neighborhoods. How well do you know, say, the person downstairs? Whom can you turn to for help? That sort of thing. If she couldn't find out anything about the apartment by the end of an hour, she'd have to try another approach. But it was bound to work—if anyone was at home.

She pressed the buzzer of the apartment on the floor below. No answer. Then she tried the one above. Again nothing. She pressed the buzzer for Bridey Murphy, who was on the top floor. Her curiosity about this occupant was almost as strong as it was about Lora. Her ring was answered and she quickly pushed the front door open before it locked again. She walked into a neatly carpeted hall and up the stairs. The Deane apartment had the same hand-lettered sign on the door as on the mailbox. She went up two more flights. Bridey Murphy's door was ajar, chain in place.

"Yes, what do you want?" a voice quavered.

Faith went into her routine.

"Well, I don't understand all you're saying, but I've lived in Boston neighborhoods my whole life. You'd better come in."

Bridey Murphy was a little old lady.

Faith resisted the temptation to say, So this is what became of Bridey Murphy—hoax or no hoax. Instead, she started to explain why she was there, or ostensibly why she was there. It really wasn't necessary. Bridey was obviously lonely and ready to talk to anyone about anything.

Her apartment was spacious, although crowded with furniture—a large couch, easy chair, ottoman, end tables, bookcases, a formal oak dining-room set, the china closet crammed with plates, figurines, and cups. Lace curtains hung at the windows, doilies were in abundance, and hand-colored family photos from the twenties and thirties decorated the walls. Over the small fireplace, there was a large, elaborately framed chromolithograph of a little stone cottage nestled in the green hills of County something.

"I grew up in the West End. It's gone, of course. They just leveled it for the hospital, you know. Mass General. But that would be before your time. Now, the West End—that was a neighborhood. If you had a scrape and your own mother wasn't home, you could go into anyone's apartment and they'd give you a bandage and a cookie. Not like today."

She was off and running. All Faith needed to do was direct the course toward the present.

"So, you don't feel that close to the people around here? Even in your own building?"

"Not close, no. I know them all right, but that's not to say I *know* them. Sounds silly—"

Faith interrupted her. "They're just people you say hello to in the hall?"

"Exactly. Would you like a cup of tea, dear? And I've got some nice Irish soda bread. I'm Irish, you know, both sides. I guess you could tell from the name. I've gotten a lot of comments on *that* over the years, but I just say, 'Bridget—Bridey—Kathleen Murphy. That's the name I came into this world with and it's the one I plan to have when I go out.' Not that I didn't have my chances."

Faith looked at the woman's softly lined face and bright blue eyes. Her hair was still thick, although the curls were pure white now. She was sure Bridey had had her chances. She must have been very pretty.

"Never found anyone I thought I'd want to wake up to every day, and then, my own parents fought like cat and dog. Couldn't see living the same way. Maybe I'll be sorry when I'm older, but not so far. I like my independence."

If Bridey wasn't sorry yet, Faith doubted she ever would be. The woman was close to ninety if she was a day. The cane leaning against her chair was the only sign of any infirmity.

"Tea would be fine, but please let me make it."

Over the woman's protests, Faith got the tea and soon they were sitting at the kitchen table over their cups like two old friends.

"After I lost my apartment in the West End, I moved farther up on the Hill—Beacon Hill. It was a nice place, but I hated what was happening all around me. Thank the Lord my parents didn't live to see it. They loved the West End. Everyone together. It wasn't just the Irish. All races, all religions, you name it. Everybody got along. We never thought not to.

"I was working at Chandler's in those days, the bookkeeping department. Now, that was a lovely store. When they went out of business, I went over to Filene's, but it wasn't the same." Bridey sighed deeply.

This was a woman who still wore a hat and gloves to church, Faith thought. Bridey was neatly dressed in a navy skirt, white blouse, and pink cardigan with a little enameled forget-me-not brooch at her collar.

"Then the rents on the Hill began to go up like crazy. My brother had bought this building and he told me I could have any apartment I wanted. I took this one because it was up high. He's done very well in real estate," she confided.

"What about the other people in the other apartments? Aren't you friendly with any of them? I noticed some of the names as I was ringing buzzers. There was one, for instance, Deane, just below. Their apartment must be like yours."

"Well now, that's a strange story if you ask me."

Faith was. "Yes?"

"Only here on weekends and sometimes, very rarely, for a week at a time or at night, then out the next morning, early. I know because I'm up at five myself. Never could lie about in bed, and I go down to get my paper. Something fishy, I thought, and I was going to tell my brother, but then I met her and I can't imagine she's involved in anything wrong. A nicer girl you'll never meet, that's Lora."

Lora! Lora Deane was renting this apartment herself! *And* one in Aleford!

"Has she told you why she's on this peculiar schedule?"

"No, but I've figured it out. I think she's a nurse or some kind of live-in worker and this is her permanent address. She's never had time to come in for a cup of tea, but I know she will one of these days. She always stops to ask how I am when she sees me. Brought me some cookies she'd baked at Christmas. Now, you can put that down on your form, because it is neighborliness. I'd go to her for help in a minute if I needed it. Not like some I could name. Why the Macombers have lived here for years, and if I get a nod of the head, I count myself lucky.

Faith had her information, but she stayed for a half hour longer talking to the old lady. As she left, she promised to come back and knew she would.

Away from Bridey Murphy, Faith considered this new information. Lora Deane was living a double life. Mild-mannered nursery school teacher by week, hip single on the weekends. But why was the deception necessary? What else was going on? And maintaining two places ran into money. Was this the real reason Lora didn't want to loan Joey Madsen funds for Alefordiana Estates?

Faith drove past the bowling alley on Route 2 and accelerated as she went up the hill before the Aleford exit. She'd never thought of Miss Lora as a mystery woman. But what did they really know about her—or any of the rest of the family? Faith decided it was time to pay a call on Gus, the paterfamilias. She knew him from the Aleford Minutemen activities and they'd always maintained a light, joking relationship. Gus was a bit of a flirt, but not obnoxious. He never crossed the line from art form to lech. It was a skill she admired—and enjoyed. She tried to think of some pretext. No parish calls, and ringing his doorbell for POW! was definitely out. Besides, being in the Minutemen, Gus was president of the Aleford Chamber of Commerce. As soon as she'd started Have Faith again, she'd joined. The Chamber sponsored a large cookout on the Saturday of Memorial Day weekend. All the local merchants had special sales and the event drew a big crowd. She felt a sudden pressing need to talk to Gus about the plans and what Have Faith might supply.

Ben was spending the afternoon with a friend and Faith was able to get Mrs. Hart to come over while Amy napped. The way things were going, the woman might never get to see what the child looked like awake. She almost called Pix, but she didn't want to let her know where she was going. Pix might have a lot on her mind, but she'd still remembered that Faith hadn't told her why she was asking questions about Brad Hallowell earlier.

Faith had completely forgotten her promise to tell Pix everything when she could and was a little embarrassed to reveal it had involved the phone calls Lora Deane had been getting, which were by then common knowledge in town.

"And you suspected Brad?"

"Well, an ex-boyfriend, angry, hurt."

"And that was what you couldn't tell me?" Pix said, looking Faith straight in the eye. No wonder the Millers had such honest children.

* * *

Gus and Lillian Deane lived in a large brick house at the end of a winding drive near the Aleford/Byford border. It was imposing—a three-car garage, swimming pool for the grandchildren and now the great-grandchildren. The shrubs were trimmed into round balls; those lining either side of the front walk were squat muffin shapes. There wasn't a fallen twig or leaf on the smooth green lawn. Every window was shielded from the sun's rays by an awning with an elaborate *D* in script square in the middle. She'd decided not to call first, just take the chance he would be in. She didn't want him to have time to think why else she might be paying him a visit. Supposedly, he was retired from active work and didn't spend much time on the job sites anymore.

Faith rang the bell and heard chimes.

She was in luck. Gus opened the door himself.

"Now, this is a nice surprise to find on my doorstep. Come on in, Faith."

"I had a few moments free, so I thought this might be a good time to talk about the plans for the Memorial Day cookout. It's not that far away."

Gus nodded. "Only six weeks."

She couldn't tell whether he was onto her or not. There had been an underlying note of amusement in his voice.

"Terrible weather this spring," he continued. "Hope it's better for our cookout. But then a lot can happen in six weeks."

He led the way to the rear of the house. Lillian didn't seem to be home; otherwise, she'd have been there offering Faith something to eat or drink. Gus might maintain a higher profile in town, but the house was his wife's domain.

"Lillian's over at Bonnie's. Can't keep away from the baby. Let's sit in here and you can tell me what's on your mind." He opened the door to what was obviously his den. There was a large-screen

TV at one end with appropriately comfortable seating. French doors led to a broad patio that ran the full length of the rear of the house. A desk with computer and printer indicated that the room was not purely recreational. He motioned to two chairs overlooking the garden and Faith sat down. A curio cabinet held a collection of beer steins. Some of them looked quite old. He noticed her glance.

"I started buying these when I was a young man. Can't pretend they came down in my family. Nothing came down, except maybe an attitude. I don't want to say it's special to the Deanes, but it's a way of life. You work hard, don't let yourself be pushed around, and leave the key under the mat for those coming next."

He knew damn well she hadn't come about how much potato salad they were going to need.

She sat quietly and let him go on.

"When I was growing up in this town, the same few people ran everything, always the same names. The board of selectmen—and it was only men—school committee, the library, the churches. If their families had missed the *Mayflower*, it was because they had something better to do. Times have changed."

"Thank goodness." Faith found something to say.

Gus nodded. "Wish I hadn't let Lillian talk me out of smoking. Feel like a pipe now. Anyway, where was I? Yes, it's changed." He leaned forward. "But not completely. Not completely, Faith.

"So far as some of those people—or I should say the sons and daughters of those people—are concerned, the Deanes will always be upstarts. We make more money than most of them do now and there's resentment about that. We were their ancestors' servants and we didn't stay in our place."

"But do you really think this is still true?"

"Absolutely. Now, you take this business with the bog. I don't mind telling you I'm more than a little annoyed with Joey for stirring the whole thing up in the first place. But not because I don't like to stir things up."

Faith ventured a smile.

"Okay, maybe I even *like* to stir things up, but I was angry with him because he didn't think it through. It's a bad investment. He has to put out too much of his own money before he sees any return and he'll be lucky to break even, what with all the stipulations the town is going to slap him with about the roads, septic systems, what not. Meanwhile, the whole Deane family looks bad. Even people who have never been to the place are suddenly talking about the Deanes robbing Aleford of precious open space. No, I'm not happy with Joey."

Faith felt a sudden twinge of sympathy for Mr. Madsen. Gus was not a man you wanted to antagonize.

"Could have done better. Told her so at the time, but she's just like her father, just like me. Wouldn't listen, and you'll never hear a word of complaint from her, either. I don't know if she loves or hates the man at this point."

He didn't say her name, but Gus was obviously referring to Bonnie.

"Alefordiana Estates—what the hell kind of a name is that? Thinks we're in Florida or something," Gus growled.

"Well, of course I'm not happy about it," Faith said.

"Going to have a road at your back door. I'll say you're not happy about it, but here's my point, Faith." He leaned over again and this time raised his forefinger. "I may not agree that Joey's doing the brightest deal, I may not even like the man that much myself, but I'll defend him to my death against anyone who says he doesn't have the right to build what he wants on his own land so long as it's not against the law. And it's not. Not a single person in that group of yours can say he hasn't met every requirement."

"This may be true, but—"

"Hear me out—I'm not finished. Then you can have your say."

Faith shut her mouth.

"Somebody in that organization is not normal. I know I lost my temper at the selectmen's meeting and I've been hearing about it from my wife, but my property had been destroyed and my family threatened. This is the work of a lunatic. My excavator, too! You've heard about that?"

Faith nodded.

"And the Batcheldors. I don't know what Margaret, God rest her soul, was doing in our house, but she was in there with a can of gas. And now somebody's tried to do poor Nelson in. Maybe this nut was up to something with Margaret. People can believe so much in a cause that they think anything they do is justified. But I'm not going to sit back and watch the whole Deane family go up in flames."

He sat back. It was Faith's turn, but she couldn't think of any response.

"So, how much potato salad do you think we'll need this year?"

It was only after they had finalized the menu for the cookout, same as last year's and the year before, that Faith was able to swim her way back up river and introduce the subject of Lora Deane.

"We feel so lucky to have Lora as Ben's teacher. She's wonderful with children." This ploy had worked with Brad—more or less.

"She's gifted with children and I'm happy she's found a job close by. Wish she'd settle down herself, but she hasn't shown any signs of it. There was the Hallowell kid. That's over or I'd have had to put a stop to it. She wants to go back to her place, but we've been firm. She's not to move one foot until everything gets cleared up. Fortunately, she's a timid girl and listens to us. That's why she's not too popular with the guys, I suppose. An old-fashioned girl, that's our Lora."

One of them, anyway, Faith thought. For an instant she felt the urge to tell Gus about Lora's apartment in the South End and Mr. Miata. It seemed wrong to keep any secrets at all from this commanding figure, and Faith was amazed Lora could pull it off day after day. Faith bit at her lip. She'd come to get information, not give it—at least not until she'd figured things out a bit more. Until then, Gus could go on thinking that his granddaughter was up for a role in *Little Women.*

With a little time left before she had to pick up Ben, Faith went home and reported in to John Dunne about the meeting at Millicent's. Amy sat at her mother's feet, surrounded by puzzles, her favorite toy. She was babbling softly to herself and Faith listened intently for recognizable words. Amy had said *bird* yesterday. They'd be having mother-daughter talks in no time.

Detective Lieutenant Dunne came to the phone immediately. Faith hated to disappoint him.

"They may be having separate, even clandestine meetings, but if so, it's only to satisfy Brad Hallowell's theatrical inclinations. And they were both surprised when they heard about the excavator sabotage."

"I can't see Millie shimmying up the boom with a machete in her mouth," John agreed. He'd been having a good day. They'd checked prints from a particularly grisly homicide with the New Hampshire police after coming up with nothing in Massachusetts. Bingo, and the arrest had been made an hour ago. The guy was now safely under lock and key.

"How about other POW! members? You said some of them were pretty militant," he asked.

"The Batcheldors were the most militant, and neither of them was in any shape to disable a steam shovel. I can't think of anyone else." She decided the time had come to tell John about meeting Nelson and Margaret in the woods.

After she told him, he asked, "Anything else you're saving for a rainy day?"

"No—and you did say you only wanted to know about the POW! meetings."

"You knew what I meant. Anyway, we'll have a look around Beecher's Bog and see what we can find. Nelson Batcheldor is out of the hospital. Might have a word with him about his wardrobe. What about that big donation, the five-hundred dollars. Any ideas?"

"Not really. I think Pix is right and it's someone in public office who can't come out and openly support POW! Whoever it is, I don't see how it's connected to Margaret's death or the letter writing. Quite a few people in town are convinced that Joey Madsen wrote the letters and killed Margaret when he found her setting fire to his house—a crime of passion. I'm not convinced."

"Neither am I," Dunne admitted.

Amy was losing interest in the puzzles at last and using her mother as a climbing structure.

"I've got to go now, but I'll keep in touch."

"I know," John said, and hung up.

Faith put the phone down. She wasn't holding out on him, but she hadn't told him about Lora Deane or her own visit to Gus. It didn't seem to have anything to do with either POW! or Margaret's murder. Tom would have to take over her duties at POW!'s meeting tonight and report back to Detective Dunne. Given recent events and the imminence of the special Town Meeting, there might be more militancy and, in turn, more suspects. These people seemed so sure. Although Faith believed it was best for the town that the bog be preserved, she could see the other point of view. POW! didn't.

She put Amy in her car seat and looked past the church to the woods beyond, leading to the bog. Though it wasn't harvested anymore, at one time it had been a working cranberry bog. Part of the Beecher's barn was still standing, their stone walls tumbled but in place, and their old orchard bloomed in the spring. In effect, Joey Madsen would be turfing over a piece of Aleford's history. The rights of the town versus the rights of an individual. It was a tough call.

The library event was a great success and the head of the endowment campaign told Faith she had already been slipped two hefty checks and received several pledges. "It's your food, I'm sure. Puts everyone in a benevolent mood," she'd said. Faith was grateful for her praise but thought it also had to do with the excellent speaker, an eminent historian, who introduced his talk by pointing out the accessibility of libraries in the United States compared with that in other countries and suggesting everyone dig deep into his or her pocket to keep it that way.

When she got home, Tom was waiting up by the fireplace. There were two brandy glasses on the coffee table. Hers was full.

"You always have the best ideas," she said.

"And here's another," he told her, moving from the wing chair to the couch and taking her in his arms. "There's nothing like staring into the nonflickering flames of a lifeless fireplace to arouse one's passion."

"True, true," Faith said, sipping her Rémy Martin, "but first tell me what happened at the meeting tonight."

"This could kill the mood," Tom warned.

"I doubt it."

"All right." Tom had been planning to tell his wife the moment she walked in, anyway. He knew she'd be kicking herself for missing it—and it had been something to miss.

Joey had arrived at the meeting ready for blood. His lawyer

wasn't with him. He walked in, went to the front row, and sat directly facing Millicent. Her face was stony. She called the meeting to order, but before she could ask for a reading of the minutes, Joey jumped up. "You did it at my meeting, so I can do it at yours. Equal time, right? Isn't that what all you lily-livered liberals believe in? Well, I've got my rights and I'm taking them."

Tom knew why he'd come alone. Madsen was certainly not following counsel's advice.

Maybe Millicent thought the best way to deal with the situation was to be gracious. Maybe she was just plain curious. In any case, she recognized the irate builder.

"I believe Mr. Madsen has something to say before we begin. Mr. Madsen?"

"Damn right I do. First of all, whoever screwed up my excavator, I'm going to get you. If it takes the rest of my life. Now, for the rest of you, you can hold meetings round the clock and it isn't going to do you any good. My lawyers have been over the plans a thousand times. There's *nothing* wrong. Alefordiana Estates is going to happen, so you'd better get used to the idea. I'm under the impression that this is still a free country and a man can do what he wants with his own land. You're trying to take that right away from me and I'm serving notice here and now that you're going to fail. Nobody takes anything away from me that's mine."

The room was silent. Joey was running out of steam. He left the stage and walked to the doors at the rear of Asterbrook Hall. He turned and shook his fist, repeating his last words. "Nobody does me out of what's mine. Remember that!"

Faith was listening openmouthed to Tom's description of the meeting. "What happened after he left?"

"You know Millicent. A class act. She thanked the group for their indulgence and called for the minutes. The rest of the meeting went fast. I had the feeling people were itching to get out and tell everyone who wasn't there what had happened. Pix almost had me winded by the time we got here, she was so eager to tell Sam. Oh, and by the way, the Scotts are back. Louise was looking very determined, so I have the feeling it was her idea more than Ted's. But you know Ted. If he didn't think it was safe for them, especially her, to be back, he wouldn't budge. Millicent read your letter—very good—swore us all to secrecy for some reason. We're not to reveal the contents, and Louise announced she and Pix would be preparing the mailing tomorrow. I didn't volunteer you."

Faith's brandy glass was empty and it was late. It had been a long day—Bridey Murphy, Gus, the library. She was tired—but not too tired.

When you sign up for something, April seems a long way off in September, which is why Faith found herself at the end of a line of preschoolers, all chanting, "I know a little pussy, who lives down in the lane" in unison. When they got to "He'll never be a pussy, he'll always be a cat, 'cause he's a pussy willow, now what do you think of that!" for the fourth time, she thought she might have a new description of hell. An eternity of Miss Lora's annual Pussy Willow Walks.

They were on their way into the bog. Faith had on the fisherman's boots she'd purchased in Maine and the ground squelched beneath them. They'd had more rain during the night, but today was bright and fair.

"It never rains on Pussy Willow Walk days," Lora told the helper mothers. She didn't like to call them chaperones—"sounds too much like your Dad insisting on going on your dates," she'd told Faith once. Any relative of Lora's would be getting more than he or she bargained for on the young woman's dates these days, Faith thought. And how did she manage to look so full of energy and good cheer after weekends of carousing?

The helper mothers—helper fathers appeared only occasionally—were spread out through the line. Faith, at the front, was supposed to keep watch for low branches and thorny bushes. She trudged along and tried to ignore the performers behind her. They were gearing up to start the poem again—Ben's high little voice chanting as enthusiastically as the rest.

The densely growing trees, covered with thick ropes of interwoven vines, had kept the ground beneath from getting as wet as the ground immediately around the bog. Lora had made sure there were pussy willows to find, she'd reassured the mothers. They were on the other side of the woods, on a path that led to a small pond. Faith continued to reconnoiter. She was getting a bit ahead of the pack, but she told herself it was for their own good. She snapped a few branches out of the way to convince herself.

Emerging from the woods into the open, she noticed that there seemed to be a fallen log in the path. They'd have to help the children over it. She went closer.

It wasn't a log.

It was Joey Madsen. Face up, his eyes wide with surprise. There was a knife in his chest. He'd been stabbed and he was dead.

Chapter 8

Faith screamed. She couldn't help it, even knowing the children were close behind her. She ran back toward the group, which had become instantly silent. The children's faces were frightened. One little boy was getting ready to cry.

She spoke quickly. "I saw . . . I saw a poor dead animal and it startled me. I'm sorry if I startled you, too, children."

There were a few solemn nods. Ben immediately spoke up. "What kind of animal? A big animal? A fox? A deer? What is it, Mom? Can we see?"

Faith cut him off, "No, sweetheart, I think it would be better to go back now and wait until the path is clear. We need to leave him in peace."

Lora was looking at Faith in some confusion. "You're sure we should turn around?"

"I'm sure," Faith said firmly.

The other mothers began to get the children back in line and one of them started singing "Inch by Inch." Soon the kids joined in. Thank God for presence of mind, Faith thought, and motioned for Lora to step aside.

"What's going on?" the teacher asked in a low voice.

"There's been an accident." Faith could not bear to tell Lora that her brother-in-law was dead, and in any case, she couldn't let her know until the police had been there. "A very bad accident. Please call Chief MacIsaac and tell him to get here right away. Tell him to call the state police and ask Detective Dunne to meet him here."

"The state police! Faith, you've got to tell me! It's a person, isn't it! What's happened?"

"I can't say any more and I can't let anyone go any closer until the police arrive. *Please*, you have to take care of the children." Faith hoped this would distract Lora. It did. The class was almost out of sight and Lora sprinted after them.

Faith called after her, "Wait! Go upstairs to Tom's office and tell him to come as soon as possible!"

"Okay," Lora said, running to keep up with her charges.

They were gone and Faith was alone in the bog with the body. She would have welcomed the sound of any nursery rhyme, no matter how many times it was repeated.

Joey. Joey was dead. She felt dizzy and sat down on a rock. For a moment, she thought she might be sick. She dropped her head to her knees. Pine needles carpeted the ground in a thick brown mat. They smelled faintly of balsam, of Christmas trees. An ant crawled from underneath. She sat up. Joey. Joey Madsen had been murdered. She couldn't stop thinking of his sightless eyes staring up at the spring sky. Face up. Not face down.

Joey had known his killer. No one had crept up stealthily behind him. He'd come down the path, maybe his hand out in greeting. Someone Joey knew. Someone he trusted. Why were they meeting here, out of sight? Why not at the company's office or at Joey's house?

She stood up, wishing Tom would hurry. She walked back toward the body, careful to retrace her steps. Away from the dense canopy the trees made, the ground was soft. She could see the imprint of her boots, coming and going. There were other footprints, too. A ditch ran alongside the path, filled with the runoff from the pond. The water was still and covered by thick green slime.

There was very little blood. Just a stain on the surface of Joey's sweatshirt, around the handle of the knife. A large crow flew overhead, cawing loudly. She needed to stay nearby. She needed to keep the birds or other predators from desecrating the corpse. From pecking at those open eyes.

An animal, she'd told the children, to protect them from the horror of the truth. What if she hadn't been first in line? She shuddered. An animal. But Joey was not an animal. He was a proud new father, a husband, a son, a human being. She thought of Bonnie and little Joey.

Tom found her in tears a short distance from the body. She threw herself into his arms.

"Oh, Tom, it's Joey Madsen. He's dead. There's a knife in his chest. I had gone ahead. The children didn't see. Oh, what will his poor wife do!" She sobbed. Tom held her close and stroked her hair. She lifted her tear-streaked face to his. "Who can be doing all these terrible things? First Margaret, then Nelson, now Joey! Who will be next? I'm scared!"

"Me, too," Tom said.

They held each other in silence for a few minutes: then Tom asked, "Are you okay? I want to go a little closer."

Faith nodded.

"Tell me how far you went."

"See that bush by his foot? Up to there."

Tom walked carefully in his wife's tracks and knelt by the bush.

Staying where she was, Faith said her own prayer for Joey—and for the rest of the town.

Tom came back and they stood holding hands, waiting for the police.

Charley arrived first, crashing out of the woods, followed by two patrolmen. "What's going on?"

Faith pointed to the body. "It's Joey Madsen and he's dead."

"What the hell!" Charley started to go over to the dead man, then stopped. "Who else besides you two has been here?"

"Nobody, except Joey and whoever did it, so far as I know."

Charley considered the lifeless form a few feet away. "Face up," he commented out loud. "Didn't think he had anything to be afraid of, even way out here. Now what was he up to?"

The shock was wearing off and Faith had started to think along the same lines. Did his death have anything to do with his outburst at the POW! meeting last night? Tom had quoted Joey's threat: "I'm going to get you, even if it takes the rest of my life." Did whoever cut the hoses on the excavator get him first? "Joey is ready to kill somebody." Where did that come from? Lora, speaking of Joey's outrage. Was it a question of kill or be killed for the murderer? But Joey wouldn't have come to this isolated spot to confront an enemy—unless he was armed himself. And Faith wouldn't know that until the police told her—*if* they would tell her.

Charley was asking her what time she'd found the body and what she was doing here in the first place. As she began to relate the morning's events, Detective Lieutenant John Dunne arrived with his partner, Detective Ted Sullivan, and the rest of the CPAC unit from the state police. The medical examiner was on the way from the Framingham barracks, Dunne told Charley before turning to Faith. Both Sully and Dunne did not seem surprised to see her there; Charley must have told them, of course. On the other hand, neither looked pleased at her presence. John strode over closer to the body and Faith now knew exactly what a quaking bog was. He returned, conferred with Sully, who already had his camera out, then walked over to the Fairchilds.

"Taking a nature walk?" he asked Faith.

"No, I was one of the helper mothers, the chaperones, for the Pussy Willow Walk Lora Deane's class was taking."

Dunne wrote it down in his notebook. Cases where Faith was involved always introduced concepts and words he had to ask his wife about. Snuglis, now Pussy Willow Walks.

"Have you touched the body, moved anything near it?"

"No to both. I could tell immediately he was dead." The eyes. The eyes would haunt her waking and sleeping hours for a long time to come.

"Be sure to get shots of the footprints, and we'll make the casts right away," he called out to Detective Sullivan. The rest of his men were combing the area for evidence—anything. The knife handle was being dusted for prints.

"You two going to be home today?"

"We are now," Tom said, and John nodded. He knew what they must be feeling—shock, fear—and this was all before the delayed reaction.

"Did you know him well?"

"Not well, but we knew him," Tom answered.

And even more about him, Faith finished silently. She wanted to go home.

After a few more questions, Dunne told them they could leave.

"I'm sorry," he said to Faith. She knew what he was trying to say and was grateful.

"Thank you."

The Fairchilds went back up the slight slope into the woods, retracing their own steps—and the path the murderer had taken. There was only one way in and one way out. Joey had come that way, too—and Miss Lora's class. It had been a busy morning in the bog.

"You get Amy and I'll get Ben?" Faith suggested.

"No," Tom said. "I want to stay with you. We'll get them together."

They walked quickly away from Beecher's Bog. Joey had died on the first warm, sunny day of the year, beneath a cloudless blue sky. The air was filled with birdsongs. Margaret would have known what they were. She'd been alive ten days ago. Joey had been that morning. Their deaths were linked. Faith was sure of it and she knew she had to try to find out before there was another.

The Fairchild family was sitting around their large kitchen table, eating lunch. Amy was in her high chair, feeding herself after a fashion. She'd recently displayed an independent streak when it came to food, grabbing the spoon herself and taking great joy in picking up such things as linguine, one strand at a time, with her tiny fingers. While Faith was happy to note these beginnings that promised a lifelong interest in food, it made feeding Amy in a hurry difficult. Today there was no rush and the toddler was delicately picking out the peas from the chicken potpie with puff-pastry crust that filled her bowl.

Ben had finished his and asked for more.

"Did they move the animal?" he'd wanted to know earlier, as soon as he'd seen his mother.

"They will soon."

"Then we can go for our walk tomorrow?"

It was going to be a while before Faith willingly entered the bog and she'd resorted to that useful catchall, "We'll see."

Now, being together felt good. Faith had the feeling that she and Tom had gone through something akin to an earthquake or other disaster. Afterward, you just want to hold on to those closest to you. Comfort yourself. Feel blessed. She could tell Tom was experiencing the same emotions. His chair was so near Amy's that she was getting potpie on both their clothes.

Faith wasn't hungry and had been picking at her food. She was nervous, expecting the phone to ring, or a knock on the door.

The phone was first.

"Faith! My God! I just heard!" It was Pix. "We were finishing the mailing and Ellen Phyfe came bursting in, shouting that Joey Madsen had been murdered in the bog and that you'd found him."

"How did she find out?" Aleford really was incredible.

"She was in the camera store, and you know they listen to the police band all the time."

Faith did know. The group at Aleford Photo was an interesting crew, who gave new meaning to the term *moonlighting*. Bert, for example, was a licensed undertaker, had two paper routes, restored old cars, sold crucifixes and other religious articles by mail, had a houseful of foster children and his own kids—and worked in the store. By comparison, Richard was a sluggard, working only three jobs: at the store, as an auxiliary cop, and as a professional race-car photographer. If you wanted to know the latest in either photographic techniques or local larcenies, Aleford Photo was the store to frequent. They were pretty good for car advice, too.

"I have to take Danny to soccer; then I'll be right over," Pix said. "And we didn't send out the mailing. It seemed terribly inappropriate, if that's the right word."

Faith wasn't sure *inappropriate* was the right word, either. *Callous*, *unfeeling*, *dancing on Joey's grave*—all came to mind. She went back to the kitchen. Tom was cleaning up himself and Amy. Ben was in the backyard on the swings.

"It's all over town," she told him.

"Don't tell me you're surprised." He'd missed a spot and she took the wet cloth and wiped his cheek.

"It does change things, though. Pix said they didn't send out the mailing. Do you think the Deanes are likely to press forward with Alefordiana Estates? Remember, Gus wasn't too enthused about it."

Gus hadn't been too enthused about the man his granddaughter had married, either. But that was a long way from murder. Although, two men with violent tempers . . .

"I have no idea," Tom said. "Bonnie may be so upset that she'll want to continue even if it doesn't make the best business sense—in memory of her husband and because there's no doubt he would have wanted it that way."

Faith thought about Bonnie and found herself disagreeing with Tom. Bonnie might be upset, but if it didn't make sense financially, she wouldn't have any part of it. She wondered how Bonnie had viewed Joey's scheme. She had been conspicuously absent from all the presentations, but then, she'd just had a baby. This thought was qualified immediately. A woman who closes a deal as she's going into labor wouldn't shy away from important meetings after the birth—if she wanted to be there.

"I wonder what Millicent is planning to do? She's put so much time and energy into fighting Alefordiana Estates. It wouldn't be like her to abandon the cause, even if the cause is dead." As she spoke, the last word stuck in her throat. Faith picked Amy up. She was beginning to droop. Sleep, the sweet escape. Faith wished she could crawl in with her daughter.

Pix's call was just the first, and eventually they had to take the phone off the hook. Faith prepared a brief statement that she gave to the Aleford Police Department, then referred all the newspapers and other media to them. Prudently, she'd called both her parents and Tom's when it became apparent that the news would spread. She downplayed her role: "Wrong place, wrong time." Her mother, Jane, had sounded skeptical, "I did hope your last murder would be it, dear"—making Faith feel somewhat like "the bad seed."

Faith's sister, Hope, on her way to an important meeting, was more direct. "Can't you find anything else to do up there? I thought when you started the business again that would take care of things."

"It's not a hobby," Faith had protested. "I'm not deliberately finding bodies!"

"We'll talk. Got to run." And Hope was off to crunch some more numbers, and squeeze some individuals, as well.

Late in the afternoon, Tom went out for milk. He returned from the Shop 'n Save with a gallon, some Ben & Jerry's New York Super Fudge Chunk ice cream, and the news that Aleford seemed to have developed a siege mentality over night. There were very few people in the market and they weren't lingering. Even the checkout clerks looked nervous.

"It was weird. People were stocking up the way they do when a big storm is predicted, but there wasn't any excitement like there is then."

Faith was making lentil stew, more than enough for dinner. She had also felt the need to fill the larder. A few loaves of olive bread were rising on the back of the stove. She'd taken some thick pork chops out that she planned to rub with garlic and rosemary before broiling. As usual, in times of trouble, she turned to substantial food. Garlic always made life seem better.

Pix had come and gone, jumpy as everyone else. She was picking the kids up rather than letting them walk home from their various practices. Faith had asked about Samantha's latest college inclinations and Pix's face had gone blank for a moment. Samantha? College? She recollected herself and said, "Still waiting for Wellesley, and since that's the one place she hasn't heard from, that's the one place she wants to go. I'll be happy when this is all over."

"So will I," Faith said—and they both knew they weren't just talking alma maters.

Charley MacIsaac and John Dunne came by shortly after Pix left.

"Homicidal maniac—that's what people are saying," Charley commented.

"And what do you think?" Faith directed her question to both of them . Dunne answered.

"Homicidal, obviously. Maniac, I doubt. Both of these crimes have been carefully planned, nothing accidental or spontaneous about them. And all this window dressing—poison-pen letters, disabled construction equipment, harassing phone calls."

"The brick through Lora's window, the attack on Nelson, although that was probably not intended to fail," Faith reminded him. "So you think everything that's been happening this month is connected?"

"Don't you?" Cops loved to answer a question with a question, Faith had observed.

"Yes, I haven't figured out how, though."

"If it makes you feel any better, we haven't, either, which is why we're here."

"You need my help." It was a statement of fact.

Dunne grimaced. He would have done well in Ed Wood movies. However, Faith's overriding thought was John's admission that he needed her particular expertise. They were back in business.

Dunne opened his Filofax and flipped to a blank page.

"Tell me everything you know about Joey Madsen and his family. Don't leave anything out, no matter how insignificant it seems."

"Was he carrying a weapon?" Faith knew enough to get her questions in first when John was in one of these expansive moods.

"No—and before you get around to asking about the murder

weapon, it was a common, ordinary kitchen knife. Impossible to trace. He or she could have had it in a drawer for years or picked it up at a yard sale—it wasn't new."

Faith obediently filled John and Charley in on everything she'd learned about Joey Madsen and the family he'd married into. Tom added what he knew. Faith even mentioned Miss Lora's double life and her own recent visit with Gus.

"It's no secret Gus Deane didn't think much of his granddaughter's choice," Charley told them. "Tried to buy him off. Bonnie heard about it and almost didn't invite the old man to the wedding. It was quite a scandal at the time. Her father was still living and he smoothed things over."

They talked some more. Charley seemed convinced that someone connected to POW! was involved. John didn't comment, nor did Faith—out loud. Could Beecher's Bog mean so much that you'd kill for it? And no one in POW! would have murdered Margaret, a founding member! Unless someone in POW! found out that Joey had killed her, enraged that she was burning the house down, then killed Joey, taking the law into his or her own hands. It certainly avenged the one crime while preventing what POW! viewed as an almost equally heinous one from occurring. Brad Hallowell clearly viewed the development of the land this way. And what about the possibility that Margaret hadn't been alone that night? Her accomplice had gotten away but might have seen who killed her—and again, the killer might have been Joey. Faith related her theories and ended, slightly chagrined, "There are a lot of 'might haves.' "

The men, including her husband, nodded.

"But it's possible," she protested, in the face of solid male opposition, never a pretty sight.

"It's possible," Charley conceded in the tone of voice he used to humor her. She wasn't offended, just vowed to keep her theories to herself in the future. The other two didn't say anything. Dunne stood up. The kids came running into the room. They adored him. Something about his size, a Barney double. He hastily made for the door. Kids were fine in their place—his own kids at home, for instance—but they tended to make him nervous—those little feet, so easy to trip over, and the never-ending questions.

The Fairchilds ate early and bundled the children off to bed as soon as humanly possible, then went to bed themselves. By mutual consent, they didn't talk about what had happened. They were exhausted.

Faith pulled the loaded van into the winding driveway of one of Aleford's older homes—a large mid-nineteenth-century stone house that had grown over the years. It had a glassed-in conservatory and a long porch filled with comfortably cushioned wicker furniture. The porch was on the side of the house and faced gardens so magnificent that they had been included in the Evergreen's garden tour each year since the tour had started. No expense had been spared on this house and Martha Fletcher, the hostess, had given Faith the same instructions for this evening—although, she had been cautioned, nothing nouveau riche. The client had actually used the term.

It was 3:30 and Faith was glad to see Niki's car was already parked at the rear of the house. Typically, Mrs. Fletcher had invited people for six o'clock. In New York, that could sometimes mark the end of a long lunch. While not exactly in a party mood, Faith was looking forward to the event. Last night Joey's face, dead and alive, had punctuated her dreams. She was eager for distraction.

Niki opened the kitchen door. "Our hostess is indulging herself with a long soak in a scented tub. I know because she told me. She made it sound so sinful, I'm going straight out tomorrow and pick up some lavender bath salts myself."

Faith began to cheer up and told herself that for approximately the next six hours, she wasn't going to think about anything but food and drink. On the way over, she'd had trouble concentrating on the pot roast to hand; her mind, so cooperative earlier, had turned rogue and persisted in tossing about competing theories about Joey's murder. Niki helped with the resolution by giving her boss a tight hug and saying firmly, "I'm doing the fruit; you do the table. We can talk later. Nobody's going to get killed tonight."

Faith appreciated the sentiment and sincerely hoped Niki was right.

An hour later, Mrs. Fletcher appeared, pink and rosy from her bath. She was wearing her dressing gown, but her makeup was on and she'd already scattered the jewelry from the safe-deposit box in various places about her person. Some good pieces, probably Grandmama's, but the diamonds needed cleaning and Faith noticed that the catch on the gold and sapphire bracelet had been repaired with a small gold safety pin. It would obviously be in bad taste to have anything professional done to one's heirlooms. Nouveau riche again.

Martha Fletcher stood in the dining-room doorway, a tall, substantial woman with her gray hair smoothed back into a tidy, at the moment, bun.

"It looks beautiful!" she gushed. Faith had to agree. They'd knocked themselves out creating this Patriots' Day buffet. The table was covered with material Faith had found at Fabric Place—a cream background with tiny flags, eagles, and stars stenciled in navy on the heavy glazed cotton. She'd placed groupings of votive candles in various-sized brass balls with star cutouts throughout the room. They gave off a soft glow and matched her hostess's brass chandelier, suitably dimmed. They'd done a large arrangement of blue delphiniums, Queen Anne's lace, red and white ranunculuses, and several colors of anemones for the sideboard, where the wine and, later, the coffee would be served. A lower, smaller arrangement sat on the table.

"And everything smells so good already. I knew I was right to have you!" Mrs. Fletcher rambled on.

"Thank you." The aromas from the kitchen *were* mouthwatering. Faith needed to get back there and see that the hors d'oeuvres were ready to go. She excused herself. Her hostess glanced at her watch and gave a shrill cry. "They'll be here any minute! I have to make sure Prescott's ready and get dressed myself!" Prescott Fletcher, her husband, was a distinguished-looking gentleman. He had popped his head into the kitchen earlier, looked about the room with a marked degree of unfamiliarity, asked them if they had everything they needed, and left in obvious relief when they said they had. Prescott had continued to add to the bounty of his family tree as a venture capitalist, Pix had told Faith, who wished she had the time—and nerve—to pin him down and ask him what this actually was.

In the kitchen, the staff was in full gear. Instead of a first course, they were serving heartier-than-usual fare for hors d'oeuvres: crab cakes with a spicy remoulade, asparagus wrapped in paper-thin slices of smoked salmon, zucchini pancakes with salsa and sour cream, wild-mushroom tartlets, two kinds of crostini—one with a duck pâté, the other with tapenade—and cherry tomatoes stuffed with chèvre. There wasn't anything particularly patriotic about the choices, although all were made with native products. Faith had decided enough was enough after determining the main course, dessert, and decor. Her hostess had wanted the catering staff to wear period dress, but Faith had politely but firmly declined, explaining this would seriously hamper their performance. She had no intention of getting stuck in the swinging door—or roasting to death in all those layers. She wore her black-and-white chef's pants, tailored to fit, and a tuxedo-front white shirt with a black rosette instead of a tie. The rest of the staff was similarly attired, except they wore plain black pants, and Scott, the bartender, wore a tie. Faith had met Scott Phelan and Tricia, who was now his wife, five years ago. Scott had played a role in solving Cindy Shepherd's murder. It was as hard now as it had been then for Faith to keep her mind on track. If anything, he was better-looking. Take-your-breath-away looks. Old-fashioned movie-star good looks, Gregory Peck as opposed to Brad Pitt. Tricia was a beautiful girl herself and the two were very happy together. They were teasing Niki, who was frantically washing lettuce, a hateful task. She'd suddenly decided they didn't have enough for the salad—mixed greens topped with pomegranate seeds and a blueberry vinaigrette dressing.

"You're going to be an old maid if you don't watch out," Scott warned.

"It wouldn't be the worst thing in the world. Better than ending up with some jerk."

"Not all men are like Scott, you know, Nikki. I happen to *like* jerks," Tricia said, quickly moving out of her husband's reach. "Don't mess me up! I just did my hair." She held up one arm to push him off.

"A jerk, huh?" He kissed her anyway—carefully.

"I'm only making sure you don't take me for granted," she said.

This would have gone on—and had—but it was time for the party. Niki spoke before Faith could.

"Okay, okay. Enough foreplay. Get out there and do your jobs. Faith and I have real work to do here," she ordered.

When the two had gone, Tricia with a tray of hors d'oeuvres, Scott to take drink orders, Faith and Niki laughed. "Better than TV," Niki said.

"Much better," Faith agreed, "And wait until they have kids!"

Scott returned. "It's not a white-wine crowd. Mrs. Fletcher was right about ordering a lot of scotch. And of course I have one order for a flintlock; it's a good thing we brought rum. They're starving, too. Went for Tricia like locusts."

"I'd better take another tray out right away," Faith said. This sometimes happened. People knew they were going to a dinner party, so they skipped lunch or ate lightly, then arrived ravenous. Well, there was plenty. She headed into the living room.

"And he has such a temper, my dear. No control at all. Remember when he turned his desk over in second grade!" A silver-haired lady was having a good time raking somebody over past and present coals. Faith wondered who was the object of this conversation, and moved unobtrusively a little closer.

"That's where Joseph got it from, no doubt," another woman commented, mouth pursed in disapproval.

"Joseph who?" a red-faced, rotund man asked, his drink—scotch, no ice—in one hand, a well-laden small plate in the other. He was wearing the modern equivalent of patriotic patrician dress: red chinos from Brooks, the same provenance for the navy sports jacket and striped tie.

"Joseph Madsen, the contractor who got himself killed yesterday," the first speaker answered. "We're speaking of the way certain mannerisms run through the generations in that kind of family. He's exactly like Gus."

"He may be like Gus, but he's not related to him. Not that I ever heard of. Married the old man's granddaughter."

"Oh, that's right, of course. But it's all the same. They simply don't know how to behave."

"Made themselves a bundle, though." The man took a healthy swallow. "Misbehavior has its rewards, if you know what I mean."

Both women nodded. That they were above such things—well above—was written all over their faces, suffused with the sherry they were sipping—and their own blue blood.

Faith turned to another group and offered the hors d'oeuvres.

Gus had been right.

The conversation was hard to swallow—from the notion that Joey had gotten himself killed, and this was taking "blame the victim" to a new height—to the idea that these "newcomers" to our shores were unable to control their passions. A prospect not without titillation for some in the room, she was sure. The whole thing made her sick. These were not the Alefordians she knew. When she'd mentioned the job to Pix, she'd made a face. "Pretty snooty bunch. I'm surprised she's hiring you. They always use the same people from Cambridge or entertain at the club." Aleford boasted its own country club, but the Fairchilds didn't know anyone who belonged, except the Scotts, who were avid golfers and regularly apologized for their membership: "The club's so close to our house."

Faith moved to another group and offered the tray. They, too, were discussing the murder. It had been naïve to think it would be otherwise. This was a more savvy bunch, more circumspect.

"We understand you discovered the body of poor Mr. Madsen," one woman said, "It must have been quite a shock."

"Yes, it was," Faith answered. "Try one of the crab cakes, an old family recipe." It was. Faith had created it when the firm was just starting in New York.

"And the police have no idea who could have done such a thing?" the woman persisted.

"Not to my knowledge," Faith answered.

"Probably a business deal gone sour. You hear about these things all the time. Of course, not in Aleford. Shame he had to be here when it happened," the man next to her said. Faith had the impression that he wouldn't have minded if Joey had been killed elsewhere. It was the venue that bothered him. "Not in my backyard" joined "blame the victim."

Faith left the room, her mind filled with murderous thoughts, and they had nothing to do with Joey Madsen.

Back in the kitchen, Niki was arranging the slices of Yankee pot roast on a hot platter, with the vegetables and potatoes grouped at one end. The gravy was keeping warm on the stove. The sight of the meat, prime beef shoulder from Savenor's Market on Charles Street, suddenly made Faith hungry. It was a delicious dish. She took baskets of corn-bread sticks and nut bread out to the table. But the party mood had vanished. Pix had told her once when Faith had first moved to Aleford that the town was like a patchwork quilt, all sorts of patterns and colors sewn into a usable whole. The bits and pieces of its fabric didn't look like much until it was assembled; then you could see how one square complemented another. Faith liked thinking about the town this way, but tonight's gossipmongers didn't belong. Second grade! And she was damn sure that if Gus had indeed overturned a desk, he'd had a good reason.

By the time Have Faith's crew was wearily washing the last streaks of sorbet from the dessert plates, Faith had decided she would try to stick to her rule more strictly in the future and stay in the kitchen during events, emerging solely for her bow at the end. Then she could pretend that only the most sophisticated, intelligent, broad-minded people were enjoying her fare. It would keep her fantasies in place.

The Phelans followed her back to Have Faith and helped her unload the small amount of leftovers. She pressed some of the pot roast on them for the next day; then Scott walked her to her car after they had locked up.

"I know the twins, Terry and Eddie Deane. They used to race dirt bikes up in Pepperell with me. Good guys. I still take care of their cars." Scott had recently started his own auto-body business after working for someone else for years. "The Deanes will get to the bottom of all this, and, Faith, Joey wasn't the nicest guy in the world—or the most honest. I'm not saying he deserved what he got, but there's a lot you don't know."

Faith had told them in the kitchen what she'd overheard at the party.

"It could be somebody settling an old score, even a very old score. And it may not have anything to do with this bog business." Scott liked to ride his bike on the trails surrounding the bog, which upset the conservationists, so he'd stopped—not because he was convinced, but because he didn't want to get in trouble. He hadn't cared before he was married, but Tricia was not someone you made angry. Besides, he was older now.

"I know you think you're pretty good at this detective stuff, but some of the people Joey was involved with wouldn't think twice about sending you on a very long one-way trip. He's been borrowing from everybody and his uncle for the Estates thing. Could be that somebody wanted the money back and he didn't have it. Stay away from this one, Faith." He grinned at her. "Tricia and I need the work."

She appreciated the intent, but there was no way she could keep out now.

"Can you find someone to take care of your children?"

Faith was used to Millicent's habit of plunging in directly after a perfunctory "hello, how are you," but this was more of a dive than usual. She knew if she kept on the line, eventually all would be clear. Millicent also had a way of saying "your children," which laid any blame squarely at Faith's door. When she spoke to Tom, it was always "your dear little Ben and Amy."

"I can usually turn up someone," Faith replied. So long as the individual did not have a known criminal record or express intense dislike of anyone under twenty-one, Faith would hire him or her, often in desperation. Baby-sitter lists in Aleford were more closely guarded secrets than the formula for Coca-Cola.

"Good. I want you and Tom both here for an emergency meeting of some of the members of POW! this morning. We have to figure out whether or not we should go forward with Town Meeting."

"But doesn't that depend—"

"See you at ten o'clock." Millicent hung up.

Faith went into Tom's study, where he was wrestling with his sermon. The events of the past two weeks had impelled him to write his response to this community rent by fear and distrust. He looked as if he had been on the mat for real, brow sweaty and hair mussed. She told him about the meeting.

"You don't have to go just because Millicent has made it a command performance," she said.

"But I want to go. This is exactly what I've been trying to say—meetings like this make things worse. And I intend to tell them. The whole business should be dropped immediately. If the Deanes pursue the project at some later time, we'll decide what to do then, but my God, a man *and* a woman are dead because of all this strife."

The babysitter appeared with a pile of homework and Faith didn't dare tell her that both children were not the types to sit quietly at play. Motioning to a note on the kitchen table with instructions and phone numbers, she left quickly, before the girl could change her mind.

On the way over, Tom told Pix, who had joined them, how he felt.

"I agree completely. It would be unseemly to keep attacking the poor man now that he's dead. It's all become so unimportant, anyway," Pix said.

Millicent ushered them into her parlor. It was crowded with people: the Scotts, Brad Hallowell, Ellen Phyfe, and Nelson Batcheldor. He still wore a black armband, but he seemed fully recovered from his own ordeal.

Millicent took charge. "Now, what is the opinion of this body? I called you as representatives of the larger group and we'll have to do a telephone tree to confirm whatever we decide, but we should come to a decision today. People are starting to talk."

Tom stated his position eloquently and the Scotts voiced their agreement.

"There's no need to reconvene Town Meeting now, when we don't even know if the project is going forward. It would be extremely disrespectful to the entire Deane family, and particularly his widow," Louise said.

Brad Hallowell and Ellen Phyfe disagreed. Faith had expected it from Brad, but she was surprised at Ellen.

"We've worked so hard," Ellen said. It must have been all those envelopes she'd stuffed. "Don't you think we should see it through just in case?"

Brad seconded her vehemently. "Everything's in place. We can have this thing nailed down by this time next week, and I wouldn't put it past the Deanes to use Joey's death to get everybody on their side—a big play for sympathy. Then zap, we've got Alefordiana Estates and the bog is literally history."

Tom stood up. "I, for one, will have no part of any further efforts of POW! I can't condone taking advantage of a man's death, even for a cause I may have thought was worthwhile. I strongly advise you to hold off. The town is divided enough—and frightened."

"I agree with the Reverend," Millicent declared. "Nothing's going to happen overnight, and we are ready if something does. As you point out, Ellen, we have worked hard, and much of that is due to the efforts of those in this room."

"Margaret wouldn't have wanted us to stop," Nelson said in a surprisingly strong, firm voice from the corner of the room where he'd been sitting silently since the meeting began.

"Are you sure?" Faith asked. "Don't you think the murders—and the attack on you, her own husband—would have led her to the same conclusion most of us have reached? My own feeling is that we have to find out who's behind all this and solve the crimes before doing anything else. That's what I intend to concentrate on."

"Margaret hated Joey Madsen. I can't say she would have mourned him too much."

Tom was quickly losing patience with the gathering. "Margaret was a member of our church, and as a woman of faith, I would not have expected her to like the man, but I know she would not have taken any pleasure in his death. Particularly in a case where murder was involved."

Nelson seemed to come to. He looked chagrined. "Of course she wouldn't. I don't know what I've been saying."

Faith felt a stab of pity for the man.

The meeting ended with a unanimous vote to suspend activities for the present, a grudging assent on Brad's part. Everyone else seemed convinced. There was one amendment. Instead of a telephone tree, Millicent decided it was only fair to hold one more meeting to put the matter before the full membership. Faith thought she probably enjoyed these get-togethers and wanted one last night onstage. It could be a long time before POW! met again.

She stood up and pulled on the denim Comme des Garçons jacket she had worn. "The sitter is taking the kids to the big playground and I said I'd meet them there, so I have to run." It was almost noon.

The room emptied, leaving Millicent, Brad, and the Scotts to set up the agenda for Monday night. Tom was returning to his sermon. He was pleased with the way things were turning out. Faith was pleased, too—plus, she had a plan she was beginning to mull over.

The quickest way to the playground was on the new bike path. The old tracks from the commuter train that had gone to Boston's North Station had been taken up and replaced with macadam. It was so new that few Alefordians had started to use it. Any innovation, no matter how useful or pleasurable, took a while to catch on. She went through Depot Square and entered the path. Any bikers, or walkers, were busy eating lunch. She felt hungry herself and began to think what she should make. *Croque-monsieurs*, the French version of toasted cheese sandwiches, weren't the most healthy choice—cheese, butter, smoked ham—and if they had *croque-madames*, a fried egg, too—but it was what she wanted to eat today. They'd have a big salad too.

She'd come to the part of the bike path she liked best. The trees on either side would be covered with blossoms soon. It was the wildest part of the byway—no houses and no entry on or off the path. It was wooded on both sides; the children liked to explore here and they'd discovered a small pond with ducks one day that had now become a frequent destination. She began to walk more rapidly. The sky was growing overcast and she didn't have an umbrella. It had been sunny and warm when she'd left the house.

There was a sudden rustling sound in the trees to the left of her. She knew it was absurd, but she felt nervous and picked up her pace even more. The rustling increased and followed suit. She stopped. It stopped. Now she was panicky. There was no way out. No houses. No way to get off the path until the next cross street—a long distance ahead. She couldn't run off into the woods on the right side. If someone was following her, there was nothing to stop the pursuit and she'd be even farther away from help. She looked into the woods, venturing to take a step closer, but she could see nothing beyond the trees. Whoever it was stayed hidden, taking great care not to be recognized. The thought chilled her.

Faith started walking again, then ran. Ran flat out. The watcher in the woods increased speed. When and where would the attack come? Her heart was racing. If only she could make it to the street! If only someone would come along! She opened her mouth to yell for help and at first no sound came out. Then she managed a strangled cry. She was getting breathless.

Who will be next? That's what she'd wondered aloud with Tom. The question had been answered.

Faith was next.

Chapter 9

To her left, she could hear her stalker coming closer. Faith looked frantically ahead for the cross street. She had never run so fast in her life. She focused all her thoughts on her legs, pushing and straining to keep going. There was no hope of screaming now; she was gasping for breath. Any second, her attacker would be at her back. She heard a whooshing sound and turned her head, even as fear produced a fresh burst of speed.

It wasn't an assailant. It was a bicycle. A venerable lady's Raleigh with a wicker basket dangling from the handlebars.

It was Millicent Revere McKinley.

"Help!" Faith grabbed at the bike. "There's someone in the woods. Someone's after me!"

Millicent reached into the basket and took out a pocket siren. She pressed the button and produced the desired effect. Faith put her hands to her ears and sat down in the middle of the path, panting. After a while, Millicent twisted the canister and the noise stopped.

"It's not a good idea to sit there. You're smack in the way of traffic," she pointed out. "Now, what's going on?"

Faith wanted to hug her and did. It was that kind of moment. Fleetingly, she realized that this was the second time Millicent had come to her aid in a time of great peril. Faith wondered if she would have to present the woman with her firstborn or perform some kind of Herculean labor such as cleaning the moss from all the headstones in the old burial ground to even the score.

It took a moment for her to get her breath and arrange her thoughts.

"Someone was stalking me. I could hear the person but couldn't see who it was—not even if it was a man or woman. Every time I stopped, the noise stopped and whoever it was hid. But why wasn't I attacked right away? Not that I'm sorry." Now that the danger was passed, Faith was puzzled. There had been plenty of time before Millicent happened by. Had it been some sort of sadist who had been delighting in her terror?

"You're sure it wasn't an animal, a dog?" Millicent asked.

"I'm sure. An animal doesn't increase speed when you do and slow down when you do. And whoever it was kept moving closer to the path. If you hadn't come along, I don't know what would have happened." Faith's last words were sticking in her throat.

They had moved and were sitting on the grass off to the side of the path. Millicent's bike was resting majestically on its kickstand.

"I use the bike path often. Much safer than the street, but I always carry my horn. You never know what undesirables could be lurking about, and I suppose that's who it was—a tramp in the woods, some such person." She looked Faith straight in the eye.

Neither woman believed for a second that it had been a tramp.

"Maybe," Faith said. "I can't imagine who else it could have been." Which was the truth.

"I'll see you home," Millicent offered courteously.

Faith had almost forgotten she was not going straight home.

"Oh dear, the children. They're at the playground. I was on my way there."

"Then we'll go there."

Millicent got back up on her steed and rode at a stately pace next to Faith, who was happy to trot rapidly alongside. She wanted to get off the bike path as soon as possible.

"Where were you going?" The last Faith had seen of Millicent, she was deep in conversation with those who lingered on after the meeting.

"I was on my way to see Chief MacIsaac. Right after you left, we realized that we can't plan any sort of meeting until we know when the funeral will take place, and there are one or two other things I want to discuss with Charley in person. We would not want to offend anyone by having the meeting on the same day as the funeral. It would be in extremely poor taste."

Faith agreed. She was tempted to tell Millicent not to mention the incident on the bike path, but Charley might as well know sooner than later. Also, Millicent wouldn't listen to her anyway.

They reached Reed Street and turned toward the playground. Faith felt as if she was stepping back into place, back into her normal life. Kids were running around like crazy; their mothers were sitting in small groups, talking and every once in a while retrieving an overly ambitious toddler from the big slide or settling a dispute about whose turn it was for the tire swing.

Amy was in the sandbox and Ben was on the monkey bars. The sitter was halfway between, reading Hermann Hesse. Millicent bade Faith farewell, looked around at the scene with the air of someone visiting the zoo, and rode off. Without Faith beside her, she rode speedily and with expertise, negotiating hand signals and turns with aplomb. Speed. If she hadn't ridden so fast . . . Faith didn't want to think about it. She paid the sitter, thanked her, and led the children home. Amy had collected as much sand in her shoes and clothes as a day at the beach produced.

Tom was waiting for them. "I finished my sermon. It's a gorgeous day and we need to go someplace." He looked at his wife. "What's happened? Are you okay? You look—"

She interrupted him. "*Pas devant les enfants*," she said. Definitely not in front of the children. She put Amy in her high chair with a cup of yogurt and cut-up strawberries, then Ben at the table with the same. She drew Tom into the living room and told him what had happened.

He was terribly upset. As soon as she finished, he went to the phone and called Charley. Chief MacIsaac arrived in time for a bowl of squash soup, bread, and cheese.

"What do you call this? It's good."

"Butternut squash soup—good for us, too. I added lots of nutmeg and a little cream," Faith told him. She'd had some herself and was feeling better. She took the kids upstairs. Amy went down for her nap—you could set the town hall's clock by her—and Ben went to his room to "rest," protesting vociferously all the way, "But I'm not tired!"

When she returned, Charley was eating some apple crisp Tom had dug out of the refrigerator. Tom had a plate of it, too. Both portions were crowned with a large scoop of ice cream.

"But you didn't warm it up," Faith protested. "The ice cream is supposed to melt."

"Tastes fine. Now let's talk about your adventure this morning. Millicent filled me in, but I want to hear it from you."

Faith described what she now considered her marathon and ended with a new idea.

"It had to be somebody I know."

Tom nodded. "I thought of that right away. Otherwise, why

not come out immediately and why take so much trouble to hide each time you stopped? You didn't even catch a glimpse of any clothing, right?"

"No, not even the size of the person, although to make that much noise, he or she couldn't have been too small. But that doesn't give us much to go on."

Charley was getting depressed. Things were totally out of control. "I've called Dunne and should hear back from him this afternoon. What are your plans for today? Going to stay put?"

"No," said Faith.

"Yes," said Tom.

They looked at each other and smiled for the first time since Faith had come in the door.

"I have *got* to get out of the house," she said. Out of the town, too, she added to herself. Aleford had lost some of its charm lately. "I want to go someplace with lots of people, where no one knows us. Someplace indoors. No nature walks."

Tom nodded. Faith was right.

"The Boston Museum of Science it is, then," he said. "I can't think of anyplace more crowded on a Saturday afternoon than that, except the Children's Museum maybe, but we were just there, or the Aquarium, only I'm not in the mood for sharks."

"Neither am I," his wife agreed.

It was late, but Faith and Tom were still sitting up in the kitchen. They'd eaten at Figs in Charlestown, great thin-crust pizza—tonight's the house specialty: figs and prosciutto with Gorgonzola cheese.

There wasn't a sinkful of dirty dishes staring them in the face, but that was the prevailing mood in the room. The kids were finally asleep—wired after the museum, even Amy.

"Hungry?" Faith asked in a desultory voice. She knew the answer.

"No, thanks. Want anything to drink?"

Faith thought for a moment. The occasion didn't call for champagne. "Pour me some seltzer, will you? The prosciutto made me thirsty. I'm going to get some paper. Maybe if we write this all down, we'll be able to make some sense out of it."

"I doubt it, but you get the pad and I'll pour the libations."

Faith was a great believer in organization. She couldn't cook in a messy kitchen, and while she didn't always measure ingredients, when she committed a recipe to print, everything was precise. She approached crime the same way.

"All right, let's list the targets. In some cases, he or she was successful; in some, not."

"Thank God," Tom said. "But shouldn't we list suspects? Isn't that the way it's usually done?"

"Do you want to help or not?" Faith was understandably abrupt after the day she'd had.

"I want to help. It was only a suggestion. Targets it is. Much easier, too."

"That's the idea." Faith patted his hand. "Now, the first was Margaret, then Nelson, then Joey, then me."

"What about the people who received the letters, and Lora?"

"For now we'll start with bodily harm, known attempts; then we can add all the other information." She folded the paper into columns and wrote each name at the top. "Think suspects, means, motive, opportunity—all the stuff you read about. Also, anything else that comes to mind. For instance, Margaret got one of the letters." Faith wrote "letter" in the column, followed by "threat"—that "if you want to stay healthy" business. The Batcheldors' letter had been the only one to contain a threat. Faith put an asterisk next to the threat and wrote, "Same wording as Lora's calls" at the bottom of the page, after another asterisk.

She continued. "Now, in terms of suspects, it could have been anyone in Aleford. Maybe we can get at it through motive."

"The only scenario I can think of is that Joey, or someone else in the family, came across the arson attempt too late to do anything about saving the house, hit her—maybe not with the intent to kill her—then got panicky and left when it became clear she was dead."

"I agree, and therefore, the likeliest suspect is Joey."

"Okay, but what about the attack on Nelson? Let's assume it's the same person. Nelson has said over and over that he has no idea who would have wanted to harm Margaret, so what would the murderer gain from Nelson's death? Nelson doesn't know anything."

"Gain—that's what's missing. Usually there's a common link there. Who would profit from Margaret's death? Nobody. The same with Nelson's. Unless the Batcheldors have all sorts of hidden assets. Certainly they spent a fortune in bird seed, but apart from that, they never threw money around."

"True, but the link may not be gain. It could simply be to avoid exposure."

"You certainly seem to have the lingo down, darling."

"I try. I'm switching to beer. You want one?"

Faith shook her head. She wanted to keep her mind clear.

"The suspects in Nelson's case are more limited," she said. "The chloral hydrate had to have been administered sometime during the breakfast, which means it had to have been someone who was there."

"It's beginning to look more and more like Joey. He may have thought Nelson knew something—or Nelson may know something and not know he knows it. That makes more sense than it sounds."

"I know," Faith said, and wrote it down. "But Joey didn't kill himself—and he is in no condition to go scampering in the woods after me."

Tom looked disheartened. "We do have a problem. Unless Joey's killer was completely unrelated to the other two crimes and that killer thinks you saw something when you discovered the body."

"It was a person he knew," Faith mused. "Who disliked him but might have seemed like a friend, or at least an acquaintance?"

"People in the construction field, perhaps, some of the POW! members, and from what you told me about your conversation with Gus, he might be a possibility."

"If Gus found out that Joey had killed Margaret and tried to kill Nelson, would he have taken the law into his own hands? He wouldn't have wanted his family's name dragged through the courts—and the tabloids. It's also possible that it was Joey all along who sent the letters to try to intimidate POW! *and* made the calls to Lora. If Gus found all this out, he might have seen getting rid of Joey as justifiable homicide, an extreme form of citizen's arrest."

"I can't believe Gus Deane would kill anyone, though. Especially a family member." Tom sipped his beer slowly.

"He was at the breakfast, remember. And he adores Bonnie. If he thought Joey was hurting her in some way . . ." Faith was scribbling madly. "And what about Bonnie herself? She's very tough. Suppose she found out what Joey had been up to?" Faith added her name. Bonnie had been at St. Theresa's. She'd been wearing a voluminous snuff-colored skirt with a wide apron of blue-striped mattress ticking—plenty of room for pockets. Plenty of room to hide a bottle of medicine.

"And you? What would these people have against you?" Tom asked.

"I must be getting close to the truth—which leads me to my plan." She hadn't intended to tell Tom, but they were in this together now. "I want to give whoever it is another chance, but before you say anything, this time it would be perfectly safe. I'd be a decoy, let it be known that I do know something. But have John or Charley in the pantry or wherever."

"You must be out of your mind!" Tom exploded.

Faith was disappointed. She'd thought he understood.

"Tom, it's the only way to stop this. Someone else may get killed."

"And it's not going to be you."

Faith kept quiet. Tom finished his beer.

"Well, what have we learned?"

"Besides the fact that I married a crazy woman?" He tempered his remark with a long kiss.

"Besides that."

"One of our killers, if there are indeed two, was someone at the Minuteman breakfast. Although, the notion that there are two seems unimaginable."

Faith was casting her thoughts back to Patriots' Day morning, assembling the cast of characters: Gus, Joey, Nelson, Bonnie, Brad . . .

"Brad Hallowell. We haven't talked about him."

"How does he fit into all this?" Tom had slipped his arm around his wife's shoulders. She smelled good—having put Amy to bed, Faith had a whiff of the cornstarch powder she used for the baby mixed in with her Arpège.

"Suppose *he* was the person Margaret was meeting at the unfinished house on Whipple Hill. He sees Joey kill her, then tries to blackmail Joey into dropping the Alefordiana Estates plan. When Joey refuses, Brad kills him."

"What about the attack on Nelson?"

"Nelson knows Margaret was meeting Brad at the house. Maybe Brad has a ski mask, too, and was cavorting in the bog with them. Brad is satisfied now that Nelson is too terrified to say anything and is letting him live. He may be certain there's no evidence to tie him to the crime."

"And he made the calls to Lora and threw the brick?"

"Yes—and cut the hoses on the excavator. Joey would never damage his own property, unless he really did want to frame POW! But I think he would have picked something less expensive."

"All the pieces fit so far, but there's the attack on you. You guys are on the same team," Tom pointed out.

"True, but Brad knows I've been looking into things. I implied that I'm not satisfied with what the police have been doing—or not doing. I said as much at the meeting this morning."

"I remember," Tom said glumly.

"And Brad was sitting right there."

"He certainly is temperamental. I thought he was going to blow his stack when I said I'd quit if we didn't call off Town Meeting for now."

"Exactly. Lora said as much, too, when she first told us her suspicions about her caller." That night, Lora in Tom's arms, seemed a century ago. And what about Lora? Lora, the lady of at least two faces, if not a thousand. Could she have been in this with Brad and their whole breakup a smoke screen? Then who was Mr. Miata?

Faith wrote a few more hasty notes.

"Let's call it a day—or rather, it is day. It's tomorrow already, and if I'm not mistaken, it will be show time in a few hours."

Tom pulled her to her feet. "Show time? Not exactly. But I do have plenty to say."

Joseph Madsen's wake was Sunday evening. The funeral would be held at St. Theresa's early Monday. Faith put on a black linen suit from Searle and went next door to drive to the wake with the Millers. Tom had had to go to the hospital to see an elderly parishioner who'd suffered a heart attack that afternoon.

"I wonder who will be there?" Pix said as they drove to the funeral home.

"Judging from the number of cars, I'd say most of the town," Sam remarked. "You two go on in and I'll park in the Shop 'n Save lot. There's no room here."

The parking lot of the Stewart Funeral Home was full and when Faith and Pix went inside, there was a long line to get into the room where the family was sitting with Joey. Faith spied Millicent ahead of her and the Scotts. Nelson was with them. This was an occasion that transcended mundane disagreements. At least, Faith hoped so. For these two days, no one had any affiliations. Death was a nonexclusive club. No sponsor needed.

Faith had been in a great many funeral homes. It went with the job. Stewart's was interchangeable with most, except for the framed prints of the battle on Aleford Green and other famous moments from local history. The furniture was Chippendale by way of Ethan Allen, the wall-to-wall carpeting beige, and the walls themselves covered with a muted striped paper that matched the floors. As the line moved slowly forward, they passed a number of large floral offerings: Deane Construction Company, Deane-Madsen Development Corporation, Deane Properties, Deane Toyota, the Masons, the Aleford Minutemen, and, when Faith glimpsed the casket, the biggest and most heartrending of all: "Love from Bonnie and Little Joey."

"Open or closed?" whispered Pix. She figured Faith, of all people, should know.

"Closed, I would think," she answered. Yet, morticians could accomplish a great deal. They'd shut those staring eyes and cover the wound. The casket might be open after all. She thrust the image out of her mind and tried instead to think of Joey as he'd been at the selectmen's meeting.

Sam joined them. "Such a young guy." He thought of his own

children. "His poor parents. They were very proud of all he'd accomplished. He comes from a large family in Somerville and he's always been the star."

The star. Faith believed it—married well, made good money, produced a long-awaited child, another Joey at that. Joseph Madsen had had everything going for him.

They were close to the front and one of the Stewarts came along with the guest book for them to sign. It was hard to tell the various Stewart generations apart. In their somber clothes and conservative haircuts, they all looked about fifty. Faith wrote her name. She was dreading meeting Joey's parents, who she was sure were the two elderly people sitting next to Bonnie. Mrs. Madsen's eyes were red and puffy. A balled-up handkerchief was clenched in one hand. Bonnie had brought the baby, who was sleeping peacefully in her arms at the moment, unaware of the tragedy surrounding him. It was unbearably sad.

The casket was closed. Faith breathed a sigh of relief. Someday she might be able to remember him alive. Gus stood up to greet her, gripping her hand hard and pulling her into his arms.

"I'm so sorry, Gus. I know how horrible this is for all of you."

The old man nodded. He hadn't been crying, but his face was red. He looked angry. Lora was standing beside him. She hugged Faith, too. It was as Faith had expected. All thoughts of POW! and divisiveness were absent.

"We'll get whoever did this," Lora said angrily; then her face changed and tears welled in her eyes. "Poor Bonnie! Poor little Joey! He's never going to know his father." Lora had her hair pulled back and it looked limp. She was wearing her glasses and no makeup, but now that Faith had witnessed the transformation, she could detect the very attractive woman beneath the disguise. She was surprised she'd missed it before. Context is everything. The way you don't recognize the checkout people you see several times a week at the market when you bump into them on the MBTA or other places. Brad had picked up on Lora's appeal. So had the well-dressed stranger. Who else?

A young man next to Lora put his arm around her and Lora managed to make the introduction, "This is my brother Bobby. Eddie and Terry are over with the Madsens. This is Mrs. Fairchild, Bobby."

"So you're the one who found him. I'm sorry. It must have been a terrible experience." Bobby Deane was tall and successfully fighting the weight a slight heaviness at the jowls indicated could be a problem. He sounded sincere, yet car salesmen always did. He took her over to the Madsens.

"This is Mrs. Fairchild."

Faith looked back at the Millers, who were still talking with Gus senior. She caught Pix's eye and signaled for her to come to Faith's rescue—immediately. This was because as soon as Bobby said those words, poor Mrs. Madsen lost whatever composure she'd maintained and was now sobbing uncontrollably on Faith's breast.

"Tell me what he looked like! Did he say anything?"

Faith patted the woman on the back. Mr. Madsen hovered next to his wife. His face seemed to have shut down when he got the news and not opened up again. He was silent, waiting for Faith's reply, too.

"He was . . . he was at peace. I know he didn't suffer"—there hadn't been time—"and I'm afraid he was already gone when I got there."

Mrs. Madsen lifted her face to Faith's. She smelled faintly of some kind of floral toilet water, the kind you give your mother on Mother's Day when you're a child.

"Thank you."

Bonnie, who had been sitting motionless with the baby as all this was going on, stood up and guided her mother-in-law back to where they were sitting. It wasn't that Joey's widow didn't look at Faith; she looked through Faith. Pix slipped her arm around her friend and they moved on. Faith realized she was trembling.

"Dear God, these poor people," Pix said. Sam came up behind them. "Let's go get something to eat. Samantha's with the kids and you don't have to go home yet. You need a drink, and I wouldn't mind one myself."

Gratefully, Faith let the Millers lead the way. On the way out, Millicent stopped them.

"Nothing is going to be right until we find out who's responsible for all this." When she closed her mouth on the words, it made a grim line across the bottom of her face, a line sharply accented by the unvarying shade of red lipstick she favored.

Faith nodded and started walking. She really wanted to get away. Away from the fury of Bonnie Madsen's grief. The candles they were burning smelled sweet, like the incense that would be used in tomorrow's Mass. She was beginning to feel queasy.

Pix had a question, though. "Did any of the Deanes seem upset to see you or other POW! members here? Lora used to baby-sit for us and I don't think they associated us with the group, but it might have been different for you." Faith stopped to listen.

"No, no one expressed anything other than thanks for my words of comfort. I wouldn't have expected otherwise. I've known Gus all my life," Millicent replied.

Faith was feeling better. "And that would be . . ."

Millicent smiled sweetly and left.

It was hard to find food in the suburbs, unless you wanted to drive to Waltham, which had unaccountably become the mecca for innovative, excellent chefs outside Boston or Cambridge. To get a quick meal, you had to settle for a chain or choose warily from the menu at the Aleford Inn. They went to the inn. Sam ordered some scotch for himself and sweet vermouth for his wife and asked Faith what she wanted. She knew enough not to order the house wine and joined Pix in some vermouth—but dry.

The trick with the inn was to avoid anything with a foreign name or fancy sauce. No chicken à la Versailles or scrod with hazelnut sorrel cream. Scrod simply broiled accompanied by the inn's thick-cut french fries, the skin left on, was delicious, though, and all of them ordered the same thing. They opted for the vegetable of the day, carrot pennies, rather than the house iceberg-lettuce salad with Thousand Island dressing. They'd tested those waters before. When the food arrived, Faith ate hungrily.

"Remember, just a memorial service and maybe a few words at the grave," Pix was reminding Sam. The Millers had a plot on Sanpere Island in Maine, where Pix's father was buried. It was a lovely cemetery surrounded by birch and evergreens. Faith thought it might not be a bad place to end up. Her thoughts were determinedly morbid. Joey was only a few years older than Tom and she. But then they weren't going to get themselves killed. Not that Joey had chosen this course, but something he did had led to murder. His murder.

"Who do you think killed him?" she asked Sam straight out.

Sam took the question in stride. He chewed reflectively.

"I wish I could think it was someone from away." He used the term the natives on Sanpere applied to anyone not born there—a category distinct from summer people and tourists; people who lived there but weren't *from* there.

"But you don't."

"No, I'm afraid I think it's someone he knew well; someone we all know. But damned if I can come up with who that someone is."

Faith and Pix nodded their heads simultaneously in agreement.

They looked like the ornaments people put in their car's rear windows. They bobbed again. Someone they all knew.

The funeral was as sad as—and even more crowded than—the wake. Cars lined the side streets near the church. There were also a number of pickups and vans with the names of various local construction companies. Joey's colleagues had come to pay their last respects. Inside the church, Faith half-expected the pallbearers to be followed by a contingent of hard hats, uniformed like a police funeral. The police were there; both Charley and John sat in a pew near the door. As Faith and Tom walked by toward the front of St. Theresa's, John leaned out. "Are you going to be home later this afternoon?"

They would be now and told him so.

It was a long service. Father Reeves was accompanied by the priest from Joey's old church in Somerville, who drew tears when he described Joey as an altar boy, Joey in CYO. Faith tried not to think about what Scott Phelan had told her the night of the Fletchers' dinner party. Maybe Joseph Madsen's feet had strayed from the path, but they were there once, and this could be one of the reasons his mother was crying so hard.

The interment was in a cemetery in East Boston, where his grandparents lay at rest. Tom was going, but told Faith she should pick up the kids and stay home. Enough was enough.

She spent the afternoon engaged in quality time, aware that she hadn't exactly been piling up points for her motherhood merit badge. She read to Amy until she went down for her nap. Ben was doing Legos on the floor next to them. It was a baby book, he'd declared, but Faith knew he was listening intently as the Poky Little Puppy made his distinctive way through dogdom.

Tom came home. It had started to rain as soon as they reached the cemetery, of course, he told her. A sodden spring. It meant a hot, dry summer everyone said—the same people who knew the wind velocity merely by glancing at a swaying branch. The catering company was air-conditioned; the parsonage was not. Faith figured on doing a lot of cooking. She would, in fact, be doing a lot of cooking this week. They'd accepted several jobs and had a wedding the following weekend.

She looked out the front window. The rain hadn't reached Aleford yet, but Detective Lieutenant Dunne had. He was coming up the front walk, covering the distance in several fewer steps than most. She opened the door before he could knock.

"Good, you're home," he said, and walked in. "Tom, too?" There was a distinct note of hope in his voice.

"Tom, too," Faith assured him.

Tom had told Faith that Dunne had been in East Boston, as well. It was hard for him to be unobtrusive, but he'd remained at a distance from the main body of mourners.

He sat down, removed his raincoat, but refused Faith's offer of nourishment, as usual. The man must eat like a horse when he got home, she thought. Some form of nourishment was preventing any withering away of flesh from his immense frame. She'd been to the state police barracks and aside from some ancient, moldy-looking sandwiches in a machine next to one that dispensed soft drinks, there wasn't a scrap of food in evidence. She pictured Dunne's wife, who Faith had heard was a mere slip of a woman, valiantly stirring large pots and turning a spit with huge haunches of meat. Faith was so distracted by her mental images, she almost missed John's first words.

"I have to get back right away, but I want to talk to you about Saturday."

Faith figured as much.

"Are you absolutely sure you were being stalked? It wasn't an animal—or a kid playing some kind of game?"

"If it was a kid, it was a very weird one," Faith said, then went through the whole experience again—the way the person had stopped when she did, speeded up—and hid.

"It seems as if someone thinks you know something. Do you?" John's question was direct and forceful. "This is no time to hold back, Faith."

"I *do* have several theories. Tom and I spent Saturday night going through every possibility we could think of, but I'm sure I haven't missed anything and I've told you or Charley everything." It was true—and frustrating.

"So what did you and Tom come up with?" Dunne leaned back in the wing chair. It didn't creak, but it looked full.

Tom gave him a synopsis of the various suspects. "Nothing makes sense. Murder doesn't make sense. It's an act against nature, against the divine order of the universe, but the most likely possibility is that there were two killers: Joey Madsen and then Brad Hallowell. Faith thinks Brad may have developed serious psychological problems as a result of his involvement with some violent fantasy computer games."

"He seems to view life as one giant monitor screen and doesn't distinguish between reality and RAM," she told John.

"And you think he was your would-be assailant?"

"I don't have any evidence, but yes, I think he was," she replied. No evidence yet, she added to herself. After Tom's reaction to her decoy plan, she knew what Dunne's would be. Not telling him about a future possibility wasn't, strictly speaking, withholding information—at least not in Faith's book.

John stood up to leave. "You notice anything at the Madsen wake or funeral?"

Faith shook her head. "Nothing, except a truce has been declared between POW! and the Deanes. Bonnie Madsen wasn't particularly cordial to me, but that's understandable since she might have some powerful feelings regarding the person who discovered her husband's body. I don't think it had to do with my opposition to Alefordiana Estates. Millicent has called a meeting for tomorrow night to suggest to the membership that all efforts to halt the development of Beecher's Bog cease for the present. Depending on how people react, the truce might be over."

But Joey wouldn't be around to find out. He wouldn't be around to make his fortune, either.

Tom refused to have anything more to do with POW!

"I made myself clear to Millicent and the others. No matter which way the membership votes, I'm out."

Faith felt slightly guilty. She planned to set her trap tonight, or the first phase, and it suited her not to have Tom around. Though she agreed in principle with his stand, she had to go to the meeting. Besides, she was curious. At any rate, Tom's staying home solved the sitter problem.

Maybe a hair more than "slightly." She was walking over with Pix, who didn't have any problems with guilt at all. She was still 100 percent opposed to the destruction of the bog, she'd told Faith earlier in the day.

"Of course, I don't think we should be doing anything about it now. I agree with everything Tom said on Saturday, yet it may become necessary to take action in the future. Suspending but not disbanding POW! would make that easier."

Faith kissed her husband good-bye.

"Why do I have the feeling you're up to something?" he asked.

"I don't know. Why?"

"No, you're supposed to tell me."

"That you're being silly?" She kissed him again. "Don't worry."

"Now I really will," he said gloomily. "I've heard those words before. Maybe I should go to the meeting with you after all. We can see if Samantha is free."

"Tom! Absolutely nothing is going to happen to me at the meeting, before or after. Besides, I am a grown-up. I also happen to know that Samantha is at some regional sports banquet tonight. The team made the finals, or whatever they're called. She also got into Wellesley and is going there, so I'm sure she doesn't want to change a diaper tonight or play Candyland with Ben."

"Neither do I." Tom was being unusually truculent. "The two of us haven't been out alone in ages. Let's go out next weekend."

"That would be lovely, darling. Friday night? Rialto bar and a movie?" The bar had the same incredible food as the Cambridge restaurant, but the Fairchilds preferred the service and ambience at the bar, more casual, also more attentive—besides, they could eat well and get to a movie this way.

"Okay. I'll look and see what's playing. What do you want to see?"

"Sweetheart, this is Tuesday. We have all week, and Pix is waiting. I have to go."

"Fine, fine, leave me here all by my lonesome."

Ben called plaintively from his room, "Daddee, Daddee, are you going to read me a story?" Tom wouldn't be lonesome at all.

Again, Asterbrook Hall was crowded. Pix and Faith didn't get front-row seats, but they found two together, even though they were late.

"Look, Joey's lawyer is here," Pix said, expertly scanning the audience for a head count and to see who was there. "What do you think he's up to?"

"Same thing he was doing at the other meetings, collecting information for the Deanes." But the lawyer hadn't been at the last POW! meeting. Joey had been alone. Faith took a deep breath. She was waiting for the right moment.

The moment came late in the meeting. It had been an acrimonious one at times and the lawyer would have plenty to report. Distrust of the entire Deane family was in the air. Although no one actually attacked the company, the innuendos were less than subtle. One of the things that was making the majority of the people in the room uneasy was the fact that the Deanes had started renovating the old Turner farmhouse on the property—the house Joey had referred to as "the jewel in the crown" at Alefordiana. He had told the selectmen the house would be "lovingly restored" and promised that not an inch of original clapboard would be sacrificed to a Palladian window or any other anachronistic architectural detailing.

"I want to know why they've started to work on the house when they haven't received the permits for the rest of the plans. What do they know? Have the selectmen given a secret go-ahead behind our backs?" Ellen Phyfe's voice was shrill as she raised these points. Several people in the audience clapped. Angry faces turned to confront the lawyer, who remained impassive. The seats to either side of him were empty, as if he carried some dread disease. But it wasn't contagion that the Aleford residents at the meeting feared; it was association.

"Fortunately, we have a member of the board here tonight. I asked Penelope Bartlett to come as a personal favor. Mrs. Bartlett?"

" 'Personal favor'—I'd say more like arm twisting," Pix whispered to Faith. Indeed, Penny did not appear overjoyed to be there.

"Come up here, so everyone will be able to hear you," Millicent directed. Penelope Bartlett was made of stern stuff, however, and whatever means Millicent had used to get her there did not extend to Penny's performance once she was in the hall.

"Everyone can hear me perfectly well from where I am, Miss McKinley. Let me start by saying that I am saddened and appalled that any citizen of Aleford should think the board of selectmen would make secret agreements with anyone! This indicates a serious lack of trust and I intend to bring it before the board at our next meeting and hope that Mrs. Phyfe and others who share her views will be in attendance." Since Ellen Phyfe's husband was a member of the board, everyone immediately began to look forward to another good episode.

Penny continued. "The late Mr. Madsen applied for and was granted permits to restore the old Turner farmhouse earlier this winter. The planning board, the Historic Commission, and the building inspector all advised the board to approve his plans, which we did. The meeting was open, of course, and some of you who are here tonight were there then, so I'm surprised this has come up. Obviously, the Deane-Madsen Development Corporation, to whom we granted approval, had to wait for the weather to improve, and this was our understanding at the time."

Penny sat down. Millicent smiled. "Thank you, Mrs. Bartlett. I believe that clears things up."

"No, it doesn't." Sherwin Greene jumped to his feet, no easy task for a man carrying as much weight as he did. "Why were they starting work before the rest was approved? And why are they continuing?"

Ellen called out, "That's right. I saw the trucks there today."

"I'm afraid I'll have to ask those wishing to speak to wait to be recognized," Millicent said. She had thought Penny's presence and reply would do the trick, but more was needed.

Help came from an unlikely corner. The lawyer had languidly stretched his long arm into the air. Millicent recognized him immediately. He didn't bother to stand.

"The Deane-Madsen Development Corporation is undertaking the restoration of the property known as the old Turner farmhouse because it owns it and has received the appropriate permits. The company intends to sell the property irregardless of the outcome of the plans pending for the area known as Beecher's Bog."

"Thank you very much. Now I think we're all clear on this matter."

Of course "we" all weren't and there was further discussion that went around the same circles in endless and boring detail. "I've lost all feeling in my right buttock," Pix whispered. "If I don't get out of here soon, the left one is going to go, too." Faith bit the inside of her cheek to keep from laughing. She was getting punchy—and numb.

Finally, Millicent offered a compromise.

"It's clear that there are two very distinct positions: those who feel we should dissolve the organization and those who oppose that. I'd like to put a motion before the group that we effectively disband but keep a core executive committee who will monitor all matters dealing with the disposition of Beecher's Bog and activity at the old Turner farmhouse. This group shall be composed of the original signers of the letter in the *Chronicle* and those who worked on the mailing, to be more specific: myself, Nelson Batcheldor, Louise and Ted Scott, Pix Miller, Brad Hallowell, Ellen Phyfe, and Faith Fairchild. I will now take five minutes of comments from the floor in favor and five minutes opposed."

Surprisingly, there was almost no opposition. Maybe everyone was getting pins and needles. Sherwin Greene got up during the time allotted for the opposition and everyone expected a blast. Without naming the Deanes, he had repeatedly referred to "untrustworthy, greedy, bloodsucking land developers" during the previous debate.

"I assume you will keep the membership's names and other information on file, as well as other material we might need to make a sudden response to an attack?"

"Certainly," Millicent replied. "Perhaps Brad could speak to this issue."

Brad Hallowell stood up. He had been strangely silent all evening; then Faith realized that of course he'd already known about Millicent's watch-and-wait motion. She'd presented it as a compromise, yet it had been the plan all along. Brad had no quarrel with it; he'd still be in the game.

"Everything's on my computer with backup discs. We could get a mailing out or start a telephone tree of the membership for a meeting in no time at all."

Sherwin stood up again. "That's all right, then, but what about reconvening Town Meeting? Would we have to collect the signatures again?"

Millicent had been doing her homework. "Since we did not actually set a date, the signatures we have will suffice. I checked with Lucy Barnes yesterday." Lucy Barnes was the town clerk.

Sherwin sat down, Millicent took the vote, and the motion passed.

"If there is no further business, I declare this meeting a—"

Faith's hand was up. Millicent looked peeved.

"Mrs. Fairchild?"

Mrs. Fairchild rose and addressed the room.

"I'm afraid I will have to decline the position on the executive committee, honored as I am. My work has recently increased. We're moving into the wedding and graduation season. I'm also shorthanded at present because my assistant is taking a pastry-making course, so I'm alone at the company. Tomorrow night, for instance, all by myself I have to make beef bourguignon for seventy-five and bake a hundred meringue shells—some always break." Faith was deliberately rambling. She knew she sounded nutty, but she didn't care. She was speaking loudly and clearly. "I won't even be able to get there until seven because of the kids. . . ."

Millicent had had enough. "I'm sure this is all very interesting"—her tone suggested "interesting to persons totally unknown to Millicent Revere McKinley"—"and we are sorry not to have your"—there was a pause, Faith waited—"help." There was no adjective in front of the word, such as *competent, able, invaluable.* Miss McKinley gathered the papers in front of her into a pile. "I now declare this meeting adjourned." So much for Faith.

Pix was giving Faith a funny look as they filed out of the room and up the aisle. "Now what was that about?"

"You know how stretched I am without Niki. I don't have time to be involved in POW!"

"But POW! isn't doing anything right now," Pix pointed out logically.

This was why Faith had been glad Tom had stayed at the parsonage. She was beginning to wish Pix had stayed home, too.

"Millicent and Brad, probably the others, too, are going to want to have a meeting every time the Deanes replace a piece of rotted board. They'll be meetings of the inner circle all the time."

"I hope not," Pix said. "I'm busy myself." She seemed to have dropped the subject and began to discuss Danny's problems at school. "I know next year will be better. We just have to get through these last few weeks."

But when she left Faith at her door, it was clear she wasn't dropping the subject. "Do you want me to help you tomorrow night? I'm not sure what I could do—beat egg whites?" She sounded willing but dubious.

"It will take you twice as long as it takes me. Don't even think about it. Besides, it's nice to be by myself sometimes. It happens so rarely."

"Pretty soon, Ben and Amy will be off to college and you'll wish for less time alone," Pix commented sadly, although even with a future empty nest, all of her volunteer activities made time alone a remote possibility.

"Good night," Faith said, then, for the second time that evening, added, "Don't worry. I'll be fine." And she was sure she would be.

* * *

Niki *was* taking a pastry course and Faith *did* have to work Wednesday night making beef bourguignon and meringues. Faith spent the day making sure as many people in town knew these two salient facts. She even managed to work it into the conversation when she picked Ben up at school. Miss Lora, the professional that she was, had not let her personal grief intrude on her classroom demeanor and the children had spent a happy morning with papier-mâché. The large room smelled of wet newspaper and wallpaper paste. Ben was encrusted from head to toe and displayed a huge creature of some sort, sadly too wet to take home; besides, he had to paint it.

"It's a triceratops, Mom." At last, something she could recognize.

"He has a very serious interest in prehistoric life," Lora Deane told Faith, indicating that it was past time for the Fairchilds to get the brilliant child whatever encyclopedia and computer software he might need to further his study.

With children in tow, Faith spread the word at the library, the market, Aleford Photo, and ultimately the post office. If the post office didn't do it, nothing would.

Tom surprised her by coming home early. "The Lord does work in mysterious ways. A meeting I had to attend has been canceled. If you want to take off, go ahead. I'll handle things here. I know you've been stressed about getting everything done without Niki."

Guilt, guilt, guilt.

"Oh, Tom, that would be great."

"I also have an ulterior motive. This way, you'll be home sooner."

Faith sincerely hoped so.

Have Faith's kitchen was on the outskirts of town. She drove over, parked the car in front, then unlocked the door to the premises and went in. It was five o'clock. She'd told the world she was getting there at seven. That gave her two hours to get some work done. It was true. She was concerned about doing the work herself. Niki's class was three nights a week for the next month, and Niki had always had a part-time day job at a restaurant in Watertown.

But before she did anything else, Faith made her calls. First one to Charley.

"I'm going to be working at the company tonight and think you should be here at six-thirty."

"What's going on, Faith?"

"I want to talk to you about the murders, you and John. Be sure he's with you. Something's come up and we may be able to solve this thing." She liked the collegial way that all sounded.

"All right, I'll meet you there," Charley said. "I'll call Dunne, too."

"Six-thirty. Don't be late. I have to get home." Faith didn't want to give Charley any more hints of what she was up to. He'd be over in a minute and mess things up.

Satisfied, she started separating dozens of eggs, reserving the yolks and putting the whites into a large copper bowl. She hummed to herself. The meringues would be heaped with her homemade vanilla ice cream, then topped with a boysenberry puree and fresh raspberries. It was one of the desserts she'd created for the Patriots' Day dinner, then had abandoned when she couldn't get boysenberries last week.

She began to beat the egg whites with a balloon whisk. It was a satisfying job. Soon the white peaks began to stiffen. Things were going along beautifully.

The door opened. She heard footsteps. Charley hadn't waited. She looked up in annoyance. But it wasn't Charley.

Faith gasped. "You're not supposed to be here yet."

It was the murderer.

It was Nelson Batcheldor.

Chapter 10

Nelson?

Faith would have assumed he had stopped by for a cup of sugar, except for the fact that he was pointing a gun at her chest.

"Don't worry, I'm not going to shoot you," he said in an almost-jovial tone. Where was the bereaved widower?

"I should think not! Please put that gun away right now and tell me what you're doing here. I'm afraid I don't have much time to talk; I'm very busy," said Faith, trying to bluff her way out.

"Oh, I do have to kill you, just not shoot you." Nelson showed no inclination to follow Faith's request or lead.

There was a stool next to Faith. She grabbed it.

Nelson?

Nelson Batcheldor had killed his wife—and Joey Madsen?

"I've always been so fond of you and Tom, but you've been seriously interfering with my plans. I had hoped to get everything settled last Saturday on the bike path, but then Millicent had to come along and stick her oar in." Nelson was annoyed. Nature lover, bird-watcher, vestryman, librarian, handyman—these were naught compared to the dramatis personae unfolding.

"And tonight I have a POW! meeting at seven-thirty. I was afraid I was going to have to be late, since you told us you wouldn't be here until seven. Then I said to myself, Nelson, why don't you take a little run over there and see if she started work early. You never know. So I did. Your car was out front, and here we are."

Faith had been right. POW! *was* having meetings all the time, but that did not seem important at the moment, since, as Nelson had so aptly put it, here they were.

"Nelson, sit down. Why don't we both sit down? I'll make some coffee and you can tell me what's going on. You seem upset, and of course I want to help. All this talk of killing. Haven't we had enough? Think of poor Margaret."

Two thoughts were pounding in her brain. The man was completely insane and the police wouldn't be coming for almost an hour. Insane. An hour with a homicidal maniac—Aleford had been right. Her head was close to bursting.

"I did think of Margaret. Often. I've wanted to get rid of her for years," he said peevishly.

Faith felt incredibly stupid. Where is the first place you look for a suspect? The face on the pillow next to the victim—or, in the Batcheldors' case, on the pillow down the hall. But they'd all been deceived by the attack on Nelson, staged by Nelson himself in some way. The man had been extremely clever and a consummate actor.

He was facing her across the broad metal counter where she'd been working. Nelson was slender and tall. His large, round, black-framed bifocals and the tufts that sprouted from his eyebrows gave him an owlish look. Perhaps this had attracted Margaret. He was dressed, as usual, in baggy tan pants and a rumpled button-down oxford-cloth shirt. In the winter, the shirts were covered by ancient Shetland pullovers, much mended, but inexpertly. Faith had always assumed the man was simply wearing his college wardrobe until the threads gave out, a common practice in Aleford and one from which she had had to wean her own husband.

Except for the gray in his bushy hair and the line through the middle of his lenses, Nelson Batcheldor had probably looked much the same at eighteen as he did now at forty-nine. He did not look like someone who had killed two people and was preparing to do away with a third. But then, murderers seldom did look other than completely ordinary. Few drooled or rolled their eyes.

Nelson was speaking very matter-of-factly about his desire to rid himself of his wife. "There were all sorts of opportunities, but I kept putting it off. I'm afraid I have a tendency to procrastinate," he said apologetically. Faith hoped this tendency was rising to the surface now. "I never had a pressing reason until last fall, and it also seemed sinful to take her life before it was really necessary."

"Necessary?" Faith had missed a chapter.

"I couldn't remarry with Margaret alive," Nelson explained patiently, much the way he'd explained the mechanics of a drill to Ben during the work on the classroom. Faith broke out in a cold sweat and the inside of her mouth got dry.

"Margaret wouldn't give you a divorce?"

"I don't know. I never asked her. No one in either of our families has ever been divorced," he said with pride.

"Look, let me make the coffee." Faith was sure Nelson would want to tell her all about it, and if she could keep refilling his cup, she had a chance of either being rescued or thinking of some way out of the situation herself.

"I don't have much time. Millicent doesn't like to start the meetings until everyone is present, and it's also going to take a while to set up your suicide."

"My suicide!" Faith screamed.

Nelson jumped. He cocked the trigger. She realized she mustn't startle him.

"What suicide? I'm not planning on killing myself," she said in what she desperately hoped was a calmer tone of voice.

"I know," he whispered, "but I'm planning on it. I have to." He raised his voice slightly. "You were bound to find me out sooner or later. You said so at the meeting, and that would have spoiled everything. Destroyed my only chance for happiness. I think we'd better get down to it right away. You've been overwhelmed by work. The whole town knows it. You simply cracked."

No problem with procrastination tonight.

"Now wait a minute," Faith said, relying on whatever natural authority her position as his spiritual leader's wife might give her. At the moment, she was grasping at anything. "First, I think you owe me an explanation before I die. And second, I believe I'm also entitled to a last request. And I want a cup of coffee." Nelson wasn't your run-of-the-mill criminal. She hoped her bizarre appeal would be matched by his own quirkiness. The code of the Batcheldors or whatever.

He sighed and looked at his watch.

"All right, but I'll try to be brief. Why don't you get the coffee while I talk. You see, I plan to knock you out and put your head in the oven. It is gas, I hope. Then, I need to stay around for a bit to make sure it's working."

Faith knew all the color was draining from her face. She decided not to tell him that, although the burners were gas, the ovens were electric—a better combination. She didn't want him to opt for something short and sweet such as a pistol shot before burning the place down. He'd used the same basic method before.

Nelson perched on the stool across from her and eyed the large copper bowl. "What's that?"

"Egg whites for meringues. Are you hungry? I have some cookies—or I can make you a sandwich."

"Margaret didn't like to cook. I'm afraid she wasn't very domestic. Of course I knew that when I married her. That wasn't the problem."

Faith slowly ground some coffee beans. "What was the problem, then?"

"Not a very interesting story, I'm afraid. We married too young. I was just out of the service, the Vietnam War. Thank goodness I didn't have to go over there. I can't stand hot climates, and the jungle would have been the end of me. That's where I got my gun, though. Margaret never knew I saved it. I won a medal for marksmanship. For a long time, I thought I would shoot her, but it's so difficult to cover up that sort of thing. All my friends were getting married. No excuse, mind you. But I've always been a bit of a follower. Margaret did know that."

The last phrase was spoken bitterly.

"I never even got to choose the color of my own socks, let alone make a big decision. Never even got to open my mouth. She wanted to live here. I wanted to live farther out in the country, but her family was from here. So Aleford it was. I wanted children. She didn't. And those damn birds. I would have liked to sleep late just once. Since she died, I haven't gotten up before eight."

Faith found herself in the extremely odd position of feeling sorry for the man who was about to end her mortal life.

"You should have talked to Tom or his predecessor. Tried to work things out."

"Talk about our personal life to an outsider? No, I don't think Margaret would have liked that. I know I wouldn't."

Faith was boiling water. The kettle whistled and Nelson was startled again. She quickly turned it off and poured it into the coffeemaker that sat on the counter to the left of the stove. It hissed as it hit the grounds and filled the room with a pungent smell. She set out two large mugs and waited before pushing the plunger down, straining the grounds in the glass cylinder.

"None for me, thank you," Nelson said. "It keeps me awake."

Keep him talking.

"All right. You killed Margaret, but why Joey Madsen? I assume you did, right?"

Nelson nodded. "I may not have shared Margaret's passion for ornithology, but I agree about Beecher's Bog. The man's plans were reprehensible."

"You killed him to save the bog?"

"No, of course not. I killed him because he was blackmailing me."

Faith poured herself a cup of coffee she didn't want. Even if she threw the scalding liquid at his face, he'd still be able to get her before she could reach the door—if not by racing after her, then with his gun.

"Why don't you start at the beginning?" She hoped this new appeal to his reference librarian's inherent sense of order would work.

He looked at his watch.

"A synopsis. You know Margaret was feeling incensed about Alefordiana Estates. I realized I could capitalize on that fervor, and we began to plan little forays into the bog to drill, as it were, should it become necessary to confront the developers head-on, disable their equipment, whatnot. You surprised us one day and were no doubt surprised yourself by our uniforms. Margaret thought they lent verisimilitude. I was able to convince Margaret that Joey was writing those anonymous letters and that the threat to the land was increasing. In fact, I wrote the letters myself. The library was getting rid of a great many of its outdated magazines and it was quite easy to find the appropriate means."

Nelson had always taken pride in his work. Faith remembered the way he'd shown her and Miss Lora the finished shelves and storage areas he'd built for the school.

"We decided that we had to send a strong warning to the

Deanes, and burning down the new house appealed to Margaret. I'm afraid I fanned the fires of her conviction a bit, overriding her objections with some of Machiavelli's old arguments. Margaret had never been a part of the radical movement, since I'd been in the army and she thought it would be disloyal. She always thought she'd missed out on something. She certainly entered into my plans with gusto. We were going to destroy their excavator together, but it didn't work into my schedule. I was sorry she missed it."

All Faith's prior sympathy for the man plummeted, leaving a leaden weight in the pit of her stomach. Poor Margaret, duped to death.

"We took the gas can to the house and as she was pouring it, I hit her on the back of the head with a wooden cudgel one of her ancestors had brought back from an Amazonian adventure. I made sure to place it in a pool of gas, and presumably it was destroyed in the flames."

Along with your wife, you bastard, Faith said to herself. All the while Nelson had been talking, she'd been surreptitiously glancing about the kitchen, seeking a means of escape.

"So, Joey saw you at the house?"

"No, I was very careful. I disposed of my clothes—they smelled of gas and smoke—in the small pond on the way back to our house, taking the shortcut. No one saw me. Who would be about at that hour? I took a bath and went to sleep. Joey didn't see me the night of the fire; he watched me take the chloral at the Minuteman breakfast. He figured things out after I was stricken."

It was on the tip of Faith's tongue to ask why Madsen hadn't gone straight to the police, but she had her answer. Joey needed money, a lot of money. Blackmailing Nelson was going to help pay for Alefordiana Estates. Simple—and Joey would have gotten a kick out of the whole thing, too. Making Nelson foot the bill for something he abhorred.

"Margaret had been having trouble sleeping a number of years ago and the doctor prescribed chloral hydrate. I substituted cherry cough syrup and an over-the-counter sleeping pill. It wasn't as effective and the doctor kept giving her the chloral in greater strengths. I was able to put quite a bit aside. My plan was to kill her with it, but then Alefordiana Estates and POW! came along. Really much better."

Faith was confused. "But weren't you afraid that you might overdose yourself?"

"I *am* a librarian, you know, and I thoroughly researched the drug and its effects before trying it out. As I mentioned, I had been able to put plenty aside, so I ran a few tests. To get the timing right."

"But how did you manage to get it into the breakfast? The police searched the trash at the church and all the bins on the green. There wasn't a bottle or other container, and there wasn't any chloral in your flask. And how could you have taken it right under the eyes of the state police?"

Nelson permitted himself a self-congratulatory smile. Most murderers were extremely egotistical, Faith had heard, and Nelson was no exception.

"I filled a sturdy balloon with the dose and carried it in my shot pouch. My flask simply held water, as it might have on that famous day. Before leaving for the green, I told my bodyguard I had to relieve myself. Then I went into the bathroom, where I quaffed the chloral, then flushed the empty balloon down the toilet." Nelson seemed to be reverting to 1775 speech. "I also drank two nips of vodka to help the chloral work faster. I was sure the police would not find those out of the ordinary, although I did not see any other liquor bottles in the trash at the time. And it worked perfectly. Except, unbeknownst to me, Joey Madsen was in one of the stalls, watching."

It hadn't worked perfectly for Margaret, or for Joey. And not now for Faith.

It still seemed like an enormous amount of trouble to go through to get rid of someone who perhaps nagged too much. What were those references to marriage and things changing last fall?

Nelson was still reminiscing about Patriots' Day. "I felt a bit groggy, but I knew that everything would be all right. If I died, then it would be God's will and my love would not have proved as pure and holy as I had believed."

At some point soon, he would be coming around to her side of the counter to knock her out, with the pistol butt probably. He wouldn't expect her to put her own head in the oven. There was a smoke alarm. It was hooked up to the alarm company. If she could set it off, help would arrive quickly, but perhaps not fast enough. And setting it off would involve starting some sort of fire. Nelson would not stand idly by while she burned some newspaper and held it to the alarm.

"I love the reenactment. It's one of my favorite days of the year. She looked so lovely in the morning mist. A goddess."

The only possibility was to get to Nelson before he got to her. It would have to be when he came near. Faith had often thought what an ideal setting a kitchen would make for murder. *Batterie de cuisine* could easily become battery by cuisine. Knives, heavy pots, pans, cleaning fluids, the oven—Nelson's own choice. . . . She tuned back in to what the man was saying. She thought she had a plan. Under his watchful eye, she backed toward the coffee and poured another cup. Quickly she turned the burner next to the pot on simmer.

"It was a shock when Joey called me and said he'd figured out that I had killed my wife and staged the attack on myself. But I wasn't too worried. I played along and gave him three thousand dollars in cash to start. He was to collect another seven and we arranged to meet at the bog. I'd been keeping some cash on hand for some years. You see, I wasn't sure exactly what I might need. I was glad I had been so foresighted, because this has been rather expensive. I had to give five hundred dollars to POW! Anonymously, of course. The last thing I wanted was for the group to disband due to lack of funds. Then Joey's blackmail money, although I didn't even bother to bring the second payment. I used that for the ring."

"The ring?" Faith was paying close attention now.

But Nelson was off on his own tangent.

"Blackmail. A terrible thing. And if a man can't have privacy in the bathroom, where can he, I ask you!" It was a rhetorical question and he did not pause for an answer; although at this point Faith would have agreed with anything the man said just to keep him talking.

"He had such a smug expression. I expect he thought he could bleed me dry. I'd have had to sell my house, although I do hope to move. Sauntered down the path to meet me. 'Got something for me, Nelson, old buddy?' he said. As if we could ever be friends. I grabbed his hand—he'd actually had the nerve to extend it in greeting—then inserted the knife. The library had a wonderful medical text I was able to study at length. I had never realized that you could employ a knife with such a relatively short blade—one a little over four inches, and we happened to have exactly the right size at home."

It was as Faith had imagined, even down to Joey's greeting. She didn't think she could stand to hear Nelson say any more, but the hands on the clock had barely moved. Unless Charley and John decided to come early, too, she had to keep the conversation flowing.

She asked her question again. "What ring, Nelson? You mentioned a ring."

"The engagement ring for Lora. Didn't I tell you? We're getting married."

Faith sat down on the stool. It was that or fall down. Her knees had buckled beneath her.

Nelson spoke dreamily. "I think I must have always loved her. You know how she is with the children. We plan to have a large family. She comes from a large family, but I've never known the pleasure of siblings."

Some siblings might dispute that characterization, but Faith wasn't about to interrupt.

"Of course, I'd seen her in town. Watched her grow into full womanhood, but it wasn't until last fall that I knew my destiny had arrived. I had a kind of epiphany the day the Story Lady came. It might be interesting to talk to your husband about this sometime. It was a religious experience."

Faith thought now would be as good a time as any, but was sure that Nelson would not.

"The Story Lady?" Her questions had been brief ones throughout Nelson's monologue. It was so unbelievable, more complex inquiries eluded her.

"Lora has a friend who is a professional storyteller and actress. She came to entertain the children one day. I'm surprised Ben didn't mention it," he said accusingly.

In her son's defense, Faith spoke at greater length. "I do remember now. Ben was very upset at missing the visit from the Story Lady. The children talked about it for weeks afterward. But he was home with chicken pox. Amy had it, too." Faith had soaked them in so many Aveeno baths that the skin on her own arms had never been softer.

Nelson was mollified. "I'm sure she'll come back. A wonderful performer. She brought a suitcase filled with costumes and had the children act out the various stories with her. At the end, she spun a tale about a beautiful enchanted princess whose heart had been turned to stone because no one loved her. The Story Lady loosed Lora's lovely hair. It fell to her shoulders in a gleaming cloud." Nelson was quite the weaver of tales himself.

"She put a gold crown on Lora's head and draped her in a purple velvet cloak. Lora took her glasses off and sat in the story chair." At least Faith knew what this was—an oversized rocker where the children gathered to hear Lora read.

"The princess could only be rescued by true love. The Story Lady had the children think of all their favorite people and things. One by one, they expressed their thoughts to their teacher. It was a very moving experience. As they went around the circle, Lora began to glow, lifting one arm, then the other. Her eyes opened wider. She smiled. Their love was working. I directed all my thoughts toward her from the corner where I had been working. I'd stopped when the program began. At the end, Lora kissed each child. I thought for an instant she might kiss me, too, but that would have given us away."

Lora with her hair down, Lora without her glasses, Lora with a crown—Faith knew what all that would have looked like. The Story Lady had unwittingly signed Margaret's death warrant.

But Lora and Nelson? What would Lora get out of the relationship, although it was clear that the Batcheldors had more money than Faith thought. You could get quite a decent diamond for seven thousand dollars, especially at the Jeweler's Building in town, but Nelson would have gone to Shreve's. He was a man who stuck to tradition.

He looked at his watch and uncocked the gun. Quickly, she tried to stall with another question.

"Have you set a date for the wedding? We're pretty booked, but it's possible we could fit it in. Niki does a beautiful cake—and it tastes good, too. Lots of butter-cream frosting with a hint of orange and—"

"You've finished your coffee."

The innocuous phrase had never sounded so chilling.

Nelson stood up and moved toward the end of the counter. She couldn't act too quickly—or too late. He wasn't saying a word now and was holding the gun by the barrel, ready to strike. He seemed much taller. She watched him intently. He was coming around the edge. Dozens of eggs were lined up in their cartons. He knocked into one with his elbow but didn't look away from his prey.

When he was almost next to her, she jumped off the stool and pushed it straight in his path. At the same time, she kicked some of the large pots stored under the counter out onto the floor. They made a loud clattering sound. He stumbled, as she hoped he would, and the pots added to his confusion. He leaned down slightly to push everything out of the way, shoving the stool aside with his foot.

Using her apron as a pot holder, Faith immediately grabbed the heavy copper skillet she'd planned to sauté the beef in from the burner she'd turned on. The pan was red-hot. She brought it down on Nelson's head as hard as she could, letting it rest a moment. Her fingers were burning. He screamed in agony. The smell of his singed hair was nauseating. She hit him again full force and he fell to the floor.

"I thought you might need help," a voice at the door called out.

It was Pix.

Chief MacIsaac and Detective Lieutenant Dunne were punctual men. Faith had said 6:30, so 6:30 it would be. They were sharing some supper at the Minuteman Café—meat loaf—when their beepers went off. They jumped in John's car and arrived at the kitchen with several other officers of the law, sirens blaring—and Tom.

The first thing Pix and Faith had done was to make sure Nelson would not be mobile should his unconscious state prove brief. They did a thorough job of trussing him with twine Faith kept for the purpose, although in the past it had bound poultry and beef. Pix was good with knots. Then they called the police, Sam, and Tom, in that order. Sam walked into the parsonage to watch the kids just as Tom was hanging up, frantically wondering what to do about them.

"I'm not sure I'm made of the same stuff as Charlotte—you know, the one who continued to cut bread and butter as her lover was carried past the kitchen window stiff and cold on a shutter. Nelson wasn't my lover—far from it—but I still don't feel much like cooking tonight. It's going to be a while until I forget the sight of his body on the floor, and I may have to get rid of this perfectly good skillet."

"Early days yet," Pix advised. "We can wash the skillet and Twinkle its bottom." It was at this point that the police arrived.

"Copper cleaner," Pix explained. Then Faith explained a whole lot more.

Nelson wasn't dead, for which Faith was profoundly grateful. They took him out on a stretcher and he was already stirring.

Tom took Faith over to the end of the room. They sat in Ben's beanbag chair, with Faith on her husband's lap. The picture they presented would have been laughable if the situation had been comical.

"Faith, Faith, Faith . . . I almost lost you!" He held tightly to his wife, as he had since his arrival, rushing wide-eyed through the door.

The terror was over and Faith was beginning to breathe normally again. She was aware that her heartbeat had slowed. Nonetheless, she didn't mind the position she was in and was happy to cling in return.

Pix was starting to clean up, but John Dunne stopped her.

"I know you're trying to help, but this is all evidence and we have to do some work here. I want to make sure this guy goes away for a long, long time."

"I don't think there is much doubt of that," Pix replied somewhat acidly. She didn't want Faith to have to deal with the eggs and dirty dishes in the morning—and she doubted the police would tidy it all away. "He's killed two people and tried to make it three."

"Why don't I call you when we're finished?" He smiled at her. She wasn't as used to his appearance as the Fairchilds and found herself instantly obedient.

"We should get Faith home now, anyway."

"Good idea. Charley and I will drop by in a while."

"Maybe we'll take her to our house. My husband is watching the children at the parsonage and my daughter is coming to take over. She can feed them and put them to bed. No need for them to see their mother upset." They both turned toward the end of the room, where Faith and Tom were still ensconced in the beanbag chair. They looked comfortable, but Charley and Pix couldn't see Faith's face. Pix put herself in her friend's shoes for a moment and knew she would need a drink and a whole lot of people to talk to right away.

It turned out to be what Faith wanted, too, and they went straight to the Millers'. She was happy to let them take charge of her life for the moment, only specifying pot stickers instead of the pu pu platter they were ordering as an appetizer from the local Chinese restaurant.

While they waited for the food, the seats at the Millers' long harvest table gradually became filled with people. Pix had been busy making calls. Millicent arrived with Brad, followed immediately by Gus, his wife, Lillian, and Lora. Sam phoned for more food and told his wife to stop alerting the populace. "We've got a quorum or whatever, and with Charley and John, there won't be any more room."

Faith was sitting at the head of the table. She was feeling slightly dissociated. All around her, people were chattering away, expressing shock and relief. An hour ago, she had been on her way into her own oven.

"You okay, honey? Want to go home?" Tom asked anxiously.

"Not yet. I have too many questions. And I'm hungry."

By tacit consent, everyone was waiting for the food and the police. Pix had given them a rough idea of what had happened at Have Faith when she'd contacted them, but no one was approaching the subject directly now.

Lora Deane got up from the table. She had followed her grandparents in, subdued, and been sitting quietly ever since. Looking at the young woman, Faith realized most of the questions that remained unanswered had to do with Miss Lora—both Miss Loras.

Lora bent over Faith's chair as she passed by. "I'm so glad you're all right! And I think you're incredible. I would have died with fear on the spot or fainted or something." She leaned close to Faith's ear and added in an urgent whisper, "*Please* don't say anything about the apartment." Faith looked at her in surprise. Lora explained, "Bridey told me about the 'student' who'd been by and described her so well, I knew it was you. I'll meet you wherever you say tomorrow and tell you everything." Lora straightened up and went on her way, presumably in search of a bathroom.

Faith was happy to comply with her request since it meant Lora Deane would tell all. Opportunities such as this didn't come along every day, and Faith could wait. She had a pretty good idea what the apartment was for, anyway.

The doorbell rang. It was the food. Opening the containers and serving the food caused some good-natured commotion. It wasn't exactly *Eat Drink Man Woman*, but the dishes smelled inviting. Gus and Lillian wanted fried rice. Millicent was reaching for the family-style spicy tofu. "Cleanses the blood," she informed the table. Sam wanted some of everything and Danny wandered in, complaining they hadn't ordered any spareribs. Sam heaped a plate with food and sent him back to the computer and MYST.

"Is this the no-MSG place? Changhai?" Brad asked.

"Of course." Pix was indignant. The young man was lucky he had even been asked to dinner. There was no need to cast aspersions on her culinary judgment. She had picked up a thing or two from her employer. They had stopped using the place that drenched everything in red dye number two sweet sauce months ago.

Charley and John arrived, creating another round of confusion. Contrary to usual practice, Detective Dunne was ready for food. He and Charley had had to leave a perfectly good meat-loaf dinner, barely touched, on the table at the Café. He grabbed a container of rice, one of pork with black-bean sauce, and dug in, first carefully removing his Sulka tie.

"What have we missed?" Charley asked.

"Nothing," Faith answered. "We've been waiting for you. Is Nelson conscious?"

"Yes, but he's not making much sense. You hit him good and hard. He seems to think he's getting married on Saturday—to you, Lora." Charley was sitting across from the Deanes. He added, somberly, "Seems to believe it absolutely. Says he gave you a ring."

All three Deanes dropped their forks.

"You were getting married and you didn't tell us!" Lillian wailed.

"He's old enough to be your father!" Gus thundered.

"Stop shouting at me! I don't even really know the man!" Lora protested. "Somebody tell me what's going on?"

John had wedged a chair next to Faith's. He was annoyed with her for setting the trap. They'd suspected Nelson Batcheldor for some time and were trying to collect evidence. It was true they hadn't come up with much, but Dunne did not approve of ordinary citizens taking police matters into their own hands, especially at considerable risk. But then, Faith wasn't an ordinary citizen. He reached for another container. He wasn't picky when it came to Chinese food. This one had some kind of chicken with fruit. It tasted like oranges or tangerines.

He and Charley had agreed not to tell the Fairchilds Nelson's other babblings, most of which concerned all the things he planned to do to Faith to get even. John hitched his chair closer to Faith's. With Dunne on one side and Tom just as close on the other, she was beginning to feel as if she'd acquired an extremely mismatched set of bookends.

"Between the two of us, we ought to be able to answer Lora's question, don't you think?" he said to Faith. She'd had a few pot stickers and that was all she felt like eating for now. Her appetite had deserted her when the police arrived and she'd realized they'd be going over the events of the evening.

"Shall I start?" she asked. He nodded. His mouth was full.

"Nelson Batcheldor was deeply unhappy in his marriage to Margaret. He was also an extremely disturbed person with a distorted view of reality. That meant he didn't do any of the things another man in his position might have—seek counseling, get a divorce. Instead, he developed a rich fantasy life revolving around getting rid of Margaret and replacing her with his ideal mate. I'm afraid that turned out to be you, Lora," Faith explained.

"Me! Why did he pick me! And how could he possibly have thought I'd be interested in him? He was old and not exactly what I'd call attractive."

Faith knew what Lora called attractive and she agreed silently. Nelson Batcheldor was not it. Now the old part, that was debatable, especially as the years were passing. The young woman's reaction had chased away any lingering suspicions Faith had had about her involvement in Nelson's schemes. He had sounded so definite about their plans, as if they had been spending every spare moment planning their future together.

"He wanted children," Lillian Deane informed them. "And wasn't he doing all that carpentry work at the school? He must have seen how gifted you are with them," Lora's grandmother said with pride. "The only reason I know how much he wanted to be a father was a remark he made many years ago. I was pushing you in your stroller, Lora." She paused as the irony of the situation was duly registered by everyone present. "He stopped me and told me what a beautiful baby you were, which was true. Such lovely soft curls and big blue eyes. 'You're a very lucky woman, Lillian,' he said. 'I'll never be a father—or a grandfather. It's the tragedy of my life.' I tried to reassure him. Of course, he and Margaret were quite young then. He cut me right off, 'It's out of my hands.' Those were his very words. He smoothed your hair and tucked the blanket around you and left. I remember thinking what a good father he would have made. It's a shame. I always thought he meant they couldn't have children."

No one had interrupted Mrs. Deane's lengthy reminiscence. They weren't used to hearing so much from her, especially when Gus was around. Faith resolved to get to know the woman better.

"Always thought it was some sort of plumbing problem," Gus commented. "Didn't like to pry."

"Margaret didn't want children. That was one of the things he held against her," Faith explained. "But that wasn't the only thing wrong—the only thing he held against her."

Nevertheless, Pix, Lillian, and Lora exchanged meaningful glances. Not want children! Faith felt compelled to come to the defense of friends, relatives, strangers who'd decided otherwise.

"Children are not for everyone."

"Amen," said Charley. "Now let me get this straight, Lora. He didn't give you a ring. Didn't approach you in any way?"

"No, he was rather shy. I don't think we ever had a conversation about anything except the size of the bookshelves and the weather. No, wait, he was there when my friend came and acted out some stories with the children. He was very impressed by her and came over to talk afterward."

Faith told them about the Story Lady and her transformation of Lora into Lorelei.

"I can never let her know." Lora was aghast.

"If it hadn't been then, it would have been another time. When you were singing 'Wheels on the Bus' or reading *Love You Forever*—that's a real tearjerker. Nelson saw his devotion to you as a pure and holy thing. It justified everything else."

"We had our suspicions that he may have staged his own poisoning, but we weren't sure how," John said. "We'd found some vodka nips with his fingerprints on them in the men's room trash at St. Theresa's. Alcohol intensifies the effects of chloral hydrate. But we couldn't figure out how and when he'd taken the drug itself. He was lucky he didn't kill himself."

"It would have been lucky for Joey," Gus said sternly.

Faith realized she'd have to reveal Joey's blackmail activities to his in-laws. She wasn't sure this was the time or place.

"He'd practiced on himself," she told them, then described the way he'd brought the chloral into the hall.

"A Minuteman for twenty years. It's hard to fathom," Gus remarked. Like Millicent, uncharacteristically remaining in the background, Gus believed certain avocations produced unassailable moral fiber.

Before the talk ventured into Joey Madsen's activities, Faith brought up her question.

"Nelson confessed to sending the letters and cutting the hydraulic hoses on the excavator—and the murders—but he didn't say anything about the calls. Did you ask him about them—and the brick through Lora's window?"

Lora flushed and looked at Brad. He sat up and swallowed hastily. Somehow most of the smoky chow foon rice noodles with beef and peppers were finding their way to his end of the table.

"Hey, I didn't call you! You made it perfectly clear that you never wanted to hear from me again. Or made it clear to my answering machine, I should say. And why would I throw a brick through your window? Why would anyone?"

His anger intensified his good looks. A bit of the moors—of Heathcliff—swept into the room.

"That was insensitive of me, I'm sorry. I should have spoken with you in person, but I wasn't sure I'd go through with it then."

Gus appeared to be fearing the rekindling of a flame he had considered doused, the ashes raked into the ground. "We're wandering here. If Hallowell didn't make the calls, who did?"

Dunne answered. "Nelson again." He regarded Lora with pity. She was going to have a great deal to work out. "He just wanted to hear your voice."

There wasn't much to say after that—or rather, there was, but no one wanted to voice the sentiments. It was sad, horrible, scary. Millicent broke the mood.

"So, Gus, what are you going to do about the bog?"

Before Gus could reply, Sam intervened. "You don't have to answer that, especially not in my nice, peaceful house."

Everyone laughed. Gus put the tips of his fingers together. He regarded each face in turn. Faith knew what he thought about the project. She wondered what he would say—if anything.

"The bog. The damned bog, as far as I'm concerned. Joey would still be alive. Probably not poor Margaret, but it gave her crazy husband a way to do her in. I'd just as soon never see the bog again or hear about it. But we own it. It's ours."

Millicent wasn't one to back down. "I know that, but you don't have to go through with Alefordiana Estates. There are other options."

Gus nodded. Lillian was poking him in the ribs. "Don't worry, Mother, I'm not going to embarrass you. You're right, Millicent. We have lots of options, but they're *our* options. I don't mind consulting with you, but not with that group you got up. That's got to go. Divides the town into warring factions, and we have enough natural divisions." Gus reached across the table to shake Sam's hand. "Thank you for your advice and for dinner. This is the first time we've been invited to your house." Pix turned scarlet. "Now, Pix, don't feel bad. We haven't invited you to ours, either. And all of us have lived in Aleford since we were hatched. We have a lot of work to do."

Faith knew she was witnessing an occasion as historic as the events celebrated each Patriots' Day. But she was tired. Someone had tried to kill her and come very close. She wanted to kiss her sleeping children. She wanted to make love with her husband.

"Tom, let's go home."

"I couldn't sleep a wink all night."

Lora and Faith were having a late lunch at Geoffrey's on Tremont Street in the South End. When Faith considered the local options for their tête-à-tête, none had seemed suitable. A picnic at the bog, and anything reminiscent thereof, was out. So was The Minuteman Café or the inn—too public. The Fairchild kitchen meant constant interruption. And obviously, meeting at the Deanes was impossible. Lora did have two apartments, but Faith wanted the teacher off her own turf, vulnerable, and ready to spill her guts. Geoffrey's had great food and was close to Chandler Street. After meeting with Lora, Faith planned to visit Bridey. She felt she owed the woman an explanation, and besides, she wanted to see her again. With Nelson securely behind bars, Tom was happy to watch the kids and give his wife an afternoon out. Niki was making the bourguignon and meringues, with Pix as *sous*-chef. All bases were covered—a rare occurrence. Faith had driven into town, a little light-headed, and entertained a fleeting thought of keeping on going—that primal urge to run away from home that most women experience at times. "Why, I could just keep on driving."

Lora had been waiting at the restaurant and started talking before Faith even sat down. They ordered and Lora picked up where she'd left off.

"I kept wondering whether all this would have happened if I had gone to the police in the first place, as you and Reverend Fairchild wanted me to."

The same thing had suggested itself to Faith—as soon as Detective Dunne had revealed the source of the calls.

Resisting the urge to say, "I think there's a lesson here," Faith settled with, "I think I understand why you didn't want to go to the police, but the phone calls themselves were a crime and shouldn't have been covered up. Charley would have helped you get the phone company to trace them."

Behind her glasses, two big tears welled in Lora's eyes. Her hair wasn't pulled back and she did have some makeup on, but otherwise she looked like her everyday self.

"I could have saved Joey's life. I'll never be able to forgive myself."

There was enough guilt in the world. Lora wasn't a parent yet, but she had a mother. Faith couldn't let her sit there and suffer, weeping into her grilled-vegetable sandwich.

"You should have reported the calls, but remember, you didn't tell us about them until that Wednesday. You went away the following weekend, which we'll get to in a minute, and Nelson must have known that. He didn't make any more calls, so there would have been nothing to trace. Then Margaret's death was Monday night, or, strictly speaking, Tuesday morning. You got a brick through your window, then moved to Gus and Lillian's house."

"You're right! I never got any more calls. He must have been too nervous to call. I didn't recognize his voice, but I'd never talked to him much, and he may have used a handkerchief. I've seen that on TV. I bet he thought grandfather would, though."

Or he was too busy cutting up magazines, filling balloons with chloral hydrate, attending his wife's funeral—no idle moments for Nelson, Faith thought.

"But I still don't get it. Why was he threatening me if he was in love with me?" Lora asked.

"It's hard to say. Maybe somewhere deep inside, he was conflicted about his attraction to you and wanted the temptation removed? Or more likely, he hoped if you moved away, he'd be able to see you without the whole town knowing."

"He probably doesn't know himself. Kind of an approach-avoidance thing." It seemed Lora was reading more than Dr. Seuss.

Faith took a bite of her southwestern chicken salad. Lora had perked up considerably during their foray into the unconscious. Now was as good a time as any.

"Why have you been living in two apartments?"

Miss Lora blushed.

"This is very embarrassing—especially because you're one of my mothers." Faith presumed she was referring to the preschool and not any special devotion on Lora's part.

"I have a certain image in Aleford. 'Miss Lora'—she's so good with kids, never gave her parents or grandparents a moment's worry. Will make some nice man the perfect little Betty Crocker wife someday. Sure, she's a bit homely, but some men don't care about those things."

All of it was true. Each item had crossed Faith's mind at some point or been introduced into conversation. There was no doubt—in Aleford's collective conscious, Lora Deane was Miss Goody Two-Shoes come to life.

"I love to dance. When I went off to college, I discovered that music did something to me, released something, and I felt so free. One of my roommates was really good with makeup and clothes. She encouraged me to get contacts, but I don't see as well with them as with my glasses. Still, well enough for a date. Well enough to dance."

"But why the double life? Why not just be who you are all the time?"

Lora appeared to be about to go into her "give me a break" routine, but stopped. She sighed instead. "First, I would have caught hell at home. My dad was still alive, and he was just like his father. My brothers are the same way. They all actually thought it might be a good idea for me to be a nun when I was deciding where to go to school! Then Dad died so suddenly and everybody was a mess. I couldn't upset them then."

"And the money? Weren't you afraid Gus might not give it to you if he disapproved of the way you were behaving?"

Lora hesitated. She pushed a piece of eggplant that had escaped from the overstuffed sandwich around her plate with a fork.

"Well, yes, that did cross my mind." She ate the eggplant. "Okay, I thought about it a lot and it didn't seem fair. He never said anything when my brothers sowed their wild oats, and believe me, it was quite a crop. When I got the money, I used some of it for rent here and I really did use some for tuition. It's true that I'm working on my master's."

Faith was glad to hear it. Miss Lora *was* so good with children.

"And no one knew about Chandler Street?"

"No. I left a letter in the box where I keep all my important papers in the Aleford apartment—in case I got hit by a car or something."

There were so many somethings going on lately that Faith thought an explanatory letter showed foresight.

"What are you going to do now?"

"I'm not sure. I don't want to keep deceiving people, especially my grandparents. But I don't want them to get mad at me, either. My mom won't care. She has a whole new life and she'd probably be glad I was having one, too. She used to get a little fed up with being one of the Deanes all the time."

"And you?"

"I'm proud of the family, but we are pretty old-fashioned."

It was time for Miss Lora to grow up and become Ms. Lora.

"Why don't you start by telling them you want to leave the Aleford apartment and move into the city. Say that you found the perfect place." Faith didn't think Lora had to be too precise about when she had found it.

"Then gradually start changing your appearance. Wear the plum-colored dress, then immediately go back to a jumper the next day. After a while, everyone will have forgotten how you looked before. They might say, 'Have you cut your hair?' or 'There's something different about you; I can't quite put my finger on it.' " Faith thought she had worked the whole thing out rather neatly.

Maybe not.

"How do you know I have a purple dress? I've never worn it in Aleford."

Faith gave a hasty and abbreviated account of the day the Fairchild family shadowed Ben's teacher, then suggested dessert.

"I'm not seeing Eduardo anymore. Things were getting too heavy. Maybe I should go back with Brad. What do you think?"

Faith had a strict rule about giving advice to the lovelorn, and she stuck to it now. The person involved usually ended up blaming you if it didn't work out, and sometimes if it did. She had the same policy when it came to discussing husbands.

Lora was eating a huge piece of chocolate truffle mousse cake. Faith was drinking espresso with a twist of lemon.

"The only thing we don't know is who threw the brick."

"I suppose there has to be some mystery left," Lora commented complacently. Mrs. Fairchild knew all about her now. It hadn't been too weird.

They went to see Bridey Murphy, who expressed great delight in the drama of the situation. She'd read about the murders in Aleford and seemed to feel she had played a small role in solving them. Faith wasn't sure of her reasoning, yet she did not disabuse her of the notion. Bridey was a wonderful lady. Then Lora insisted that they both see her apartment and advise her about window treatments—advice Faith did feel comfortable offering. And she always liked to see where other people lived.

Lora's apartment was more sparsely furnished than Bridey's, but bright and cheerful. There were stuffed animals on the bed and in an old rocking chair Lora had painted blue. Combining the animal collection from the two dwellings might pose a serious design problem.

Faith got home about five. After being greeted by her family, somewhat picturesquely engaged in planting a flat of Johnny-jump-ups along the front path, Faith went inside and noticed the light on the message machine was blinking.

It was Brad Hallowell. "Um, this is Brad. Um, Brad Hallowell. Could you give me a call, Mrs. Fairchild? Faith, I mean? Um, maybe I could come over? Or you could come here—no, that wouldn't be good. Look, just call me, okay? I want to tell you something."

Apparently, this was the day for true confessions. Faith dug out the Aleford phone book from the stack in the cabinet next to the phone. Brad had either forgotten to leave his number or assumed that she knew it by heart. She didn't.

He answered after the first ring.

"Hello, Brad? This is Faith. I got your message."

Never one to mince words, he dispensed with any small talk. "Look, this is kind of embarrassing." She'd heard that before today, too. Was Brad Hallowell also leading a double life? Maybe he actually hated computers and was secretly holing up in a garret in Cambridge writing his coming-of-age novel in longhand.

"I know I should be telling the police, but . . . well, it's my mother, and she didn't mean any harm."

Mother, harm, police. This was getting interesting.

"What has she done?"

"She threw the brick through Lora's window."

"Your mother!" Faith couldn't help herself—her voice rose near a screech.

"After I left the Millers' last night, the brick thing kept bothering me. I mean, everybody there thought I did it. I guess I was pretty steamed by the time I got home, and Mom was waiting up for me, as usual." He sounded resigned but not pleased. "I told her all about what had happened to you and also about the brick business. She got terribly upset and told me she'd done it."

"All because Lora broke up with you?"

"Basically, yes. I had been taking it badly, especially at first. I knew she was mad at Lora and I guess she just kept thinking about it. She was edging a new bed she'd put in the garden and somehow got the idea that heaving a brick at Lora's house would make her feel better. She didn't intend to break the window; Mom has terrible aim."

Faith was pretty sure Mrs. Hallowell's aim was much better than her son believed. But then, apparently he was willing to believe anything.

"Let me get this straight. Your mother was out putting bricks in her garden in the dark of night and had an extra, so she drove over to Lora's and let it fly?"

"We have floodlights in the back. Mom often gardens late at night. She likes to hear the crickets."

No more mysteries. Except for a few that would forever surround Mrs. Hallowell.

"She's outside now; otherwise, I wouldn't be able to talk. She doesn't want anyone to know about this, but I don't want the cops, or Lora, to go on thinking I did it."

So much for Mom.

"I'm glad you called me, but shouldn't you be telling this to Chief MacIsaac?"

"I have the feeling he's a little antagonistic toward me. You know I kind of lost it at the selectmen's meeting that time."

This was true, and now Faith knew what was coming—and why Brad had called her.

"I was hoping you could talk to him. Maybe Mom wouldn't even have to know." He was wheedling and sounded exactly like Danny Miller when he wanted to get out of doing his homework.

"I'll talk to him—but your mom will have to know," Faith told him.

No more mysteries.

Chapter 11

The morning of one's child's birthday always dawns with joy. There's a moment of thanks, a moment of quiet reflection: looking back over the years, anticipating the years to come. Then the day comes galloping in, starting in Ben's case with a flying leap into his parents' bed. "Happy Birthday! Happy Birthday to me!"

Night brings a return of that morning mood and the supine position. May tenth was drawing to a close and Ben was five years old. Faith was lying down on the couch. Tom was in the study working on a sermon entitled "Beginning Anew." "I can work in spring *and* the quality of mercy," he'd told her.

Sticking to the formula of one guest for each year of the child's life, Faith had still found Ben's birthday party more enervating than the large society wedding she'd catered recently. The children seemed to multiply and were everywhere at once. Fortunately, it had been a beautiful, warm day and the party was outside. Tom had been on the other end of the camcorder most of the time—why he was working now. Pix brought the dogs over at Ben's request, as a special treat, then left with them soon after, when one child reacted with terror, not delight.

Faith sat up. Ben would start kindergarten in the fall. It was going too fast. Although, in a few more years, she wouldn't have to worry so much about day care. . . .

She missed Tom. It had been sixteen days since Nelson had tried to kill her. She had found herself counting immediately afterward and hadn't stopped. She and Tom had instinctively been spending as much time as possible together and with the kids. Maybe he'd like a beer. Maybe he was ready to go to bed.

She walked into his study and came up behind his chair, kissing the top of his head.

"That's nice," he murmured, then stood and took her in his arms. The study door burst open. They sprang apart like guilty lovers. It was *déjà vu* all over again, except the woman in Tom's arms *was* his wife and the woman at the door wasn't.

It was Millicent Revere McKinley.

"You'll never guess!"

That was obvious.

"Oh, the front door was open and I saw the light on in here when I came up the sidewalk. I assumed you were working." She gave them both a reproving look. "Such wonderful news!"

Faith didn't mind playing along. It had to be pretty important for Millicent to come barging in like this.

"What is it?"

"We own Beecher's Bog! That is, the town owns it, always has!"

"But why didn't we know before?" Tom asked.

"I'll start from the beginning. Apparently, the town only leased the land to the Turners. Originally, it was going to be the site for the Poor Farm, which was why the town didn't want to sell it all. The Turner family could build a farmhouse on the small lot they did own and would retain ownership of that, but the rest was to revert back to the town after Roland Turner's death. He could leave his house to his heirs, but not Beecher's Bog and the surrounding fields. He was farming it in those days and getting cranberries from the bog. Later descendants made quite a profitable business of it."

"How could it have taken so long to discover this?" Faith was extremely disappointed in Millicent—Millicent, who had ferreted out virtually every detail of Aleford life since the town was incorporated in 1713.

"Roland lived to be a very, very old man. Ninety-eight or ninety-nine. By then, the Poor Farm was located elsewhere. Anyway, during his life, neither he nor anyone else in his family brought up the life-tenancy question, in the hope that the town would forget about it, which it did. During the war, many papers were destroyed and there must have been a great deal of confusion." When Millicent said "the war," it was not WW II, the Big One, or the Vietnam War, but the one and only one as far as she was concerned—the War of Independence.

This was all very interesting, but Faith was still in the dark.

"It would certainly have changed things if we'd known about this sooner," she said bitterly.

"But they only found the papers today!" Millicent protested.

"Who found what papers, where?" Tom asked.

"The Turners were too honest, or too nervous, to destroy the papers detailing the agreement. They hid them in the house, in one of the kitchen walls. You know the restoration work has been continuing. Today they were replacing some of the plaster and found the tin box with the documents."

"You mean the men working for the Deanes?" Faith was astonished.

"I mean Eddie Deane himself. Gus just called."

There was a Bronze Musket plaque in here for somebody, maybe the whole family.

"Now, I have a million more people to tell. Isn't it thrilling?" And she was off into the night to spread the news, not unlike her illustrious ancestor.

Faith and Tom went back to what they had been doing. After a while, Faith observed, "That does it, then. The bog has been saved. The identity of the poison-pen writer and murderer revealed. The mystery of Lora's double life solved. The only thing we'll probably never know is what was in Millicent's letter, her guilty secret."

"I think I can help solve this one, if you promise not to get mad at me for not telling you sooner. Believe it or not, the whole thing completely slipped my mind."

"I believe it. Now tell! I knew Charley was giving you all sorts of inside information!"

"The letter contained no words, only a number, Seventy-four."

"Of course. I should have known. Her age! Seventy-four. Her guilty secret! She should be shouting it from the top of her gabled rooftop. Besides, these days it's nothing. Millicent will still be Millicent twenty years from now."

Faith paused a moment to reflect on this daunting thought—with the happy realization also that Millicent's secret was hers. No more vague allusions to the 1940s as dark ages.

She settled back into Tom's arms, another thought uppermost in her mind.

"You know, we made a very good team, darling, although you tended to be a little too cautious—and forgetful."

"A team?"

"As in Nick and Nora Charles, for instance."

Tom made a face. "I could never drink that many martinis and still function, but now that the kids are older, we might consider getting a dog—say a wirehaired terrier?"

Faith smiled. Definitely a very good team.

Excerpts from

Have Faith in Your Kitchen

by Faith Sibley Fairchild

A Work in Progress

Faith's Yankee Pot Roast

2¾ pounds beef bottom round, tied
⅓ cup olive oil
3 large carrots
4 medium potatoes (Faith likes Yukon Golds)
3 medium onions
3 cloves of garlic
½ teaspoon thyme, more if using fresh
Salt and pepper
1 bottle Samuel Adams lager, cream stout, or the equivalent

Preheat the oven to 350° F.

Brown the meat in the oil on all sides in a large casserole with a lid or in a Dutch oven.

Peel the carrots and potatoes. Cut the potatoes and onions into quarters and the carrots into two inch pieces. Mince the garlic. Layer the vegetables around the browned meat and add the thyme, salt, and pepper.

Pour the beer into the casserole and bring it to a boil, uncovered, on the top of the stove. After it boils, turn the heat off and cover the casserole. Place it in the oven and cook for one hour. Remove and let cool. Refrigerate overnight.

This tastes best when made a day ahead. Skim the fat from the top, cover, and reheat in the oven. Remove the meat, slice it, and arrange with the vegetables on a warm platter. Sprinkle with finely chopped parsley. Heat the juices on the top of the stove. You may want to add some flour to thicken. Adjust the seasonings and serve the gravy separately.

Aleford Baked Beans

4 cups Great Northern beans or pea beans, dried
Pinch of salt
3/4 pound well-streaked salt pork
3 tablespoons Dijon mustard
3/4 cup molasses
3/4 cup dark brown sugar
1 1/2 teaspoons salt
1 1/2 teaspoons fresh ground pepper
1 cup boiling water
1 large yellow onion

Soak the beans overnight and drain. Add a pinch of salt and enough water to reach two inches above the beans. Bring to a boil and simmer for an hour. Drain and reserve the liquid. The beans should be barely tender.

Preheat the oven to 400° F.

Scald the salt pork by letting it sit in boiling water for ten minutes. Cut two thin slices and place one in the bottom of your bean pot or casserole. Cut the other into small pieces and set aside. Score the rind of the remaining piece with a sharp knife and set aside also.

Mix the mustard, molasses, brown sugar, salt, and pepper with the boiling water. It's easiest to do this in a large glass measuring pitcher.

Layer the beans in the pot with the pieces of salt pork and the mustard/molasses/sugar mixture, burying the onion in the middle. Place the large piece of salt pork on the top, rind up, and pour the remaining liquid mixture over it. If there is not enough liquid to cover the beans, use some of the water you reserved when you drained the beans. Be careful not to use too much liquid. You can always add more as the beans bake.

Put the lid on the pot, or cover on the casserole, and bake the beans at 400° F. for thirty minutes. Turn the temperature down to 200° F. and bake for six to eight hours, checking to see that the beans do not become too dry. Uncover the container during the last hour of cooking.

Baked beans were the Puritans' answer to the Crock-Pot and provided them with a tasty meal during the Sabbath. The pot would be placed in the fireplace on Saturday morning, or handed over to the baker, who would call for it and place it in the community oven, usually in a nearby tavern. After cooking all day, the beans were ready for Saturday supper and Sunday breakfast. Traditionally, Bostonians eat their beans with brown bread, but Faith has served them straight from the pot with everything from focaccia to corn bread. Beantown's pot is earthenware with a narrow throat, but this recipe tastes fine cooked in any deep casserole with a cover, such as a Dutch oven.

This makes a great many beans. For the next meal, add barbecue sauce, drop a poached egg on top, or give some to your neighbors.

Cardamom Raisin Bread

1 quart milk
1½ cups sugar
½ cup butter
1 teaspoon ground cardamom seeds (or 1 tablespoon of preground cardamom)
2 cakes compressed yeast or two packages of yeast granules
1 teaspoon salt
1 package seedless raisins
1 package golden or muscat raisins
2 eggs, beaten
12 cups flour (approximately)
1 egg yolk, 1 teaspoon vanilla, 1 tablespoon sugar, mixed together for the glaze

Preheat the oven to 350° F.

Heat the milk and sugar, then add the butter and cardamom. When the butter has melted, cool the mixture to lukewarm in a large mixing bowl. Add and dissolve the yeast. Add the salt, raisins, and beaten eggs. Mix together well and then add enough flour to make a firm but elastic dough. Cover the dough and let it stand in a warm place until doubled in bulk. Then knead it well and form into two round loaves—or four standard-sized bread loaves. Place these in greased pie tins or loaf pans and let rise until doubled again.

Bake for one hour. Brush loaves with the mixture of egg yolk, vanilla, and sugar when they come out of the oven.

Once you've made it, you'll get the knack. It needs to rise for a long time and you also have to watch that the top doesn't get too brown or burn in the oven. You may have to cover it with foil near the end. You can also make the dough in a braid.

This cardamom raisin bread is a Norwegian recipe from the real author's grandmother. We've always made it for Christmas. In Norwegian, it's called *Julekake*, "Christmas cake." I now make it year-round.

Patriots' Day Pancakes

½ cup milk
2 tablespoons melted butter
1 egg
½ cup sour cream
1 cup flour
2 teaspoons baking powder
4 tablespoons sugar
½ teaspoon salt
¼ teaspoon vanilla
½ cup raspberries
½ cup blueberries

Mix the milk, melted butter, egg, and sour cream in a bowl until smooth.

Sift the dry ingredients together in a separate bowl and then add all at once to the liquid ingredients. Stir until mixed. The batter will be a bit lumpy. Add the vanilla and stir again. Fold in the berries.

The pancakes cook more evenly if you can find blueberries and raspberries of approximately the same size.

Cook on a hot griddle over medium heat. Serve immediately with a dusting of powdered sugar. (Some people also like butter.)

Makes eighteen to twenty-four pancakes, depending on size. You may also wish to add more fruit, but not too much or the pancakes get mushy.

In the book, the children pour syrup on them, but they taste far better without it.

Chocolate Crunch Cookies

1/2 pound unsalted butter
1 cup brown sugar
1 egg yolk
2 cups sifted flour
1 teaspoon vanilla extract
1 1/2 cups dark or semisweet chocolate bits combined with 1/2 cup toffee bits
1/2 cup toffee bits for topping

Preheat the oven to 350° F.

Cream together the butter and sugar. Add the egg yolk and beat until smooth. Add the flour, mix, then add the vanilla. At this stage, Faith uses her hands, as the dough tends to be crumbly. Knead until smooth.

Spread the dough in a greased nine-by-twelve-inch baking pan and place in the middle of the oven. Again, Faith finds that it is easier to pat the dough evenly into the pan using her hands.

Bake for twenty-five minutes and take the pan out of the oven.

Distribute the combined chocolate and toffee bits evenly over the cookie layer and bake for four minutes more.

Remove the pan from the oven and immediately spread the

melted chocolate and toffee bits. Sprinkle what is now the frosting with the remaining toffee bits.

It is important to let the cookies cool completely in the pan before cutting into squares.

This is a decadently rich cookie and makes either twenty-four or thirty-six cookies. It's up to you.

Note on Recipes:

As with Faith's other recipes in *The Body in the Cast* and *The Body in the Basement*, all these will taste just fine with healthwise modifications such as Egg Beaters, low-fat sour cream, 1 percent milk, butter substitutes, and the like. Unfortunately, the cookies definitely need the real thing—the best chocolate bits you can find and real toffee bits. Think of them as a reward for all those rice crackers you eat.

Author's Note

Next to eating good dinners, a healthy man with a benevolent turn of mind, must like, I think, to read about them.

—W. M. THACKERAY

Faith and I would add "and woman" to the sentence, but Thackeray was definitely onto something. We enjoy reading about food. And for many of us, reading about food *and* murder is the real frosting on the cake. Why is the pairing of gastronomy and crime so seductive?

Dorothy L. Sayers delights us with her descriptions of Lord Peter Wimsey's meals, with perhaps the best title in the annals of culinary crime: "The Bibulous Business of the Matter of Taste." That short story describes a six-course dinner, with the emphasis on the identification of the wines accompanying each course. Only the real Lord Peter is able to correctly name all of them. I like the breakfasts best and entertain fantasies of Bunter appearing at the door of my bedchamber, tray laden with tea, kippers, coddled eggs, and a rack of toast.

Meanwhile, across the Channel, Madame Maigret is taking excellent care of her husband, preparing traditional French dishes that Simenon writes about in mouthwatering detail. It is no wonder Maigret tries to get home for lunch so often. I would, too, if someone was whipping up *coq au vin* and a *tarte à la frangipane* (a particularly sinful custard pastry) for me.

On our own shores, we have Nero Wolfe, whose attention to food is as obsessive as his devotion to his orchids. He and Fritz Brenner, his chef, range over a number of cuisines in the pursuit of their art. Fritz is so gifted that he even makes milk toast "superbly." Why on earth would Archie ever look for his own apartment? Would you?

It would be simple to say that each author uses food as a way of characterizing each sleuth, a way of extending our knowledge of the kinds of people they are, and leave it at that. An idiosyncrasy perhaps? But it's more. We get hungry when we read these books, and I'm sure the authors did, too, as they wrote. How could it be otherwise, given the emphasis they place on the joys of the table? Food is important. It makes a statement on its own. Whodunit is irrevocably joined to whoateit.

Faith doesn't have a cook, nor do I. If we want something tasty, we have to make it ourselves—something, fortunately, both of us like to do. We hope you will enjoy these recipes, and when you're ready to sit down to the fruits of your labor, prop a good mystery up in front of your plate!
